Ju
F
K16   Kaufelt, David A.
        Silver rose.

Ju
F
K16   Kaufelt, David A.
        Silver rose.

SILVER ROSE

Books by David A. Kaufelt

SIX MONTHS WITH AN OLDER WOMAN

THE BRADLEY BEACH RUMBA

SPARE PARTS

LATE BLOOMER

MIDNIGHT MOVIES

THE WINE AND THE MUSIC

SILVER ROSE

SILVER ROSE

a novel by

DAVID A. KAUFELT

DELACORTE PRESS / NEW YORK

Published by
Delacorte Press
1 Dag Hammarskjold Plaza
New York, N.Y. 10017

Manufactured in the United States of America

First printing

Designed by Judith Neuman

Library of Congress Cataloging in Publication Data
Kaufelt, David A.
    Silver rose.

    I. Title.
PS3561.A79S5   813'.54   82-5135
ISBN 0-440-07945-3   AACR2

For Robert Gerald Thixton

1

She hoped they weren't waiting for her. That her name wasn't on one of their innumerable lists. That one look at her passport wouldn't give, as they said in England, the whole show away.

She hoped, fervently, that they would think she was too smart to come back.

Though fear normally made her sleepy, she had been up all night. She had tried to save money by booking a second-class berth, even though she knew better. The crossing had been predictably miserable. Two middle-aged, middle-class sisters, French, had shared her cabin and had alternately talked and snored their way across the Channel. Customs had taken forever, and the train had been delayed while officials in white-plumed hats argued over a coffin. It had traveled from London without proper papers.

She arrived in Paris an hour too late, the North Train having already left for Berlin. The fear and the lack of sleep made her feel hopelessly muddled. The agent behind his ornate brass bars had treated her as if she were mentally deficient, in the end passing her on to a subordinate who had been sympathetic. He arranged for her transfer of tickets, had seen her to a taxi. He had even suggested a respectable hotel called the Jacob, not far from the Eiffel Tower.

"Perhaps," he suggested, "the mademoiselle might do some sight-seeing."

She was halfway across Paris before she told the driver

that she didn't want to go to the Hotel Jacob, that she wanted to be taken to the Ritz.

He turned to stare at her, lifting one eyebrow as the two sides of his mouth curled down in a typical Parisian grimace. "The Ritz Hotel?"

"Yes," she said, looking directly at him. She was so tired of surly clerks, of cheeky drivers. "The Ritz Hotel."

He shrugged and continued to drive, his back eloquent with sardonic amusement. She knew, of course, that she didn't look like Ritz material. When she had made the decision—to leave the safety of London, to return to Berlin— she had decided to travel as inconspicuously as possible.

She had gone to the Lyons Store near Marble Arch and bought herself an outfit designed to make her look like a secretary. She cast herself in the role of a German secretary with several languages, going home to Berlin on holiday with the possibility of finding a new position.

She had purchased a brown suit, a dark brown coat and a tan slouch hat into which she stuffed her hair. She had borrowed a pair of cotton hose from the girl she shared the flat with and had put on a pair of brown low-heeled shoes. She wore no makeup, no jewelry. She had succeeded. She looked inexpensive, serious, a young woman interested in the economic miracle Hitler was performing in her homeland in the fall of 1938. A German girl returning home after a disappointing sojourn abroad.

There was plenty of time, she told herself as the taxi rattled over the cobblestoned streets, to be nervous now. She had a day's reprieve. There would be plenty of time to be anxious about German Passport Control. An entire day.

Still, she knew herself well enough to realize that a small wallpapered room in a solid tourist hotel would make her desperate. She needed just what her father would have prescribed: a bubble bath at the Ritz.

But she didn't want to think of her father. Not yet, she didn't. The taxi pulled up to the Ritz's Place Vendôme entrance, behind a black Hispano Suiza. Her driver winked at the doorman and the boy who took her old weathered suitcase. She undertipped the driver enough to let him know she wasn't to be intimidated.

She stood at the edge of the silk carpet that signaled the formal beginning of the Ritz lobby and breathed in the expensive air for one moment. It was a touch chilly, Madame Ritz not believing in central heating until mid-November. The blond ladies, holding tiny dogs, wore Russian sables over their tea gowns.

Perfectly aware of her garbardine coat and the slouch hat, *pour le sport*, she walked across the enormous carpet to where the concierge was waiting behind a mahogany desk. He had that pinched look on his face superior hotel men wore when confronted with someone who doesn't belong. He looked as if he had been eating lemons.

"Mademoiselle?" he asked, putting his hand on top of the green leather ledger, as if that gesture were enough to inform her that she should find more suitable lodgings.

"Rooms over the gardens," she said, airily.

That stopped him, but only for a moment. "I am terribly afraid ..."

"Ah, Mademoiselle Jablonski," a familiar voice said. She turned to find the ancient little *sous-directeur* coming out of his office to meet her, to press her hand, to smile volubly at her. His absurdly long cutaway made him seem like an extra in an American comedy, a Marx Brothers film. "It has been so very long," he said, his eyes reproaching her as if she were a wayward daughter.

He had appointed himself her father's personal representative at the Ritz years before. "How are you, Marcel?" she asked, wondering if she were going to cry, knowing that would be unforgivable in the Ritz lobby.

"Oh, *très, très bien*, mademoiselle. And you?"

"A little tired, Marcel."

He barked something at the concierge, snapped his fingers

at the boy holding her suitcase, and led her across the lobby, past the blond, furred women, to the gilded elevators.

"Rooms over the gardens," Marcel said, ignoring how sad and tired and poor she looked. He pulled a set of keys from the hook in the elevator where Ritz room keys always hung. "The house has never been so occupied," he confided. "Refugees—the right sort, you understand—pour in from Eastern Europe on their way west."

There were three rooms. Tall, austere French windows were framed by heavy pearl gray satin curtains. The furniture was carefully placed. It was light but formal Louis XVI.

She suddenly felt less frightened, more tired. She had the maid run a bath and fill it with tiny beads that turned into bubbles when they hit the water. She ordered a light supper, half a bottle of Moselle. She lay in the bed in her bedroom at the Ritz, under the satin comforter, and though she didn't want to—though she longed to savor the tangible luxury of that reminiscent atmosphere—she thought of her father.

From the beginning, Nikolaus Jablonski had refused to leave Berlin. He was amused, he said. Even when they threatened him. Even when they destroyed his car and wounded his driver. Even when they took *Der Tag*, his newspaper, away from him and gave it to Julius Streicher to incorporate into his obscene anti-Semitic *Der Stürmer*, he refused to leave.

He was still, he said, amused. Genuinely amused. The Nazis, he told his friends, were only one more comic German operetta.

He had laughed too hard and too long.

Nick Jablonski had been the most influential newspaper publisher in Germany, and Dr. Goebbels had been hard pressed to get rid of him. World opinion still counted in the Germany of the mid-1930s, and the world's press knew and admired Nick Jablonski's *Der Tag*.

But Goebbels found a way. There was always a way. Rennie Jablonski hadn't heard from her father in nearly two weeks when she had found that tiny throwaway piece of news on page five of the London *Times*. Hitler, it said, was rounding up all Jews with Polish passports. Marshal Ridz-Smigly of Poland categorically refused to accept them. An incident was in the making, the *Times* implied, as if it were a very ordinary incident. As if the *Times* of London couldn't be too concerned about Jews living in Poland or Germany or high middle Ruritania.

But Rennie was concerned. Her father had lived in Germany for twenty-five years, never bothering to get a German passport. Naturally, a Pole couldn't publish a German newspaper. And a Jewish Pole at that. Certainly the world press would understand. Nick Jablonski was to be picked up in the roundup, held for questioning.

Rennie had little doubt that if he were picked up, held for "questioning," he would ever reach Poland. People— Jews—held for questioning in Germany rarely ever reached anywhere.

But Nikolaus Jablonski was a survivor. He still had friends, as it were, at court. Rennie counted on those friends, on her father's ability to sidestep catastrophe. She had known enough not to try to telephone him. She had learned on her last trip to Berlin, during the Olympics, that telephones were being tapped, that one had to be careful about what one said in one's home, in front of servants and waiters and old trusted friends.

During that last trip home, Nick had been amused by her naïveté. "Everyone is a spy now," he told her. "There are salon spies and saloon spies and cafeteria spies and tea party spies. One can hardly go out in society if one isn't a spy." Oh, he had been amused. With his dimples and broad shoulders, his abundant ash-blond hair and effortless charm. He had laughed at her concern.

But he had been serious enough when he had sent her,

ordered her, back to London and told her to stay there.
Certainly he had been serious enough when he had said to
her, during the Olympics, as they stood up in the cheering,
*heil*ing stadium, where there was too much cheering and
*heil*ing for any of the spies to overhear them, that she
mustn't come back to Germany for a long time, if ever.

"Enjoy London. Study. Become a great and famous artist.
Find yourself a young man. Forget about Germany and
your father for a time. We're both going through a difficult
period. I'll be certain to let you know when we're through
with it."

"Through with what?"

"This temporary—one hopes it's temporary—insanity
Germany and I are going through."

She hadn't found herself a young man because what
young man could live up to her father's dimples, his charm?
As for her art, she wasn't brave enough to take the chances
which would make her famous or great. She had skill, and
perhaps something more, that was obvious. But, as her
favorite teacher said, it would take time to see if that was
enough.

Time. She lay in her bed at the Ritz, eyes open. She took
her watch off the night table and wondered if it had
stopped. But no, she heard the ticking. Relentless ticking.
She wished she had not missed the morning's train to
Berlin; that she was already through German Passport
Control; that she was safe. Well, as safe as she could be in
NSDAP Germany.

She wondered if she was going to be able to go through
with it, after all. If her hand wasn't going to shake at the
moment she had to hand the passport over; if she wasn't
going to cry out when the border guard registered her name.

Usually, she was up to the occasion. It was the moments
leading up to it that did her in, that made her stomach turn
to aspic and her mind to jelly, incapable of rational thought.
But this, of course, wasn't a school play or an interview

with a professor. This was—and she dismissed the thought a soon as she formed it—a matter of life and death. Dear God, her life and death.

She wondered, forcing herself not to think of that, whether or not she had made a mistake booking a seat in a first-class compartment. Weren't they more suspicious of women traveling first class, alone? Wouldn't it have been better to be anonymous in second class? Wasn't that, after all, the purpose of the brown suit and the secretarially fashionable slouch hat? Wasn't it a sign of mental confusion that after forcing herself into that second-class cabin on the boat train she was sleeping here in the Ritz?

Rennie Jablonski was twenty-one years old, but at that particular moment in her life she felt half her age and desperately in need of her father. Her friends in England, those Mayfair cousins her father had put in charge of her, her grandparents, who only recently escaped from Austria and were now in Florida—none of them could make her feel the way her father always could: as if she belonged.

In the morning she dressed in the brown outfit, took one last look through the tall windows at the Ritz gardens, and left her rooms. A pale sun had dimly lit the gardens, and she took this as a good sign.

Still, she hadn't made up, and once again she had put her hair under the slouch hat. Yes, she was determined to travel first class, but she was going to do so as inconspicuously as possible. She went back to role playing: a secretary whose boss had given her a bonus, a first-class ticket to Berlin.

She breakfasted in the dining room, where Olivier, the maître d'hôtel, saw to her himself. "We have missed your father," he said. "It was always a great pleasure to wait upon him."

She smiled up at Olivier and said that she hoped he would have the opportunity again in the very near future. She almost told him she was going to Berlin to bring her father out. But that wouldn't have exactly been discreet.

She finished her café au lait and brioche, wondering how her father had developed that easy charm that made lifelong friends of hotel employees, grand duchesses, cinema stars, philosophers. It hadn't been able to protect him from the Nazis, but the Nazis were infamously immune to charm.

She paid her bill, gathered up the odious brown purse and the cotton gloves, and stood up, realizing that someone had been staring at her throughout her breakfast. He was a man of about thirty, wearing beautifully cut English tweeds. His dark brown hair had been slicked back from his handsome, open face. He smiled, and she smiled back, tentatively. Despite his suit, she didn't think he was British, and his shoulders were too broad for him to be French.

She found herself thinking of him as the taxi took her to the railroad station. How nice it would have been to have had a friendly flirtation with a stranger met in the Ritz dining room. She held on to her fantasy. It was better to daydream than to let her mind run along the more familiar fantasy of arrest, torture, death.

Death she felt she could deal with. It was the thought of torture that made her mind go blank and turned her stomach queasy. She had read too many articles. She had heard too many firsthand accounts of Gestapo interrogation techniques in Spandau's cellars.

"Oh, you Jews always exaggerate everything," her roommate had said, after they had heard a lecture at Albert Hall by a German refugee. "I'm certain it's not nearly as bad as that fellow said it was."

They have no reason to question me, Rennie told herself, paying the driver, showing the porter her tickets. They have absolutely no reason, she repeated, buying a copy of French *Vogue* at the kiosk in the first-class waiting room. There's no law, yet, against a Jewess returning to Germany. If I don't look guilty—if I act perfectly natural—there'll be no Trouble. And I don't want Trouble. Oh, God, please don't let there be Trouble.

Trouble was that ill-defined but pervasive theory of life Tante Lizbeth—her father's housekeeper—claimed waited around every corner. The thought that she was going forward to meet Trouble head on made her stop on the platform and rest for a moment.

It wasn't too late, she knew, to turn around and go back to the Marble Arch flat in London. She could continue to go to lectures, to study drawing and painting, to have Sunday teas with her roommate's Honorable parents. No one could fault her. No one expected her to go to Berlin. In fact, no one really wanted her there. She knew, intellectually, that if her father wanted to get out—and if he could have—she would have heard by this time. She was probably bringing him more Trouble than he already had.

She knew this, but still she willed herself to get on the train. She had to see her father. She had to be with him. And she had to do what she could to save him.

The fear had made her muddled again. She found herself at the wrong end of the train, in the second-class car A. She was trying to make her way across the connecting platform that led to the first-class coaches when she dropped her *Vogue*, her cotton gloves. A well-padded conductor picked them up for her and asked, in French, to see her tickets.

"You are an inexperienced traveler," he admonished her, and she almost laughed. While she was still in her teens she had traveled around the world with her father, becoming —in the process—a great favorite of room-service captains and sleeping-car conductors.

"You come with me, mademoiselle," the conductor said, and she was happy to follow, to let him take control. He opened the first-class compartment in which her seat was reserved, and three men looked up simultaneously, all smiling in the same way. Two were playing a card game called jass while the third was pouring himself a drink from a silver flask. They were all smoking expensive cigars, and blue smoke filled the compartment, giving it a kind of spurious night club atmosphere.

"Well," the man with the flask said, looking up at Rennie without standing up. "We can stand some livening up, can't we, fellows?" The card players didn't answer but went back to their game.

"No," the conductor said. "I have made a mistake. Mademoiselle is in the next compartment."

"Then the porter made the same mistake, old top," the man with the flask said, pointing to Rennie's suitcase on the overhead rack.

"So he did." The conductor took her suitcase off the rack and led her out of the compartment.

"That was my seat," Rennie told him.

"I'm going to find you a more suitable one," the conductor said, leading her to a compartment at the opposite end of the car. A sign on its door said RESERVED in French and German. The conductor slid open the smoked-glass door. "I wonder if you would mind a companion, monsieur," he said to the man in the impeccable tweeds who had smiled at her over breakfast in the Ritz dining room.

"I was just thinking what a lonely trip this was going to be," he answered in what could only be an American's French, standing up, smiling his infectious, inquiring smile at her again.

The conductor put her suitcase on the overhead rack as she searched for money in the hated purse. She handed him five francs, but he said, "No, mademoiselle, at your service," and left, sliding the door closed after him.

Rennie sat down on the green plush seat. She closed her eyes for a moment and thought about taking off her hat and decided not to. "This is kind of you," she said, making an effort, opening her eyes, putting the magazine and her purse aside, wishing she could simply sleep.

The train gave a couple of false starts and then began to move in earnest. She looked out at the platform where a few people were waving good-bye, throwing kisses. The fear—which she had put away—suddenly came out again and overtook her. The train was picking up speed, taking her to Germany, to the border where men in blue-black boots with swastikas on their collars were waiting for her. It was a child's nightmare coming true.

"My name is Jarman," the man across from her was saying in a German that was better than his French. "Henry Vance Jarman, Jr. But unfortunately, virtually everyone calls me Butch."

Her fear was paralyzing. All her mind was capable of focusing on was the sound of the wheels against the track, carrying her to Germany. She had to say something. She had to appear natural. "I thought Henry Vance Jarman owned all the newspapers in America." It was the first possible thought that came into her mind.

"And half the magazines and a third of the radio networks." Butch Jarman coughed and, for the first time, looked uncomfortable. "He's my father."

She was about to say that her father was a newspaperman, too. But of course that was no longer true. So she said, "And you're going to Berlin to buy him another newspaper?"

He gave her his smile again. "No. I'm to take over as the Berlin radio correspondent for his radio stations."

"What has happened to his former radio correspondent?" She knew if she could keep talking, she would be fine.

"He was a rather gentlemanly Jewish fellow of fifty with half a dozen children and a ravishing Czech wife. He spoke the most beautiful Prague *Deutsch*. But he has been out of favor for some time, politically . . ."

"Racially."

"Yes. At any rate, he has developed a rather opportune 'heart' and has retired to Portugal."

"My father has a 'heart,' too," she said, immediately knowing she shouldn't have. No free clues; no personal information. She chided herself and, at the same time, wondered how her father's heart was; how he was.

"My father was against my taking the job," Butch Jarman said. "But I wanted to be where the action is. Then, of course, I'm ideally suited for it. I have a facility for languages, and German is nearly as easy for me as English. I spent a lot of time in Berlin over the years. It used to be my favorite city."

"And now?"

"It's not nearly as gay as it once was."

"No," she agreed. She opened her purse and hunted for a cigarette. It was a fragrant Nigeria. She like the smell more than the actual act of smoking and only smoked when she was nervous. Butch Jarman lit it for her, and she offered him one. He said he was addicted to Balkan cigars and would she mind? They smoked in silence as the train made its way through the grim, gray farmland. Occasionally, groups of peasants stood by the tracks at lesser stations, silently watching the North Train go by.

Eventually, she fell into a half sleep, filled with images of her father and of another, darker presence.

She jumped, some hours later, when he touched her.

"I'm terribly sorry," he said, concerned, standing over her. "I didn't mean to startle you."

She smiled, or tried to. "Train journeys always unnerve me."

"I was about to have lunch and wondered if I might bring you something? Or perhaps you'd care to join me?"

"I'm not at all hungry, thank you."

"You must eat something. Come and sit with me. It will distract you from the trip."

She went with him to the dining car, thinking that nothing could distract her from the trip, from the inevitability of that moment when she would be asked for her passport.

The tables were covered with white linen and silver cutlery, fine crystal. Though it was daytime, the glass lamps with their violet shades had been switched on, making each table a cozy oasis of comfort and intimacy in the first-class dining car. The maître d'hôtel seated them at a table for two, next to a window. Two of the men from the compartment she should have been sitting in were at a neighboring table. They barely noticed her. They were engrossed in a conversation about Rumanian oil fields. "Oil makes the world go round," one said. "If old Adolf's going to make war, he's going to need oil."

Rennie ordered beef soup and a sandwich and was surprised that she finished both, drinking tea while the men went on about oil and artificial rubber, making marks on the white cloth with their pens, eating and arguing.

She looked out the window past her own reflection at the relentlessly gray fields and farmhouses. Suddenly the train entered a tunnel, and even the little violet-shaded table lamps went off. For a long moment they were in total darkness.

"Are you all right?" Butch Jarman asked, as the lights came on and the train left the tunnel.

"When do you think we'll cross the border?" Rennie asked in a voice she didn't recognize. The sudden and total darkness had undone the good that the food and tea had done.

"Quite soon," he said, as if that would reassure her.

The oil men left, she finished her tea, and Butch Jarman insisted on paying for lunch. "I'm awfully rich," he said.

"You've been kind enough, letting me share your compartment . . ."

"Allow me to be a little kinder. Please."

She didn't argue. She needed her strength to keep up the pretense. She was an ordinary traveler, a little on edge but still with a great deal of poise. There was nothing to fear or worry about. "What did you say?" she asked, trying to concentrate on what Butch Jarman was saying, trying not to listen to the sound of the train's wheels taking her closer and closer to the border.

"I said I wanted to be rude. I said I want to tell you that you're very beautiful. Despite all your attempts to deny it, you're the loveliest woman I've ever seen. This is not idle train chatter or a declaration of love or the first step in a planned seduction. I purposely say it here rather than in the privacy of the compartment. But I did want to say it. I did want to thank you for being with me. I know you are in trouble, and if there is anything I can do . . ."

The train slowed down and then, after a series of lurches, came to a halt. Almost immediately a man in a brown uniform opened the door to the dining car. He waited until the few remaining diners had become silent and the waiters had finished fiddling with the cutlery. He waited for full attention.

"*Meine Damen und Herren*," he said, looking around, as if he were giving an oration. "Welcome to Germany. You have just crossed the border into the Third Reich. Will you all please return to your compartments and await further word? *Heil Hitler!*" He raised his arm, clicked his heels, and was gone.

Rennie was the first to stand. She walked as quickly as she could, with as much determination, to her seat. Butch followed some moments later, having to pay the bill. They were to detrain, he said. "Such a nuisance. There's a check gate everyone on the train has to pass through."

"You go ahead," Rennie told him. "I'll be a moment." She looked at the green enameled door which led to the compartment's toilet.

"You won't be able to stay aboard," he said, guessing at what she was thinking. "Men in uniform are already storming the train, *heil*ing everyone in sight, preparing to inspect the baggage."

"Please," she said, going to the toilet door. "I want to freshen up. Please! Go without me."

She stood inside the small toilet, waiting until she heard the compartment door slide shut. She knew that now she could only just deal with herself, with what she had to do. She put her head against the cool enameled wall and closed her eyes.

A moment later she heard the luggage inspectors enter the car. Avoiding the mirror, she stepped into the compartment and removed her passport from her purse. She didn't want them to see her hands shaking, trying to make the clasp of her purse work. She wanted to seem assured.

She moved past the brown-uniformed men who seemed to fill the corridors and stepped off the train. The cool, damp air, instead of reviving her, made her feel dizzy, displaced. Two lines of passengers had formed on the platform. At the head of each line was a set of brown-uniformed officers, inspecting passports. Off to the side was a man in a brown leather trench coat that sat on him as if it were a bathrobe. He wore a plain brown hat and stood in the shadows so his face was indistinct, his eyes hidden.

Rennie took her place at the end of the line closest to the train and farthest from the man in the shadows. She saw that Butch Jarman was in the opposite line, a few steps ahead of her.

She pulled the collar of her coat up around her, thought about a cigarette, and decided no, that would necessitate opening her purse, holding a match still, keeping her hands steady.

It had grown dark. She moved forward slowly, as people at the head of the queue had their passports checked, stamped, returned. It all seemed so matter-of-fact. Up ahead the inspector was examining a passport while a tall, thin second-class passenger waited patiently. The inspector was about to stamp it and then looked at the man in the shadows, who slowly shook his head from side to side. For a moment Rennie caught sight of his eyes. He seemed to be wearing a monocle, which caught the light from inside the train.

"Herr Wilhelm Joseph," the inspector said. "Herr Wilhelm Joseph," he repeated, as if he were savoring some private irony. "You must wait in the station, Herr Wilhelm Joseph."

"My passport," the man said, holding out his hand.

"Escort Herr Wilhelm Joseph into the station, Franks," the inspector said to a subordinate, placing the passport facedown on the table where his ledgers lay.

Joseph wore an odd smile as he turned to follow Franks. It was as if this had happened before; it was as if he had placed an extravagant bet on a long shot and of course his horse hadn't come in.

The line moved and Rennie, for the second time that day, dropped her purse, her gloves, her passport. She bent to pick them up, wondering if she were going to faint, when she felt Butch Jarman's hand on her arm, steadying her. "Why don't you wait on line with me, darling," he said in English, retrieving her things. "It's moving faster, I'm certain." He spoke deliberately, in the way Americans always seemed to speak abroad. As if no one else understood their language. As if they were alone. "Then we can get back to our compartment and have a drink."

She allowed herself to be piloted into his line, to stand with his hand on her arm, as if she were under his personal protection.

"Herr Jarman," the inspector, a Wehrmacht captain, said in Anglo-English, taking the proffered passport. "We have been awaiting your arrival. Oberstgruppenführer von Danzig sends his regrets. He had hoped to meet you here, but state business has kept him in Berlin."

"Just as well," Butch said, looking at the captain and then at Rennie.

The captain laughed. He barely glanced at the passport as he handed it to an aide to be stamped. "Allow me, darling," Butch said, taking her passport from her hands, giving it to the captain, who gave Butch a knowing look but then hesitated. He glanced at the man in the shadows, and for a moment there was silence. Then Rennie saw the man look at her, his eyeglass flashing with reflected light.

The captain handed her passport to his aide, who stamped it perfunctorily.

"*Danke schön*," Butch said, as he pocketed both passports.

"*Bitte schön*," the captain said, smiling. He and Herr Jarman were two men of the world and if Herr Jarman wanted to amuse himself with a young German *Mädel* during a boring train journey, it certainly wasn't up to him to say he shouldn't. The captain would have made any kind of wager one cared to make that the young woman had started off the journey with a second-class ticket. "Too thin for my tastes," he said to the man with the monocle and leather trench coat, who had joined him.

"Not for mine," he said, in a monotone.

As Butch Jarman helped Rennie back onto the train, she stopped and looked back for a moment. Though she still couldn't see his face, she was certain the monocled eye was staring at her.

"Are you all right?" Butch asked, as he shut the compartment door. "Would you like some water? Brandy?"

"You've been wonderfully kind, but if you don't mind, I think I will just shut my eyes for a few moments." She did so, falling into the deepest sleep she had had since leaving London. The image of a faceless man in a leather trench coat with a monocle in his eye came to her, but she forced it away. She was in Germany. She would be in her home tonight, in her own bed, in Berlin. She would see and touch and hold her father. Together, they would get out. Together, they would be safe.

Butch Jarman watched her as she slept. He still had her passport. He resisted, with some effort, the impulse to open it, to find out her name, her age, more about her. His father always accused him of being the "perfect little gent." Well, he supposed he was. He placed the passport next to her purse on the green plush seat and wondered what she would look like without her slouch hat, without that air of nervous desperation. But already she seemed calmer, less frightened. Soon they would be in Berlin.

2

The North Train gave a preliminary start and stop, alerting its passengers that they were about to be allowed to disembark. The distinctive sound of SS jackboots on the train's iron steps made Rennie fearful again. She wondered if they were looking for her; if they were coming to arrest her.

Butch Jarman busied himself with his hand luggage, tightening the leather straps. "Do you think we might see one another in Berlin?" he asked.

"I'm not staying very long." She was listening to find out where the jackboots would stop. They seemed to be coming in her direction.

He put his grip down and smiled at her, his green eyes sympathetic. "If you do find yourself at loose ends, I'm at the Adlon."

"I'll remember. You've been . . ." But she didn't get to tell him what he'd been, because the jackboots became suddenly quiet as the smoked-glass compartment door slid open. An SS *Oberstgruppenführer* stood looking at them.

He was everything an SS general should be: tall, muscular, with butter-colored hair and Mediterranean blue eyes. He wore the black SS uniform as if it were the most natural costume a man could wear. On him it didn't seem theatrical. Even the dress dagger at his waist and the blue-black boots polished to a mirror finish seemed expected.

Rennie almost laughed. He was so perfect. She waited for him to announce that she was under arrest, wondering that a general should be sent on a corporal's mission.

19

But he wasn't even looking at her. "Butch," he said in English, holding out his hand. "How are you?"

"Marvelous. And you, von Danzig? You look as if you should be sitting on a marble horse in the middle of the Tiergarten."

"Yes," von Danzig said, glancing at Rennie, turning back to Butch Jarman. Obviously, she was not to be introduced. "I am sorry to tell you this, Butch, but there is a reception committee waiting to meet you."

"No."

"Yes. A former ambassador. A chargé d'affaires. Two doctors associated with German-American foundations no one has ever heard of and two minor dignitaries' wives. Dr. Goebbels doesn't want your father to think we are unimpressed by his power or that we shall overlook his latest radio correspondent." He hesitated for a moment. "Will the Fräulein be joining us?"

"I think not."

"Then I shall await you on the platform. You must smile when you disembark. Photographers and newsreel cameras are being set up now. I wanted to give you fair warning."

He bowed, clicked his heels and, without looking at Rennie, closed the door behind him. "He's much too good to be true," Rennie said.

"His name is Wolfgang von Danzig. He comes from an old Prussian family and is one of Hitler's fair-haired boys. He doesn't do very much as a general. When my father and I were here last, he was only a colonel and did less, acting as our guide. Then he went off to Spain in the Luftwaffe with the Condor unit, got himself shot down on his third mission, and was returned to Berlin salons, where he belongs.

"He's loosely attached, I gather, to both the Foreign Office and the Ministry of Propaganda. He's to keep an eye on me, to make certain I am properly impressed by the Third Reich."

"You must be very important to rate your own general," Rennie said.

"It's my father they care about. If there is war, Goebbels believes my father's newspapers will either keep America out or push her in. He's still sitting on the fence, you see. He's a great believer in Lindbergh, and Lindbergh is a great believer in the Third Reich."

"And you?"

"I am the objective reporter. I give my listeners the facts and allow them to come to their own conclusions. I have no private opinions."

"That must make life very easy for you."

The train gave its final start and stop, and the conductors announced that passengers could disembark. Butch gave her suitcase to a porter waiting in the corridor. "You will remember that I'm at the Adlon, won't you?"

"Yes. Of course I'll remember. And thank you for everything."

Butch lit a Balkan cigar and sat down, intending to allow everyone else to get off the train before he went to meet his welcoming committee. As he smoked, he thought of the girl whose name he didn't know, and he wondered what she was so frightened of, why she had gone to such trouble to get into Germany. So many others were going to such extraordinary lengths to get out.

She changed money at the exchange in the station. The teller wore an old-fashioned high collar and pince-nez. "Yes, *gnädiges Fräulein.*" No, *gnädiges Fräulein.*" He was so matter-of-fact. She was just another client. She asked him more questions than she need have just because he made her feel so normal, so everyday.

She left the station reluctantly, but once outside, she stood very still for a moment, breathing in. *Berliner Luft,* Berlin's air, hadn't changed. It was as clean and delicious as it had been two years before. Well, it seemed as if nothing had changed all that much.

It was early evening, and Berliners were rushing about, catching trains and taxis. They seemed a bit more prosperous now, a little sleeker, but still the same good-humored, sharp-tongued people she had always known.

Perhaps her fears were inappropriate, foolish, based on her own insecurities. Perhaps her father's letters had been lost in the mail. Perhaps they were waiting for her now, on the refectory table in the hall in the Marble Arch flat. Perhaps she had worked herself up for nought. It had happened before.

The cool, clean air, the vibrant people, the neon lights gave her a lightheartedness, a sense that she had come home. The *Wagenmeister* in front of the station found her a taxi and refused her tip. "I never take money from a young lady," he said, bowing, shutting the door after her.

She gave the address to the driver. Their house was on the Lentzeallee in the fashionable suburb of Dahlem. She sat in the back of the taxi and closed her eyes to the public buildings draped in the red, black, and white Nazi banners. Soon everything would be all right. Soon she would be in her father's arms.

"Should I wait?" the driver asked. Her outfit didn't go with the Lentzeallee or with the huge glass and steel house he had pulled up in front of.

The house was lit up, as if a party was about to begin. She had never liked the house, designed by a Bauhaus architect. Even as a little girl she had felt that it was too cool and intellectual. Though tonight, with all those lights blazing, it seemed, finally, inviting.

She paid and tipped the driver and told him that there was no reason for him to wait, that she was home. "You don't mind, *gnädiges Fräulein,* if I eat my supper, do you?" He picked up his *Völkische Beobachter*—no Berlin driver was ever without his newspaper—and began to read it by the overhead light, one hand reaching for the sandwich wrapped in waxed paper at his side.

She walked up the path that led to the oversized door, put her suitcase down, and rang the electric bell. It was some time before it was answered. The anticipation was extraordinary. She felt if the door weren't answered soon, she would knock it down. She could visualize her father in his study reading his papers, most emphatically not the *Völkische Beobachter,* drinking a cup of the dark coffee he was addicted to, despite what his doctor said.

When finally a young woman in a black and white maid's uniform cautiously opened the door, Rennie nearly pushed past her.

"Yes?" the girl asked, clearly bewildered.

"You're new here, aren't you?"

"We're all new here. May I help you?"

"I'm Rennie," she said, picking up the suitcase. But still the maid seemed confused. "I'm Herr Jablonski's daughter." She said it with a smile, but she knew something was wrong.

"You have the wrong house, Fräulein. There is no Jablonski here."

"But there is. Of course there is. You must be mistaken. My father . . ." She told herself not to panic. She had to be calm and reasoned. But when the girl began to shut the door, she put her hand against it and shouted, "This is my house. My father's house. We live here."

"What seems to be the trouble, Hedwig?" A kind-looking elderly woman with white hair wearing a dark gown came through the foyer door. Hedwig, still holding the door half closed, explained to her mistress that the Fräulein was making a serious error, that she thought her father lived here.

"As you can see, my dear, he doesn't." The woman with the kind expression shooed the maid away. "We only recently moved in."

"From whom did you buy it?"

"I don't really think that's your concern." She started to close the door and, after a moment, relented. "We bought it from the state. Or actually it was given to my husband for certain services he rendered the party. Perhaps you would like a glass of water. You don't seem at all well. You are confused. Your father . . ."

"No. I don't need water, thank you. Yes, I must be confused. I haven't been in Berlin for a time and I'm turned about. You must excuse me."

She picked up the suitcase and went as quickly as she could back to the taxi. The driver was eating a thick sausage sandwich as he turned the pages of the newspaper.

He turned one more page, closed the catch over the light, and asked her where she wanted to go now. She told him the Nollendorfplatz.

"That's more like it," he said, and finished his sandwich as he drove back into the center of Berlin.

"He must be at Lillie's," she said to herself over and over again. He must be. The black, red, and white banners didn't seem as innocuous as they had earlier in the evening.

She had the driver let her off in front of the Piscator Theater in case anyone was waiting or watching the door which led to Lillie's flat. She remembered when she was a girl she thought the enormous plaster Amazons holding up the Piscator's marquee were enchanted princesses. Now she decided they were more doomed than enchanted.

She walked around the corner, crossed the street, and stood at the tram stop for a moment, studying Lillie's Kleist Kasino. She was wary now, no longer so certain what she might find behind familiar facades.

The Kasino, though it was in the unfashionable East End, had long been one of Berlin's most popular clubs. It took up the bottom floor of a patchwork brick fin-de-siècle building. A green cupola gave it an air of whimsy, a touch of oriental mystery.

There were two doors on the ground floor. One was dark green and led to Lillie's flat. The other, the entrance to the Kleist Kasino, had been lacquered a bright tomato red. Over it was a twirling blue neon sign reading "Kleist Kasino."

She watched two men with close-cropped hair, in brown SA uniforms, go through the red door. It was too early for the cabaret, but the bar was open. She waited a quarter of an hour and was glad that she had. She saw them as they walked up the Kleiststrasse. There were six of them, all blond, all carrying cardboard suitcases for their costumes. They were cheaply dressed and cheaply made up, but they had about them a bright, nearly happy, definitely hopeful air.

Rennie waited until they turned into the alley which led to the Kleist Kasino's stage door, and then she took off the slouch hat, finally letting her silver blond hair fall about her, and ran after them.

An ink-black man in a snow-white tuxedo stood just inside the door, checking each girl in. "Marlene, Ingrid, Greta . . ." He was absurdly tall and thin, with broad shoulders, as if a wire hanger had been left in the jacket he was wearing.

"Sorry, baby," he began, in perfect low Berlin German, barring Rennie's way. "But there ain't no openings at the moment."

"Pepsi," she said, standing in the light. "Pepsi." She put her arms around him and buried her face in his jacket. She had been afraid that here, too, no one would know her. That Pepsi and Lillie would be gone.

He shut the door after her and pulled her through the door that led to a narrow flight of wainscoted steps. "Oh, baby," he said in his gravelly voice, shutting the door after her, holding her to him. "Oh, baby, you certainly are a sight for sore eyes. The Little Princess Who Couldn't Laugh. Well, baby, there ain't much to laugh about now. C'mon. I'd better take you on upstairs and get back to the Goose

Girls." He hugged her again and then moved quickly up the dark, narrow staircase, carrying her bag.

She told herself she wouldn't cry. She told herself she had to be unemotional. She was to be clearheaded when she saw Lillie. She wanted to know about her father. She wanted to be able to take everything in the first time. The anxiety had come back, triply strong. She fought against the paralysis it usually brought.

But the sight of Lillie Froelich defeated her. Lillie, looking older and odder, smoking an American cigarette in a green jade holder, her geranium red hair going in every direction, her thin, long body encased in a midnight blue gown covered with black jets. Lillie didn't say anything. She opened her kohled eyes very wide so that her pencil line eyebrows nearly disappeared and then opened her arms. Rennie ran into them and found herself crying, allowing herself to be kissed and embraced.

"Oh, *Mutti*," Rennie said, because even though Lillie Froelich wasn't her mother—and didn't look like she could ever be anyone's mother—she had always seemed like one to Rennie. "Oh, *Mutti*," she said again.

"I refuse to cry," Lillie Froelich said in her whiskey voice. "I'll have to redo my makeup. Damn, the kohl is going to get into my eyes and I'll go blind and you'll have me as a burden for life, leading me up and down stairs in sordid sanitariums for the ill-equipped and hopelessly penurious. *Gott im Himmel*, I am going to cry. Well, I might as well have a good one." She rested the cigarette holder on an ashtray in the shape of a human skull and let the tears flow. "*Schatzi*," she said, keeping Rennie's hand, holding it to her rouged cheek, "you're the only human being of the female gender I have ever totally loved. Now come into the bedroom while I fix the damage and we'll talk. *Lieber Gott*, we've got what to talk about."

* * *

"You mustn't be seen here, you know," Lillie said later, as she sat in her bedroom in front of the taffeta-skirted makeup table, applying kohl to her eyelids, reaffirming the half-circle eyebrow lines over her huge, sad eyes. "I don't know what I'm going to do with you, but I'll have to think of something. Or Pepsi will. Turns out he's good at this sort of thing. And me, well, half the time I'm hopeless and the other I'm sheer genius."

She finished her makeup, looked at her watch, and faced Rennie in the mirror. "He's upstairs. In a few minutes you can go to him, when everyone is busy with the cabaret. There's a door in the closet. Oh, it's *très, très* Grand Guignol, but then again so are the Nazis. I know, darling, I always talk too much when I'm nervous, and I'm about as nervous as I've ever been right now. We thought you were as safe as a virgin in a convent, in London, and suddenly here you are not so safe in Berlin."

"I shouldn't have come," Rennie said, placing her hands on Lillie's shoulders. "I'm an idiot."

"Yes," Lillie said, holding those hands for a moment. "But I'm happy as a clam you're here, even though you are going to be a problem." She looked at her watch again. "Just a few more minutes, until those bloody Goose Girls go on."

"Tell me how Father got here."

"When they were rounding up the Polish Jews, Kornwasser —you remember that doctor-poet, Kornwasser—well, he's very big in the party now and he was still treating your father for his heart—even though it's illegal to treat Jews for anything—and anyway, he managed to get word to Nick that he was going to be arrested.

"Naturally Nick came here, and not a moment too soon. Yes, the Gestapo searched the house, but not as carefully as they might have because they assumed that he had already left Berlin." She looked at her watch again. She stood up, went to the bedroom door, opened it, and listened. From far below she could hear the sounds of the Goose Girls singing.

"Go through the door in the closet, which leads to a perfectly ordinary attic filled with remnants from my glorious past. At the far end of the attic there's an armoire, and inside is a door leading to the upper attic. He's in the room to the left."

She stood up and put her arms around Rennie. "I've got to go see my Goose Girls and say hello to those members of Hitler's inner circle who chose to grace my club tonight and then I'll come up and we'll have to decide what's to be done with you."

"Are you very angry with me, *Mutti*?"

"*Lieber Gott*, yes. But still, I'm glad you're here. Nick will be, too. He's ill and he's claustrophobic—who wouldn't be in that attic—and there's no chance of getting him out until this Polish business dies down, and even then who knows? We've got to wait until the passport forgers are back in business. But Nick will be happy to see you, you'll see. He'll be furious, but he'll be happy."

3

She had difficulty in finding the secret door in Lillie's closet. Ordinarily it was exactly the sort of thing she would have enjoyed—secret passages—but she was too anxious.

Finally, hidden behind a rack of Lillie's collection of bugle-beaded gowns, she found it. It led to a stairway that led to an ordinary attic, situated in the lower half of the building's cupola. A narrow window looked down on the Kleiststrasse. As she passed it, she looked down. A Wehrmacht staff officer's car—a Mercedes Compressor—had pulled up to the Kleist Kasino's red door and several officers were entering the club.

She shivered, telling herself they were coming for entertainment—not to arrest her—and made her way in the dark across what seemed like an acre of furniture Lillie had discarded over the years. She found the old armoire easily enough and the door which led up to the secret attic.

At the top of the stairs was a long hall, which connected two rooms. Her father's door was open. He was reading, as usual so involved in his book that he hadn't heard her. Rennie watched him for a moment. He was wearing a gray cashmere sweater with oversized brown wooden buttons, gray flannel trousers, suede lace-ups from London.

There was a davenport, an old Chinese rug, a green-glass-shaded lamp. Nick was reclining on a bamboo chaise longue, holding his book up to the light from the lamp. He seemed as nonchalant, as comfortable, as if he were spending a quiet evening at his house—well, his former house—in the Lentze-allee.

He put the book down and was reaching for his cup of mud-black coffee when he saw her. He stood up, not without some difficulty. "One gets stiff," he said, "sitting in one position too long."

He met her halfway across the room and held her to him. She buried her face in the soft material of his sweater. She smelled the reminiscent, comforting scent of the Russian cologne he wore. She missed the smell of his cigarettes. As they held one another, as the tears formed in her silver blue eyes, the irrelevant thought that he probably couldn't smoke in the attic occurred to her. Someone might see the smoke or smell it. He was careless when he smoked and read. A fire would be calamitous. . . . She closed her eyes and erased all thoughts, allowing herself to cry, to stop thinking, to feel safe.

She didn't know how long he held her, but eventually she became aware of a noise in the outer corridor, as if someone were pacing in shoeless feet.

Nick Jablonski disengaged himself from his daughter, smiling down at her. His eyes were bluer than hers, and for the first time she could remember there were tears in them. "Excuse me, *Schatzi.* I must shut the door." He did so, coming back to her, unashamedly wiping away the tears with an oversized silk handkerchief.

"There are other guests in Lillie's *faux* attic hotel," he said. "She's become a heroine in her late middle age. She entertains the Reich's soldiers below while she hides the Reich's enemies above."

"*Vater* . . ." Rennie began.

"Now don't *Vater* me. When you start with the *Vater*s it means you want to get around me, and you won't get around me this time." He took her hand and pulled her next to him onto the chaise longue. He looked at her and smiled. His dimples were still there and his blond white hair was as thick as ever. But for the first time in his life,

for the first time Rennie could remember, he was beginning
to look his age.

"What are you doing here?" he asked.

"I had to find out what was happening to you."

"Lillie's letter didn't reach you? That's not a good sign
for Lillie. If they're intercepting her mail . . ."

"I've come to take you out of Germany," Rennie said,
pursuing her own thoughts, realizing how absurd it was as
she said it.

He laughed, but his eyes were serious. "You can't get me
out of Germany just yet, *Schatzi*. The Gestapo have tight-
ened things up a bit in the past few weeks, raiding half a
dozen passport forgery shops. And besides, they're especially interested in me. It seems as if I'm high on their list."

"How do you know?"

"Kornwasser. You remember him. Thin hair, thick eyebrows, doglike devotion, when it suited him. He used to sit
at our table at the Romanische and pretend he was a poet
when we all knew he was a Kurfürstendamm doctor, helping fat ladies slim. Now he's an important man. Frau Goebbels goes to him. Or he goes to her. I don't suppose it makes
much difference.

"At any rate, Kornwasser keeps me informed as to my
status. Little Dr. Goebbels is intent on finding me. He's
afraid if I leave Germany I'll become a rallying figure for
the oppressed." He laughed and ran his hand through his
hair. "As if the oppressed wanted a rallying figure. The
oppressed are too busy trying to save their skins, trying to
eat, to rally."

He pulled her to him and put an arm around her. "We
mustn't worry. In a week or so the passport forgers will be
back in business. I'll grow a beard, dye my hair, and wear
smoked glasses. You'll cut your hair, wear pince-nez and
a banker's pinstripes, and pose as my son." He looked at her
and touched her hair. "I can't think," he said, becoming

serious, "why they didn't pick you up at the border. They know enough to realize that if they have you, they also have me."

"I was clever and plucky."

He pretended to put a telephone to his ear, playing a game with her that he had when she was a child, fascinated by the magic of telephones. "Good morning, Clever and Plucky."

She laughed, but even as she did so, she finally and fully realized how serious her mistake was. Now he had her to worry about.

"I'm sorry, *Vati*."

"I am, too, Rennie. I should have left long ago. If you've been foolish returning, think of how foolish I've been in never leaving. I was too amused by *der schöne Adolf* and his friends. But they're not comic, it turns out. They're like children. I forgot how serious children are about themselves. I forgot how dangerous children can be." He closed his eyes.

He was tired. And ill. "Your health?" she asked in a whisper.

"Not so bad. Lillie tries, but this isn't a spa. I'm supposed to exercise, so I share the corridor with Lillie's other guests, a Jewish family from Czechoslovakia." He saw the concern in her eyes. "*Schatzi*, I have always had, as the Americans say, a bum ticker. It needs a moderate amount of looking after. But I think it's safe to say that I shan't die of a heart attack."

He kissed her and held her away for a moment so he could study her. "You shouldn't be here, *Schatzi*. I should be wringing my hands, worrying about what to do with you. I should be furious. And yet I've never been happier to see you. I love you, Rennie, in a way I've never loved anyone else. I fell in love when you were born, and my love has grown over the years. I know why parents sacrifice themselves for their children. I'd do anything to protect you. But I feel so helpless. I feel as if . . ."

"Stop, *Vati*. Don't say any more." She put her fingers on his lips. "Please."

"Why not?"

"You're making me cry so dreadfully."

She moved away, feeling like a child who had blurted out some terrible family secret at a dinner party. She felt she should be reprimanded, punished. She felt contaminated, guilty, criminal. For if he had been in a difficult position before she came, now he was in an impossible one. He not only had to worry about getting himself away, he was responsible for her, too.

She wished he would shout at her, strike her. Instead, he came to her and put his arms around her once more, holding her to him. "I love you so much, *Schatzi*," he said.

"I love you, too, *Vati*."

When Lillie came up to the false attic, Rennie, exhausted, was sleeping on the davenport. Nick was on the bamboo chaise, watching her.

"How was the cabaret tonight?" he whispered, allowing Lillie to kiss him, cautioning her not to awaken Rennie.

"Dreadful," she whispered back. "The SA was out in full force, along with a rather nasty specimen of the Gestapo."

"High up?"

"I would say yes, but I can't be certain. He wears a leather trench coat and what I would guess is a newly acquired monocle. He's too solidly working class to have come by it naturally. He stood at the end of the bar all night, nursing a dark beer, looking as if he were waiting. It wasn't reassuring. My voice went in the middle of my song. I thought the SA were going to throw tomatoes, but I brought the Goose Girls on and that seemed to quiet them."

She sat gingerly on the edge of the davenport, resting her hand on Rennie's, looking down at the sleeping girl.

"What the hell are we going to do with her?" Nick Jablonski whispered, standing up, walking up and down the narrow room. "We'll go insane if we both have to live in this room. It's hard enough on Pepsi, bringing up the food, carrying down the wastes, but with another person . . ."

"She's not going to have to stay here."

"You have another hiding place? Is it safe? Shall I be able to see her? It's important that I be able to see her."

"Yes, Nick, to all three questions." She put her hand to her frizzed geranium-red hair and smiled at him. "I'm retiring from the performing arts. The Kleist Kasino needs a new cabaret. We need to draw new clientele. I thought of it tonight when I lost my voice: at the end of the week I'm going to introduce a new chanteuse. Fräulein Rennie . . . Nacht."

"But she doesn't sing."

"Yes, she does. She's been imitating me since she was four. She'll do my song. She'll talk it through, exactly the way I do. Only they'll like her better because she is, after all, just a little younger than me and perhaps a touch more attractive." She looked at Rennie. "*Mein Gott*, she's a beauty even when she sleeps."

"And when they ask for her papers?"

"What cabaret singer is ever asked for papers?"

"And when they ask where she's suddenly sprung from?"

Lillie stood up, put her hand on her nearly nonexistent hip, the black bugle beads on her dress swaying. "Vienna, where else? Now that it's one more provincial German city, now that the *Anschluss* with Austria is a fact, it's perfectly obvious that a girl with her looks would come to the capital to seek her fortune."

"And where is this new singing star going to live?"

"With me. She's a distant niece."

"It's too dangerous, Lillie."

"The best hiding places are the most obvious."

He shrugged and gave up the argument. He was giving up too many arguments, lately, Lillie thought. "I wish to God," he said, looking at his sleeping daughter, "that she had stayed in London. I don't want her to die, Lillie. I don't want them to get her. Can you imagine, Lillie, if they got her?"

She crossed the room and put her arms around him. "It won't do you any good to think such thoughts. Think, as my mother used to say, lovely thoughts."

"Lovely thoughts?" he repeated, taking her hand, kissing it. "Yes. I shall think lovely thoughts." He looked again at his daughter. "One lovely thought: I have to admit it is wonderful to see her again. Isn't it, Lillie?" There were tears in his remarkably blue-gray eyes and they began to spill over.

Often during that first hectic week in Berlin, Butch Jarman found himself wondering what had happened to the girl on the train.

Von Danzig hardly left him a spare moment for idle fantasies, however. Even before he was checked into the Adlon, he had met Dr. Goebbels at his Propaganda Ministry in a book-lined room overlooking the Wilhelmstrasse. The room —the carefully posed and placed photograph of his wife and children—seemed to Butch to have come from a movie set. There was something comical about Goebbels, but sinister at the same time. As if Eddie Cantor had accepted a role in a Peter Lorre film.

During those first few days he had long and exhausting appointments with Otto Dietrich, the garrulous chief of the *Reichspresse;* with Herr Direktor Schmidt of the *Grossdeutsche Rundfunk,* Germany's radio system; with any number of bureaucrats and autocrats who had any connection with the business of disseminating news from Germany.

In addition, he presented his papers to the American ambassador and paid visits to a number of diplomats, bankers, businessmen, and those journalists still in good odor with the Nazis. And always he was accompanied by the imperturbable von Danzig.

By the end of the week he felt suffocated by National Socialist dogma, by the constant and vociferous party line he was fed at every opportunity. He was beginning to hate the sight of Hitler's photograph, displayed on everything from tooth mugs to the Gloria Palast Cinema lobby walls.

By the end of the week he had a chance to see Bones Marrow, to have a drink with that refreshingly irreverent BBC correspondent, with whom he had worked in Spain.

It was Bones's last day but one in Germany. He was being "booted out," thanks to his irreverence. "Going back to gay Paree," he said, joining Butch in the red-leather-upholstered Adlon Grill. "Situation here's tighter than a nun's twat." He ordered a double whiskey and stroked the red Hitlerian moustache that he claimed to have had before der Führer. He had been to Eton and Balliol at Oxford and spoke with the intent to shock. "Goebbels says *Gesundheit* and Dietrich and Schmidt sneeze. Even if you decide Adolf Hitler is the nuts, the best invention since Buck Rogers, you're going to be subject to the censors.

"At Radio House, *mein Herr*ing, there's no such animal as spontaneous news. You have to submit a written script twenty-four hours before your broadcast. During the broadcast a Ministry of Prop man will be standing next to you in the control booth, a copy of your script in one hand, your pudd in the other. One unauthorized word, the broadcast's canceled and you're next season's soprano at Bayreuth." Bones Marrow ordered another double whiskey. "You'd better call Pater, old boy, and have him transfer you to Paris."

Butch said he thought he'd stick around for a while. "A woman, no doubt," Bones Marrow concluded. "French girlies are better than German girlies in almost every way."

Butch asked him about von Danzig. "As little influence as a Jewish hairdresser. His pater and Göring were pals.

"Officially he works for both von Ribbentrop and Goebbels—everyone in Berlin has two masters—but Hitler loves him because he looks the way they're all supposed to look and don't."

After saying good-bye to Bones Marrow, Butch went up to his room on the Adlon's fourth floor, decided not to open a cable from his father—they came on the average of two a

day—and took a long shower. The telephone was ringing
when he came out. He had a split-second fantasy that it was
the girl from the train. It was von Danzig. There was a new
singer at an East End cabaret and he wondered if Butch
was interested in seeing her. "The Kleist Kasino," von Danzig said.

"Lillie Froelich's Kleist Kasino," Butch amended.

"You know it?"

"My father adored Lillie. He used to take me nearly
every night when we would come to Berlin in the twenties."

"Neither she nor the Kasino are what they once were."

"No one is."

She had practiced all week and tonight, as Pepsi said,
was the night. "I'm so nervous," she told him as he led her
down to the dressing room.

"Baby, there would be something terribly wrong if you
weren't."

He introduced her to the three discarded-looking men
who were the band and to the plump blond girl, Marlene,
who was the captain of the Goose Girls.

"Classy," Marlene said, looking Rennie over.

Tante Lizbeth was sitting in the corner of the narrow
space called the dressing room, knitting. An obscure relative
of Nick's, she had been either acquired or discovered when
Rennie's mother died and Nick needed someone to take care
of the house, of Rennie. She had looked the same ever since
Rennie could remember: short, thin, with patchy white hair
and black dresses that reached to her ankles.

Though she understood German, Tante Lizbeth spoke in
Yiddish. "So I'm a *yiddler*," she liked to say. "You don't
like my *yiddling*, you know what you can do with it." She
heartily and vocally disapproved of Rennie's irreligious
bringing up.

Though somehow she had gotten herself, years before, a
German passport, she had come with Nick when he had

gone into hiding. Lillie had put her in the back bedroom
and closed her ears to her complaints, explaining her away
as the new housekeeper.

"You're making her look like a *kurve*," that woman said
to Pepsi, who had taken off his white tuxedo jacket and was
delicately applying silver eye shadow to Rennie's face, drawing silver half-moons over her eyes.

"Tante Lizbeth," Pepsi said, brushing silver lipstick on
Rennie's lips. "If you're going to stay here, baby, you have
to button up."

"Button up," she said to herself, applying herself to her
knitting. "So I'll button up." She both respected Pepsi and
was in awe of him. He was the first *shvartzer* she had ever
seen.

Pepsi stood back to examine his handiwork. "Stand up,"
he said to Rennie. "Be still for a moment." He pulled her
hair up over her head and put the silver lamé turban over
it.

"Now he's hiding her hair," Tante Lizbeth said, but to
herself. "Her hair is her crowning glory."

He took off the sheet she had worn to protect her gown.
It was silver lamé, cut low to reveal her slender breasts.
"Honey," Pepsi said, holding his breath for a moment, "you
could give all those Hollywood gals a run for their money
any day of the week."

"She looks, if you ask me, like a *kurve*," Tante Lizbeth
felt compelled to say. "A regular prostitute."

"She's supposed to look like a prostitute," Pepsi told her.
"A divine fallen angel, baby."

Lillie came in, wearing a black sequined gown with a cap
to match, long white gloves that buttoned all the way up her
thin arms. "*Lieber Gott, Schatzi*, that dress should have
looked so good on me." She made Rennie turn around. "You
look marvelous."

"Are there many people outside?" Rennie asked.

"A full house. Word has spread that a new singer is open-

ing, and Berlin is starved for new singers. Come and see."
She took Rennie's hand and led her out onto the dark, small
stage. The curtain was closed, separating them from the
audience.

Rennie put her eye to a small hole in the curtain, looking
at the crowded room. She stepped back. "I'm not going to
be able to go through with this, Lillie. You're going to have
to sing. I can't do it, I'm telling you right now. I'm not a
singer. I don't know what to do with my hands. I can't do
it, Lillie."

Lillie laughed. "You don't have to sing. Not the way you
look. And Pepsi taught you exactly what to do with your
hands. You're going to be wonderful, *Schatzi*. You'll see."

"What's Papa doing?"

"Eating his supper and reading Thomas Mann. He's
longing to see you perform, but there's no safe way he can."

Rennie took her eye from the curtain. "Is he going to be
all right, Lillie? He's so pale."

"He's going to be fine, *Schatzi*. It would be peculiar if he
wasn't pale, cooped up in that attic for weeks. . . . *Gott im
Himmel*," she said, as she put her own eye to the hole in
the curtain. "He's here again. Look. At the end of the bar
in the leather trench coat."

Rennie looked through the peephole and saw the man
who had stood in the shadows at the border. At least she
thought it was he. He held a dark beer in one small hand.
The other was in the pocket of his brown leather trench
coat. He had a round, gray face. Something glassy was catching the reflections of the overhead lights. It was his monocle,
and it made her feel as if he could see her; it made her feel
dirty and used.

"Tell the band to stop playing," Lillie said to Pepsi, at
the same time hugging Rennie, distracting her. "You're
going to be all right. More than all right. You're going to
be Berlin's newest sensation, *Schatzi*. You'll see."

"But I don't want to be Berlin's newest sensation, *Mutti*."

Lillie kissed her. "It's the best hiding place you could find, *Schatzi*," she whispered. She patted her own frizzed red hair. "Now I'm going out to talk to the customers. I'd give my eyeteeth to know why that one is here night after night." She left Rennie alone on the dark stage.

Rennie looked through the peephole once more. The man at the bar was still there. She felt as if he knew she was behind the curtain, as if he could see through it with his monocle . . . through her makeup, through her disguise.

She forced herself not to look at him but to look at the room. She had known it as well as she had the house in the Lentzeallee. She had first come to Lillie's Kleist Kasino as a child, proud to be on her father's arm, proud that he was her escort.

The great artists of the world had had to stop in at the Kleist Kasino when they were in Berlin. Rennie remembered seeing one of the world's great actresses standing at the bar wearing a mouton coat—dyed the worst shade of green, a sort of aspic—with her arm around the shoulder of a tiny Russian countess who never went anywhere except in white tie and tails.

She also remembered how, as a child, she had got up on a barstool one Sunday morning and begun to sing Lillie's song to all those who habitually ended their Saturday nights on Sunday mornings at Lillie's.

At first they had laughed, but Lillie and her father remained serious, encouraging her to finish, applauding her when she did.

Now she was going to have to sing Lillie's song again, but she was grown up. And her life depended upon how convincingly she sang.

She didn't want to think about that, so she looked through the peephole again, avoiding the bar, looking at the room itself. It hadn't changed much since she had been away. It was dark and low and filled with round tables and, for the most part, uniformed men. The walls, painted a bright red, seemed nearly black in the dim light. The three elderly men who comprised the band, dressed in white bolero shirts and ill-fitting black trousers, were playing American rumba music in the pit just below the stage. Boys in woolen sweaters and knickers brought drinks and sold single cigarettes—*"Zigaretten, Zigaretten"*—the smoke from which lay above the room like a second, blue ceiling.

There was still, she saw, a definite social order to the method with which Pepsi seated Kleist Kasino patrons. Working-class toughs in gray Wehrmacht uniforms and their thin girls, with dark hair and tight dresses, sat farthest away from the stage, close to the bar.

Older, harder men in brown SA uniforms, most without women, came next. The tables closest to the stage were for boyish Luftwaffe officers. They were fair, with blue eyes, bony, high Germanic faces, dressed in the startling blue uniforms Göring had personally designed for them. One of them was almost too beautiful, with transparent skin and a sulky, drunken manner. He bought a cigarette and lit it carefully as the lights dimmed, and the three-man band abruptly stopped playing.

"You'd better get it off the stage, kid," Marlene said, not unkindly, as the Goose Girls came onstage. "La Froelich's about to introduce us." She looked at Rennie and shook her head. "If I only had what you have, kid."

Rennie took a final glance through the peephole and saw Butch Jarman and his SS officer friend being greeted by Lillie. She was shocked at first. Had Butch Jarman told his SS friend about the border incident and had he come to arrest her? That didn't appear likely. He was, it seemed, on good terms with Lillie. They talked as if they knew one another quite well. Under her fear, Rennie realized, was curiosity. The SS officer, she decided, was too handsome by half, as they said in England. He was kissing Lillie's hand when the stage lights began to come up. Rennie left the curtain reluctantly, returning to the dressing room. Tante

Lizbeth sat there knitting what looked like the same gray piece of work she had been laboring over ever since Rennie could remember.

"I *can't* sing," Rennie said to her image in the mirror.

"If you sing loud enough, *tatela,* no one will ever know," Tante Lizbeth said, without looking up.

"*Meine Damen und Herren,*" Lillie—standing in a blue spotlight in front of the curtain—was saying in her whiskey voice. "Lillie Froelich's Kleist Kasino is proud to present the Bremen Goose Girls in a program of their own composition. Without further ado, I give you the celebrated, the renowned, the invincible Bremen Goose Girls."

The worn black curtain parted to reveal half a dozen youngish women dressed as Bavarian peasants. They had thick blond braids, dirndls, blouses with wide, deep, square décolletages. The band accompanied them as they performed a parody of a folk dance, making suggestive gestures as they twirled one another around, their round blue eyes wide with saucy pertness. At the end of each verse they turned their backs to the audience, lifted their skirts to reveal ample and bare rear ends while the audience shouted out the final line of their song with them: "Götz von Berlichingen," a German schoolchild's euphemism for "kiss my ass."

"Charming," Lillie said, as she and Rennie watched from the wings. "Is it not charming, this return to tradition? This National Socialist approved art form? It's so charming it makes me want to vomit. Still, one has to please the customers, those discerning arbiters of Third Reich esthetics." She put her long thin arm around Rennie, and hugged her. "You're on now, *Schatzi.* I know you're nervous. It would be odd if you weren't. But use that nervousness. Put it into your song."

Rennie didn't hear the words Lillie used to introduce her. She was just aware that the three-man band had retreated to the small nickel-plated table in the wings to play skat, drink schnapps, eat pretzels. Pepsi had maneuvered Lillie's old white baby grand onto the stage and had begun to play the opening bars to Lillie's song as the curtain opened.

But Rennie realized in those few seconds before she stepped out onto the stage that it was no longer Lillie's song. It was her song and she was not the charming little girl who had stood on the bar, singing to a crowd of indulgent adults. No, she was quite suddenly and finally responsible for the song, for herself. The audience was going to judge her as a woman; and so, now, was the world. She felt both fear and the awful pain of responsibility as she moved out onto the stage.

The room became quiet as she forced herself to step into the circle of blue light waiting for her. For a long moment she was paralyzed, and then, taking a breath, she turned deliberately and struck a pose, her hand on her hip, her face in profile. Suddenly the fear was gone, because she sensed that she had everyone's complete attention.

With infinite nonchalance, she put her hand to her head and removed the silver turban, allowing her hair to fall down around her head, like a piece of shimmering cloth. Her hair was both blond and silver in the blue light, with a life all its own. There was an audible, collective sigh from the audience.

While Pepsi continued to play the sad, minor-key introduction, she took the short, stubby cigarette, with its brown-paper wrapper, that she had carried in her hand, put it to her silvered lips, and lit it, carelessly throwing the match on the floor. Inhaling deeply, she let the smoke escape slowly through her nose.

The pure, youthful line of her profile, contrasted with the gnarled stump of a cigarette, illuminated by the blue spotlight, created a perfect image of an old Berlin preoccupation: spoiled youth; corrupted innocence.

Quite suddenly, she turned and faced the room, walking

to the front of the stage. Her head was held back; both hands were on her hips; the cigarette was clenched between her teeth. It was a Friedrichstrasse prostitute's pose: feet firmly planted in stiletto-thin silver-heeled sandals, her body thrust forward. After a moment she removed the cigarette, knelt down, put it out carefully on the stage floor, and then stowed the stub in the top of her stocking, for later. She stood up and once more faced the fascinated audience.

And then she began to sing. She talked rather than sang, in a husky voice. She sang to no one. She gave the impression that she had already counted the house, that she had appraised every man in the audience and found them all wanting. She was singing, her gestures made clear, not for them but for herself.

> I am the Silver Rose of Berlin.
> A flower a trifle past first bloom.
> I meet a man,
> We make a deal.
> I take him to the bed
> In my cellar room.

> I am the Silver Rose of Berlin.
> And once I had a golden flame.
> But he lasted just three nights.
> You see
> He didn't like neon lights.
> And anyway,
> He found himself another, less tarnished dame.

> I am the Silver Rose of Berlin.
> A little dangerous,
> A little rash.
> Oh, come, take the chance.
> I'll sell you love but I promise: no romance.
> All it costs is a bit of cash.

I am the Silver Rose of Berlin.
Someday I'll take a stroll
Into the Tiergarten, where it's dark.
I'll use a pistol (don't worry,
I shan't miss my mark).
And that will be the finale for
The Silver Rose of Berlin.

As the song ended, the audience was perfectly still for a moment, and then they began to cheer, standing, shouting "bravo." She waited until they quieted down and then, taking a painted silver basket filled with paper roses dyed blue and silver—the sort sold in the little shops in Wittenbergplatz—she made her way down the stage steps. She moved with a combination of grace and insolence, swinging the basket, pouting her lips a little, staring at the soldiers seated at the front tables.

"Now who will buy my roses?" she asked, as Pepsi reprised the song. "Five marks? Ten marks? Fifty marks. It all goes to a very good cause, I can assure you."

It was too much for the pretty Luftwaffe pilot. He stood up and pulled Rennie to him. "I don't want the roses," he said, trying to kiss her. "I want you." He waved a fistful of marks with his free hand as he attempted to pull her to him. "And it's your patriotic duty to give yourself to me. Our leader says so."

Before anyone else moved, the gray-faced man in the leather trench coat was at the pilot's side, removing Rennie from his arms. "What in the hell do you think you're doing?" the boy asked, but the leather-coated man placed his small hands on the boy's epauletted shoulders and, with effortless strength, pushed him down into his seat.

"Take a rose, my young friend." He took the boy's money and placed it in the basket as he removed a rose and threw it on the table. The young Luftwaffe pilot didn't protest.

His comrades were silent. The man in the leather trench coat had a strength that wasn't only in his hands.

Rennie picked up the basket and disappeared through the leather curtain at the rear of the bar. It had been put up to protect the dressing rooms from drafts and didn't. But it provided a useful exit so she didn't have to work her way back through the crowded room to the stage.

At the same time, Pepsi hustled the forlorn trio back into the pit, where they began to play their Hawaiian song, the ukulele player singing in a reedy baritone, *"Grüss' mir mein Hawaii, ich bleib' . . . dir treu . . ."*

The Luftwaffe pilots left quietly. Lillie, who had been sitting with von Danzig and Butch Jarman, glanced at the bar. The hero in the leather trench coat was no longer there. "I can't bear this," Lillie said, looking at the trio with distaste. "Give me a moment and come upstairs. You can have schnapps in your coffee and we'll talk of better times."

"The future, *gnädige Frau?*" von Danzig asked, standing.

"The next thousand years, *mein Generälchen,*" she said, giving him her gloved hand to kiss.

A few moments later Pepsi came to their table to tell them that Fräulein Froelich would be detained longer than she had supposed. A surprise visitor. The gentlemen could either wait or take a rain check. The gentlemen said they would wait. Both men were interested in getting another glimpse of the Silver Rose of Berlin.

5

Rennie sat at the taffeta-skirted dressing table in Lillie's bedroom, removing her makeup. She felt tired and not a little relieved. She had liked the applause, but the incident with the drunken pilot had unnerved her. All she wanted to do was go up to her father, but that wasn't going to be possible, Pepsi had warned her. Not until the Kleist Kasino closed for the night, not until everyone—the band, the waiters, the Goose Girls—went home.

They had already fallen into a routine. Early each morning she would go to him. They would play rummy—a game they had learned in America together—and talk about the past.

"I remember when I first arrived in Berlin," he had told her. "The Kaiser's only daughter was being married. They decked the facade of the Adlon with flags and scented the air with violets. The most beautiful women danced with handsome Guards officers to the strains of *Der Freischütz*. It was the first time I saw your mother, and then I had eyes for no one else."

He didn't complain about his prison. "I have my books. Pepsi brings *Currywurst*, albeit slightly cold, and beer, slightly warm. Lillie looks after me with nearly more solicitude than I can deal with. And you are here. What more could a man in my position want?"

She knew of the family living in the other room in the attic. A mother, a father, and a boy. But she never saw them. And her father wouldn't speak of them. "The less you know, *Schatzi*, the better. That's not usually the case, of course, but in this instance, it is."

He was so pale and thin. The gray cashmere sweater with the wooden buttons was far too large. He never reproached Rennie for coming to Berlin. He took it all in good spirit, as he did most everything else. "It will soon be over," he reassured her. "Kornwasser will get us papers, passports. He promised. The moment things quiet down."

She removed the silver lipstick as Lillie came into the room. "You'd better hurry," Lillie said. "Did that. brute hurt you?"

"Who?"

"The Luftwaffe lout."

"No, not at all."

"Good. Listen. I want you to change your clothes. Sincere and simple is the theme, *Schatzi*." Lillie went to her closet, riffled through her gowns, and pulled out, after a moment, a white satin dressing gown with a collar like a Russian commissar's. "We have a visitor."

"Who?" Rennie asked, trying for a nonchalance she didn't feel.

"I don't know exactly. My guess is he's middle-level Gestapo. It doesn't matter. He obviously has the power to do us in, whatever level he's on. But you mustn't worry. If he were here for your father, we'd have long since been stripped and searched and the house ransacked. I don't know why he's here, but I want you to be ready, in case he does decide to search.

"You're my niece from Vienna, remember. A hardworking girl who's dog tired and not overly impressed by her first-night success." She laughed. "Who would have ever thought you'd do so well?"

"What if he asks for my papers?" Rennie asked, her heart beating too fast and too loud.

"He won't." She put her lips to Rennie's cheek and went

to the door. Rennie had stepped out of the silver gown. There were red marks on her arm where the Luftwaffe pilot had grabbed her.

"You're certain that little monster didn't hurt you?"

"Not so I noticed."

"Lieber Gott," Lillie said, giving Rennie one more kiss, leaving the room. *"Lieber Gott,"* she said to no one in particular, locking Tante Lizbeth's door.

Tante Lizbeth had survived pogroms and persecutions all her life. Little could frighten her. Certainly not the Gestapo. She had her faith, her "mother and father's religion," as she called it. And she was fiercely protective of Rennie. Lillie knew she was quite capable of storming into the drawing room and telling the Gestapo man to "stuff it." Tante Lizbeth rarely thought of consequences except when they had to do with her carefully kept traditions, her faith. Lillie thought she was quite capable of almost anything except breaking Judaic law.

Pocketing the key, Lillie walked back along the corridor, praying, according to the tenets of her own ill-defined faith, for Nick and for Rennie. Most of all for Rennie, because she sensed what her visitor was after. She stopped, took a breath, and stepped through the black beaded curtain.

"I am Kimmel," he said. He didn't stand up. He sat in a morris chair with his feet firmly planted on the Oriental carpet, his legs wide apart, his leather trench coat flowing around him.

He seemed perfectly at home in Lillie's drawing room, unaffected by its peculiar decoration. French sofas commemorating Napoleon's return from Egypt vied for space with tubular Bauhaus tables, Russian icons, and above the chair in which he was sitting, an ornately framed life-size portrait of Lillie as a young woman. In it she wore a gown the same color as her hair and there was a secret smile on her face.

"And I am Fräulein Froelich," she said, and though she hadn't intended to, she sat down, across from him. He stared at her for a moment and then concentrated on extracting from his trench coat pocket a tin of colored candies. They were *Lutschbonbons,* hard candies, with swastikas imprinted in their glycerin coating.

He placed one carefully in his mouth and with equal care replaced the tin in his coat pocket. He looked a little to the left of Lillie while he moved the candy about his mouth. He kept his small, square feet firmly planted on the carpet; his small, yellow, immaculate hands on his knees. The heavy leather trench coat, unbelted, fit him like a bathrobe. Under it he wore a dark, cheap suit, the sort government workers wore on holidays.

Just from the three words he had said—"I am Kimmel" —Lillie knew he had been born and reared in one of Berlin's working-class neighborhoods. Wedding or, more likely, Neukölln. He had that yellow-gray potato-faced poor fat look about him. Though all of his features were undistinguished, round, without angles of any sort, he gave no impression of being soft. On the contrary.

"Sorry to have kept you waiting, Herr Kimmel, but I had to put off other visitors." He still didn't say anything and didn't look as if he were going to, so she went on. "General von Danzig and an American radio correspondent."

He smiled, slowly. He had thin, damp lips, and suddenly Lillie was terrified. He was so very much in control. In charge. He could do virtually anything he wanted. With her; with her cabaret; with Rennie and Lizbeth and Nick and that sad family in the attic. There were no laws to stop him; the laws protected him. General von Danzig's name only made him smile. That terrible smile.

Who exactly was he? He had begun coming to the Kleist Kasino the night Nick had so suddenly appeared. She had hoped that he had decided, coincidentally, to make the Kleist Kasino his *Lokal,* that he was interested in Marlene or one of the other Goose Girls. If it were anything more serious, if he knew Nick was hiding in the cupola, he would have acted before this, Lillie decided. And he wouldn't have gone about arresting them all in this absurd, paying-a-cordial-visit manner.

For he had brought flowers. Genuine but artificial-looking red roses. Pepsi had crammed them into a narrow vase so they already seemed dead. He had also brought chocolates. Kranzler chocolates in a gold and silver foil box.

"How kind," Lillie said, glancing at them.

His small, square feet were shod in brown leather military-looking shoes. He was, she thought, like a *Hausmeister* seeing to a large middle-class building on one of the wide streets in Charlottenberg. She wished he would take off his coat. She wished he didn't look quite so antiseptic. So clean. As if he had no odor.

She wished he would get on with it.

"Perhaps, Herr Kimmel, if you could tell me why you wished to see me?" she began and then let the words drop off. He was going to tell her in his own good time.

He scrutinized her as if she were a laboratory sample, as if she were another form of life. He gave her his thin, un-joyous smile as he moved the *Lutschbonbon* from one side of his mouth to the other.

He wore his eyeglass in his right eye. It was the one false note, the one memorable characteristic about him. The glass was both rimless and ribbonless. It looked as if it had been snatched from a recalcitrant aristocrat during a cellar inter-rogation. It was as if Kimmel had had it attached to his face by surgical means.

Lillie stood up, crossed the room, inserted a cigarette into her jade holder, and lit it. "Cigarette?" she asked.

He shook his head, waiting for her to return to her seat. She did so quickly. Her knees were weak. She had weak knees, she knew, only when she felt overwhelmingly sexual toward a man—or when she feared him.

Nick had said it was the same thing, but she hadn't wanted to accept that. Certainly she feared Kimmel. It's the *goyim* who don't smell you have to watch out for, Lizbeth had warned her. The ones who don't have titles or uniforms or chauffeured drivers. They're the real enemy.

He enjoyed taking his time. It was clear he enjoyed her discomfiture. He folded his small yellow hands and rested them on his paunch, reminding Lillie of a butcher on a Sunday outing, visiting his wife's poorer relatives in the country. He was so complacent, so righteous. "I am here to make an offer, Fräulein Froelich," he said in his monotone.

"Not of matrimony," she joked. Her mouth was dry but her words were clear, her voice—she was happy to note—steady.

"No. Not of matrimony, Fräulein Froelich. I am already married. To a good, simple woman. We married when we were quite young." He paused, took the tin of *Lutschbonbons* from his pocket, and hunted around with his forefinger, locating a red one, placing it in his mouth. "She worked in a factory in Neukölln, making china dishes for export. I was only just out of the army, out of a job. I decided to look for work in Munich. Naturally, at that time in Germany, there were no jobs. Except for Jews. But I found what I was looking for in Munich, nonetheless." He moved the *Lutschbonbon* around his mouth, thoughtfully. "After the Putsch, I was put in jail.

"I was in jail for over two years, Fräulein Froelich. My wife never complained. She went to her job every day, and when the factory folded, she went on the streets.

"But in those days every woman in Berlin was on the streets. The foreigners and the Jews with their money had their pick. They didn't want my wife. She was too solid, too square. She would have starved to death had not a Jew dressmaker taken pity on her. He gave her a job. You know what the job was, Fräulein Froelich? It was picking up pins in the back room where his dresses were made. He gave her a little red and yellow magnet, a child's toy, and all day long she went around on all fours, picking up pins for this Jew tailor who gave her a meal for this service.

"And still, my wife never complained. She was waiting for me. I am, admittedly, not much, but I am all she has. So now I don't turn my back on her. I never turn my back on those who help me, Fräulein Froelich."

"Where is the dressmaker today?"

"Old Goldblatt? Who knows? Perhaps in America by this time. Perhaps in a work camp, picking up pins on all fours for the good of the Reich. Or maybe old Goldblatt's dead. Or maybe he wishes he was dead. Forget Goldblatt, Fräulein. To tell you the truth, I don't forget Goldblatt. But you, you should forget him."

He smiled his thin, damp smile and stared at her with his colorless eyes, the glass picking up the candlelight, making him seem blind in one eye. "Most people think I am not a talkative man, you know that? You can tell them different, hey, Fräulein Froelich? I like to talk when given the opportunity, and you, graciously, are doing just that.

"But I will not take up any more of your time, *gnädiges Fräulein*. I feel you are impatient. You have had a long day. An emotional day, perhaps. Seeing old friends. Dealing with your cabaret business. You have other thoughts, other problems. I am in your way, a mere government official calling at an unseemly hour. No. Do not protest. I am, at long last, coming to the point: I should like to offer you my protection, Fräulein Froelich."

"I have no need of your protection," she answered, not knowing what he was getting at.

He looked at her for a long moment. "Since you say not, I won't contradict you, Fräulein Froelich. You know best. However, I shall amend my offer. I should like to offer my protection to your niece. I have completed some investigatory research. Fräulein Nacht is a young woman who most certainly needs protection. Or do you not agree?"

"It isn't up to me . . ." Lillie said, confused. She stood up and turned away from the stubborn glare of his eyeglass. "Of course not, Fräulein Froelich. Your niece is of age. We are living in the new Reich. We should have the young woman, herself, decide. Please. Do not bother yourself. My associate shall call her."

A man in civilian clothes who had evidently been standing in the outer foyer strode directly across the drawing room and through the curtained door as if he knew the flat intimately.

"Yes?" Rennie called out, too loudly, when she heard the strange knock on the bedroom door. "Who is there?"

The man opened the door. He looked like any young man in a gabardine raincoat. He said, politely, that her presence was requested in the drawing room. She didn't ask who requested her presence or for what purpose. He held the door open for her as if this were the most normal procedure in the world. Rennie nearly thanked him as she passed in front of him and walked along the corridor, the white satin Russian-style dressing gown making an inappropriate, luxurious swishing sound. They've very nearly succeeded, she thought, in making fear commonplace, socially acceptable.

She stepped through the black beaded curtain, saw Lillie first and then the man sitting in the morris chair. He seemed, if not like an old friend, certainly like an old acquaintance. She had seen him at the border and again in the cabaret. She was suddenly, overwhelmingly, frightened again.

Instead of looking at him, she stared at Lillie, who came to her, putting her arm around her shoulders. "Herr Kimmel has brought you flowers and chocolates," Lillie said, and Rennie wondered if she were going to laugh, to be hysterical.

"*Danke schön*," she said, in a perfectly natural voice, keeping her eyes on Lillie, attempting to find a clue as to what role she should assume, what attitude she should take.

"I've also brought you an offer, Fräulein Nacht," Kimmel said, dismissing the young man in the garbardine raincoat, smiling, remaining seated, his small, square feet firmly planted on Lillie's blue and white carpet.

"Theatrical?" Rennie asked, wondering for a moment if he might not be a producer, someone who booked cabaret acts.

"Personal. From my point of view, *gnädiges Fräulein*. Possibly political from yours." He placed his hands on the chair's thin arms and pushed himself up to a standing position. He looked into her silver blue eyes, and Rennie felt herself shiver. "I offer you my protection, Fräulein Nacht."

"Protection?" She wanted to turn and run to the bedroom, through the closet door, to her father for protection. She didn't want to have to deal with this inhuman, frightening person whose every word was threatening.

"Yes. It would include a flat at the western end of the Kurfürstendamm in a new building. With a private bath and central heat and a woman to do for you. Also, there would be a small auto with an Aryan license plate number, so essential these days, *nicht wahr*?

"And certainly my protection would cover freedom from the anxiety of anyone inquiring into your past." He coughed and folded his hands, completing the picture of a suburban house agent, detailing the assets of a suspiciously vacant villa. He looked up at her and then away. "You would only have to suffer my company three nights a week."

He turned and stared at her again through his eyeglass, as if he couldn't believe what he saw, as if he were still surprised that he could find one woman so desirable. The monocle shimmered as he spoke, opaque one moment, transparent the next. "You are the loveliest woman I've ever seen," he said, staring at her as if she were naked, whispering as if he would take her then and there.

It was frightening and bizarre, seeing so much passion, so much ardor, in such a plain potato of a man. "Oh, I know what I am," he said, seeing her expression, sensing what she was thinking. "I do not ask for a grand passion. Not from you." He turned away, forcing himself to speak in his usual reasonable monotone. "I simply offer, Fräulein, an arrangement that could be advantageous to us both. Advantageous to those about you as well, I might add."

He stepped forward, as if to take her hand, but she moved back, away from him. "It would be a business arrangement," he told her, smiling.

"I am sorry, Herr Kimmel," Rennie heard herself say, as if she were in an amusement park's echo chamber. "I wish to thank you for your offer. But I am not in *that* business." She turned and somehow left the room, stepping through the beaded curtain, standing against the dark corridor wall with her eyes closed. She refused to think. She couldn't move. She simply waited for the ordinary young man in the gabardine raincoat to come and get her, to take her to Kimmel.

"You might talk to her, Fräulein Froelich," she heard Kimmel say, finally. "Plead my case as it were. Tell her how faithful I can be to my friends. Tell her how terrible I can be to my enemies."

She heard him rattle the tin of *Lutschbonbons* in his leather trench coat pocket as he moved toward the door. "Talk to her, Fräulein Froelich," Rennie heard him say, and she realized he knew she was listening.

"We have a sign over all our work camps in the Reich. ARBEIT MACHT FREI. Work makes you free. Tell her that her choices are limited. Tell her she should think of my offer as work, a job that will set her free. Tell her I give her three days before I shall make further inquiries . . . before I shall again take up my investigations.

"Tell her, Fräulein Froelich, that she must give me an

answer by then. In the end, I am telling you, Fräulein Froelich, your Silver Rose will either work for the Reich or for me. And I am an easier taskmaster than the Reich. Tell her that, Fräulein Froelich. *Heil Hitler*, Fräulein Froelich."

6

And still the night wasn't over. "There are two men who have come to visit me and see you," Lillie told her. "I know. This is very hard on you, *Schatzi*. You were marvelous with Kimmel. But still, the fact remains that my plan for hiding you has backfired. We've got to get you out of Germany before Kimmel comes for his final answer. Three days. Seems like an awfully long time, doesn't it? Perhaps our visitors can help. One of them is an American, the son of an old and important friend of mine."

"An American?"

But Lillie wasn't listening. She, too, had had a difficult night, and her mind was going over the possibilities as she stared at the fifty-year-old stranger in the dressing-table mirror. She realized there were too many possibilities at the same moment she recognized the stranger in the mirror as herself. She turned her attention back to Rennie. "The other's an SS general. Wolff von Danzig. I've known him since he was a boy. He comes from one of Germany's great families, though he was broke like everyone else during the twenties.

"One of the barmaids he slept with used to sneak him into the Kasino, hand him an empty glass, and allow him to watch the cabaret. He had a dinner jacket. He was extraordinarily handsome. He spoke passing English. So the bouncers let him stay, thinking he was a gigolo."

"He might have been a customer," Rennie said, taking the brush from Lillie's hand, working at the wild, frizzed hair herself.

"No respectable German—at the time—could afford the Kleist Kasino." She closed her eyes, giving herself up to the luxury of having someone else brush her hair. "He'll help us if he can," she said. "He's smitten, as they used to say in my day."

"With whom?" Rennie asked, giving Lillie the hairbrush, watching her apply the too-red rouge she wore.

Lillie took one last glance at the disappointed woman in the dressing-table mirror and stood up. "*Schatzi*," she said, taking Rennie's hand, leading her out into the corridor, "you couldn't be that naïve or that unaware. Not being Nick's child, you couldn't. I'll chalk it up to the urgency of the moment." She stopped and kissed Rennie and held her for a moment. "He's smitten with you. They all are. Now come and be charming and just a little distant, *Schatzi*. The American is looking for a movie star and the general wants a damsel in distress and you've got to be versatile enough to play both parts. Come, darling. It's the last performance of the evening, I promise you."

The two men stood up as Lillie—like a variety show magician—drew Rennie into the drawing room through the black beaded curtains. She remembered Butch, of course. He smiled but made no other sign that he recognized her. It took a moment for her to realize that von Danzig was the officer who had come to meet Butch on the North Train.

They were both dressed in black. Butch in faultless evening clothes. Von Danzig in the black dress SS tunic, blue-black leather boots, silver swastikas. He stared at her with his smiling blue eyes, clearly not recognizing her as Butch Jarman's companion on the train from Paris. He bowed, as Lillie introduced them, clicking his heels together in the best Prussian-approved manner, a gesture that always made Rennie—even at that moment—want to laugh.

It's so odd, she thought to herself. Jews hiding in the attic; SS generals being received in the drawing room. She thought then that she was going to laugh—or weep—when

Butch Jarman said, "I nearly didn't recognize you." For a long moment, she couldn't say anything. She thought, for that moment, that he was going to give her away to von Danzig, who—despite his butter-yellow hair and convincing blue eyes—would have immediately begun an investigation. She was Lillie's Viennese niece. Not a girl on a train from Paris. "You don't look like the same girl who just sang on the stage," Butch went on. "I'd never have recognized you without your makeup. It is a great pleasure to meet you off-stage, Fräulein."

"Thank you" was all she could manage.

"You were wonderful," von Danzig said. "I felt it was ten years ago and Lillie Froelich was on that stage, singing."

"She's far more effective than I ever was. And far too sleepy to hear all these compliments. Try again tomorrow when she's more alert."

"Perhaps a drive along the Avus in an open car would help," von Danzig said.

"Just the thing," Lillie said, before Rennie could say she didn't want to go driving along the Avus with an SS officer. That despite his innocent good looks, the sight of his uniform and his swastikas made her sick with fear. "She's been working too hard, rehearsing. She needs the fresh air. You may call for her at noon; give her lunch but have her back by three. She needs her rest." Lillie turned to Butch.

"And since you're such a slow worker—so unlike your dear father, who was almost too fast—you get the consolation prize, Herr Jarman: you may take me to lunch tomorrow."

Butch laughed. "I'm delighted. The Kempinski?"

"No, I think not the Kempinski. I'd prefer Horscher's."

"Then Horscher's it is."

The two men said good night. "Lillie, I don't want . . ." Rennie began, almost before they were out the door.

"It doesn't matter what you want, *Schatzi*. Not at this moment, I'm afraid. I know. He's a Nazi, but there are—

odd as it may sound—some Nazis who are not very bad,
only very dumb, and I think von Danzig is one of the dumb
ones."

"Still, he's a Nazi."

Lillie looked at her and smiled. "I don't know what experience you've had with men, *Schatzi*. You're always so closed
about such matters. So you probably don't know this yourself yet. But you weren't avoiding Wolff von Danzig's eyes
because he's a Nazi. He has the same sort of sex appeal
your father has, and he's only half aware of it. He's dangerous not because he's Joseph Goebbels's show Nazi but because he's a naïf. Rather like you, *Schatzi*. You and Wolff
both appear to be cosmopolites, sophisticated, certain of
yourselves. But just a little under the facade, one can find
pure innocence. It's what makes you both so attractive,
above and beyond your looks."

"I don't know what you're talking about, Lillie."

"I daresay. But that's neither here nor there at this moment. The truth of the matter is that I should have kept you
in the attic with your father and I didn't. Now we've got
three days to make use of limited assets. One of them is
von Danzig. Your going driving with him will certainly be
noted and reported and might make Kimmel think you have
friends in high places, which you certainly don't."

"There is another option," Rennie said, moving to the
window looking over the Kleiststrasse.

"And that is?"

"I could always accept Kimmel's offer," Rennie said in a
small voice. She felt trapped, as if there was no move she
could make that would help. "Father would be protected
until he got his papers. Perhaps Kimmel might even help."

"Don't you believe it for a moment. Kimmel would sleep
with you at night and torture your father by day." She
went to Rennie, putting her arms around her. "I am going
to get your father out, *Schatzi*. And I am going to get you

out. Believe me. I will go to everyone. Butch Jarman to start with. And who knows? Perhaps even Oberstgruppen-führer von Danzig will be of use. I promise you, *Schatzi:* I am going to get you both out of Germany."

Later, after they had gone up to the secret attic, after Rennie, exhausted, had fallen asleep on the davenport and Tante Lizbeth had been dispatched to her room, Lillie told Nick about Kimmel.

"We've got to get her a new passport," he said, taking Lillie's hand, smiling at her. "Of course we've got to get her out. We always knew that. You mustn't blame yourself for Kimmel. If it hadn't been him, it would have been an informer in the Kasino or an alert Gestapo man seeing a chink of light from the street."

"All right. I'll blame myself later when there's the luxury of time. But we have just three days. Where do we find a forger now, when they've all so recently been cleaned up?"

"I think I'm going to have to pay a visit to Herr Doktor Kornwasser. My heart, you know." He looked up at the woman standing over him. "Will you make the appointment?"

"It's too dangerous, Nick."

"Make it for the day after tomorrow. That will give Kornwasser just one day to get papers, to help us. Kornwasser always performs best under pressure." He looked at his daughter, curled up on the davenport in the far corner, her hands under her head, her silver blond hair spread out on the old pillow she clung to.

He turned back to his card game, laid out in front of him on the cardboard table. "What do you think we should do with the knave?" he asked.

"You ask me, *yonkle*," Lizbeth said, from the hallway, where she had been standing and listening, "it's too late now to do anything."

* * *

It was nearly noon when Rennie woke. Her father was asleep in his chair, yet another patience laid out in front of him. In the light from the green-shaded lamp he seemed not older but somehow faded. It was as if he were gradually disappearing, not just from his old life but from all life. She switched off the light, kissed him, and thought that she had been incredibly foolish to come. She had wanted to be with him and now they hardly saw one another.

She held his hand for a moment. The gold signet ring he wore was loose. Though Pepsi brought him meals, he didn't eat most of them, except for his beloved *Currywursts*. Those spicy, brown sausages, even cool, were the only food he ate with anything approaching appetite.

Living here in the dark he might as well be in prison, she thought.

Pepsi appeared at that moment. "You'd better get it downstairs, missy," he told her. "You've got a date with an SS angel and La Froelich wants to supervise your costume and makeup."

"I'll be right down, Pepsi."

As Pepsi retrieved her father's wastes, she kissed her father once more and went out into the corridor, where a sudden noise startled her. She glanced down the corridor leading to the other room. A young boy stood looking at her, back lit by a dim light from the second room. *"Guten Tag,"* he said, with a heavy Yiddish accent. He took off his cap, a cheap brown and white houndstooth affair. *"Guten Tag, Fräulein."*

"Guten Tag," she said. He looked so frightened with his big, staring black eyes and pale, unhealthy skin. He looks, she thought, as frightened as I feel.

"Tatela," a woman's voice—nervous and shrill—called out in Yiddish. The boy turned and ran to the door of the other room, his thin legs in their short trousers sad and pathetic.

He stood at the door and watched her for one last mo-

ment. *"Auf Wiedersehen, Fräulein,"* he whispered before
going into the room.

She wondered what he and his parents were escaping
from. She wondered why they had brought him. What did
he do to amuse himself all day and night in that dim attic
prison?

"No tears," Lillie ordered her, when Rennie reached their
room. "No tears. Not today. You'll wear the black slacks
and the turtleneck you brought. . . . You must stop crying,
Schatzi. Your eyes will be all red."

"I can't, *Mutti.* I'm such a terrible coward. I'm ashamed,
but I'm frightened all of the time now."

Lillie drew Rennie to her, putting her arms around her.
"Tell you the truth, I'm feeling a touch cowardly myself
these days." She kissed the silver blond hair. "But you have
nothing to worry about. I'm going to get you out of Germany. You only have to be a little patient.

"And we'd better get dressed. I'm having lunch at Horscher's with a young man and you're going driving with a
young Nazi, and we only have one wardrobe between us.
SS officers require their women to be punctual." She stopped
for a moment. "It is important that he likes you, Rennie."

"How important?"

"You don't have to sleep with him, but I know how you
can be when you're nervous. You can be very off-putting."

"I'll try not to be off-putting, *Mutti.*"

She hadn't brought enough clothes with her. She had
thought she would spend a night in the house in the Lentzeallee, have a long, cozy chat with her father, and in the
morning take him with her on the train to Paris. She had
been a dreamer. She had woken up a bit during the past
week.

She had put on the black trousers and turtleneck Lillie
had chosen along with a pair of low black heels Lillie had
used the last of her clothes ration to buy for her.

Lillie insisted that she wear the silver blue fox jacket and hat, calling her into the drawing room, forcing her to model them. The drawing room was filled with flowers from Rennie's new unknown admirers.

"I don't want to wear the furs, Lillie. My brown coat will do," Rennie said, pushing aside the red roses, the cream-colored roses, the pink roses, the inevitable white roses tipped with silver.

"Why do all German air aces send flowers and chocolates?" Lillie asked, brushing out the furs. "Why don't they send limousines or diamonds or tiny perfect black pearls?"

"I really don't want to wear your furs, Lillie," Rennie said, allowing the jacket to be placed on her shoulders.

"He's bound to come in an open car," Lillie said, straightening the shoulders of the jacket, standing back for a better look. "It's a sickness with German officers: open cars in November. *Gott im Himmel*, you look marvelous. When I wear it I look like a traffic sign. I give it to you. Don't argue. Your father gave it to me, so I'm free to dispose of it as I wish. I am one of those sad women who only look well in chinchilla."

She remembered the day Nick had given her the furs. They had celebrated too long the night before. It was her birthday, a chilly April day. It was the sort of birthday one celebrated and then tried to forget. They had slept most of the morning and then Nick had decided the only way to cure their hangovers and her birthday blues was a walk along the Ku-damm. He thought a walk along the Ku-damm would cure almost anything. When they passed Steiner's, he saw the jacket in the window.

"It's you," he said.

"It's far too young for me," she had told him, refusing to be cheerful. "It's for a young woman."

He had dragged her into the shop, forced her to try it on, forced her to accept it along with the rakish, theatrical hat. And suddenly she had forgotten how old she was, that

it was a birthday most women choose to overlook. As so
often happened during those days, all she could think of
was Nick as she left Steiner's with her new furs.

She took the commissar-style hat and placed it on Rennie's silver hair, cocking it at an angle. "You are ravishing,
Schatzi."

Rennie took off the hat as she pried open one of the
elaborately gilded boxes of candy that had been sent to her.
She found a huge chocolate in the shape of a swastika. "Am
I?" she asked, breaking off a piece, taking a bite, looking up
at Lillie, trying to smile, as her silvery blond hair fell down
around her face, her eyes more silver than blue.

There was a knock on the outer door at that moment, and
after some hesitation Marlene, the lead Goose Girl, entered
the drawing room rather tentatively. Lillie didn't encourage
visits from the Goose Girls. But Marlene had come to tell
Fräulein Froelich that she felt ill and consequently didn't
think she could "do" the evening performance.

"You appear disgustingly healthy to me, Marlene," Lillie
said, looking at the girl with her fat, milk-white arms and
her knowing farmer's daughter's face. She stood there, a
little shy and a little insolent, taking in the drawing room,
her blond hair unkempt in the latest fashion, her puffy
cheeks white with cheap powder, her sensuous lips painted
with a dark red lipstick. She was popular with the lesser
ranks, but Lillie knew Marlene wanted an officer. "If you
want the evening free, take it," Lillie told her. "No one is
going to worry whether there are five Goose Girls or six."

"*Danke schön,*" Marlene said, letting her glance turn to
Rennie, who was standing at her favorite spot, the window
overlooking the Kleiststrasse. She had replaced the hat on
her head. It was tilted, stagy, insouciant. The fox jacket
rested on her shoulders. Her arms, under it, were crossed,
protectively. She looked elegant and fine, a film star casually
waiting for her call.

For that one moment, Lillie felt something like pity for

Marlene, the solid Goose Girl in her short-sleeved white
blouse, her brown skirt, her cotton stockings, her Alexanderplatz shoes. Marlene's aspirations, in another woman, would
be acceptable, even agreeable. As it was, they seemed cheap
and unwholesome.

"Going out?" Marlene asked Rennie, wistfully.

Rennie turned and smiled. "Yes. For a ride in an open
car. It will probably rain."

"No," Marlene said, for the first time since she entered
the room, confident. "With your luck, the sun will shine."

"She should know of my luck," Rennie said, after Marlene left.

A few moments later von Danzig arrived, wearing a soft
dark suit, a pale shirt, a blue tie. It was the first time
Rennie had seen him out of his SS uniform. He did not
carry a coat or hat. His butter-colored hair fell across his
forehead. He looked startlingly young, anxious to please, a
prosperous country boy courting a city girl, eager to make
a good impression.

"What shall I do with all the flowers?" Lillie called as
Rennie and von Danzig went down the red-painted steps.

"Send them to the Jewish cemetery in Grosse Hamburger
Strasse," Rennie said, looking up at Wolff to see how—or
if—he would react. He merely bowed his head slightly,
acknowledging but not accepting her challenge.

Marlene stood in the Kasino foyer, looking out through
the open door, watching the street as she chatted with
Greta, her best friend and fellow Goose Girl. Rehearsals
were over, and it was dark in the foyer. Greta had borrowed
Marlene's lipstick and was holding up a compact mirror,
attempting to apply the deep red color in the dim light
from the street. "It's a two-seater," Marlene said. "A dark
blue Mercedes with a rag top. The top is up, though. She
needn't have worried."

Marlene continued to watch as von Danzig opened the

car door, as Rennie's absurd fur hat toppled off when she got in. Marlene watched as von Danzig retrieved it, and she saw him laugh. She thought he had awfully good teeth.

She wasn't jealous, she assured herself, watching Greta make a mess of her face. Absentmindedly, she nibbled at the remains of the chocolate swastika Lillie had given her. It was only that she wouldn't have minded going for a ride in a Mercedes for once, with a general who looked like von Danzig. She wouldn't have minded, she told herself, if the rag top were up or down.

And then Pepsi came out of the club and shooed them out of the foyer into the street, locking the doors behind them. She would have bet a week's salary that von Danzig wouldn't take her to some out-of-the-way bit of park and maul her until she gave in and then not talk to her afterwards.

7

"Why Horscher's and not the Kempinski?" Butch Jarman asked, when Lillie had joined him at a corner table in the dark, comfortable restaurant. "It's kept me up half the night: why Horscher's and not the Kempinski?"

Butch was teasing, but Lillie looked at him in a way to indicate that she wasn't amused. "Because the Kempinski," she said, placing her long white gloves next to her gray leather purse, arranging herself decorously in the stiff-backed chair, keeping her big brown eyes focused on his overly green ones, "has a sign in its window. It's a discreet sign. Neat, modern type on polished brass. Most Americans never notice it. It's not for Americans, anyway. It reads JUDEN SIND HIER NICHT ERWUNSCHT, and though I'm not Jewish, I don't choose to dine where Jews are not served."

She continued to look at him, waiting for his reply. She was wearing a veiled black concave hat, a long black coat, a dark red dress. Her bright red hair—the exact shade of geraniums in Berlin window boxes—frizzed out over her head. Her penciled eyebrows—half circles above her heavy-lidded, kohled eyes—made her seem permanently and cynically surprised.

Lillie Froelich, Butch realized, was someone to contend with. He answered her unspoken question by circumventing it. "You must not dine out very often."

"Virtually never. But this, Herr Jarman, is an *occasion*." She waved the waiter away, then called him back and ordered a bottle of champagne. "It's not really champagne at all. Only what Heil Hitler chooses to call champagne, but still it sounds festive, and if you're anything like your father, it will put you in a more pliable mood."

"I'm nothing like my father. And why do you want me to be pliable?"

"I'm going to ask you a great favor."

"You'd better tell me straight off what it is," he said, sipping at the German champagne.

Instead, she looked around her. The restaurant was filled with men in a variety of uniforms and ladies in near-expensive furs. The noise they made was loud enough so that whatever she said wouldn't be heard. The truth was there wasn't very much difference between Horscher's and the Kempinski in regard to Jewish policy. If a restaurant wanted to stay in business, it couldn't serve Jews. The truth was that Horscher's was louder and therefore more private than the Kempinski.

She turned back to Butch Jarman and looked at him. It was nearly a shame that his eyes were so distracting, because they didn't give one the opportunity to see the rest of him. He was like his father. Handsome, civilized, a gentleman. "I want you to take Rennie Nacht out of Germany," she said, finally.

"She's told you about our shared train experience?"

"More. She's told me how helpful you were."

"This is a dumb question, but why can't she take the same train out?"

"That, dear Butch, I'm not going to tell you."

"Oh, yes, you are, dear Lillie. I'm perfectly willing to help you. You obviously know that. But I'm not going to take a chance on being booted out of Germany—or possibly, worse—just when I've finally gotten here. At least I'm not going to take that chance without knowing why."

"You won't be running much of a risk. She'll have papers."

"Is it something to do with the strong-arm boy in the leather bathrobe?" Butch asked, allowing the waiter to fill his glass again. "The one who saved her from being mauled last night?"

Lillie waited until the waiter had filled her glass and moved off. She sighed dramatically, lifted the veil on her hat, and moved her gloves and purse from one side of the table to the other. "His family name is Kimmel. He is reputed to have been with der Führer in Munich during the 1923 Putsch. I haven't been able to find out his given name or his official title, and I'm not at all certain I want to. He is not a person you should be acquainted with, Butch."

He asked for and received permission to light a Balkan cigar. "Filthy American habit," he said, sitting back, inhaling. "Smoking during meals." He smiled at her, and she thought that perhaps he was a little less of a gentleman than she had thought and that was all to the good. "All right. I don't want to know Herr Kimmel. And all right, I do want to know Fräulein Nacht. Tell me who she is, Lillie. And I'll buy the next bottle of ersatz champagne."

"You're smitten, I take it," Lillie said, while it was being uncorked and poured.

"More than smitten. During that unnerving train trip, she made me feel like Charlie Chaplin playing opposite Garbo. She has poise."

"Ha. She was as frightened as a goose on Christmas Day, but it would take another woman to see that."

"I didn't say she wasn't frightened. She *was* frightened. But she had poise all the same. It's a combination I find irresistible. Then of course there's her looks."

"It's only fair to warn you now, Butch, that she's not smitten with you. Not yet. Nor perhaps ever."

"Von Danzig's more her type?"

"Though he shouldn't be. He is, after all, a Nazi."

Butch laughed. "Dark hints won't do it, Lillie. I won't help her until I know who she is."

Lillie took another long sip of the champagne, shuddered,

sighed, and gave in with a theatrical gesture of her hands. "All right. I shall tell you, but only because I trust you. She's not Viennese, obviously. You can tell a kilometer away that she's not Viennese."

She hesitated, but Butch Jarman folded his hands like a student in school, waiting to learn from a lecture by a delightful teacher. Lillie obliged. She began by telling him about Rennie's mother, a great Jewish Berlin beauty, Viktoria Langheimer, whose father, Oskar Langheimer, had been the most influential publisher in Germany. He inherited his newspaper, *Der Tag*, from his father when it was an agricultural journal and turned it into a popular democratic daily commentary in a matter of months.

Der Tag was a great success. It was intelligent. It bowed to no one. Which was perhaps why it didn't make money, but the Langheimers had already made their fortune in cattle farming and coal mines, and Oskar Langheimer didn't have to worry about money.

He supported the Kaiser during the war. "The Langheimers," Lillie told Butch, "were Germans first, Jews second." Oskar's eldest son was the first German officer killed in action. There were three more sons, and they too were "given" to the war effort. Oskar's only living child was Rennie's mother, Viktoria. She was a famous beauty.

"Not at all like Rennie, even when it came to the coloring. Viktoria was golden whereas Rennie is silver." She had very blond hair and gray eyes and the thin lips Lillie always associated with London's National Gallery. "There was an under-glass quality about Viktoria. She had that Gainsborough look. A little horsey. Some men find it irresistible. There was a portrait of her in Nick's Dahlem house that made her seem ethereal. Ethereal is one quality I can't stand in a woman. But the men were mad about her. Old boulevardiers liked to sit around the Romanische, get drunk on brandy, and talk about watching Viktoria Langheimer steer a coarse black horse through the Tiergarten."

Lillie sipped at the champagne while Butch waited. "Naturally, Oskar spoiled Viktoria."

When Viktoria announced, in 1917, during the heart of the war, while Oskar mourned his dead sons, that she was going to marry a cosmopolitan Pole named Nikolaus Jablonski, horror filled the Langheimers' Wilhelmstrasse house.

"The fact that Nick was a Jew didn't help." Oskar had had a long, cherished dream that his daughter would marry into the aristocracy. Nick had worked for Oskar, writing editorials which were widely discussed and admired for their grasp of the convoluted political situation.

But Oskar wanted a prince, not some Jewish journalist whose former income reportedly came from unsavory sources. Nick Jablonski had spent a year in New York and another at Oxford, where he fell in with the Cliveden set, which eventually became pro-Nazi.

It was said he was the only Jew in London to be regularly received by the Queen Mother. It was said that the money he lived on during his New York and English forays came from women. He was, in effect, a gigolo.

There was a highly dramatic and not so elderly Polish princess whose name came up fairly often. His early income certainly didn't come from his father, who was a professor of Romance languages at the University of Warsaw.

Wherever the money came from, it ran out in London. Nick Jablonski decided then to move to Berlin. Berlin was cheaper, during those days before the war; and it was more exciting than Paris, where everyone took Art and Food too seriously. Nick was an instant success in Berlin, appreciated by women and certain men.

"What does he look like?" Butch asked, relighting his cigar, waving the waiter and the menus away for a third time.

"He was, is, the most beautiful man I've ever seen." She described his thick, ash-blond hair, shades darker than

Rennie's but still as striking. She lingered over the details of his dimples when he smiled and the sort of blue eyes that seem hand-painted.

"I'm a little tipsy now, so I'll confess that when I first met him I had trouble being alone with him in the same room. I hope I don't shock your American sensibilities when I tell you that the third time we met, my knickers were down around my ankles in thirty seconds flat. He has that effect on a good many women."

"You love him?"

"With all my heart and soul. I would have gladly taken a stiletto and plunged it into Viktoria Langheimer's shriveled artichoke of a heart if I thought it would have done any good."

Oskar's main objection to the match—aside from its terrible timing—was that Nick spent more time at the cafés, arguing politics, than he did at the office, writing about them.

To prove himself to his prospective father-in-iaw, Nick offered to manage *Der Tag* for six months without salary. He wanted to prove to Oskar Langheimer, a man he admired, that he wasn't a *Heiratsschwindler*, a then common phenomenon in Germany: a man who promised marriage in order to run off with his fiancée's savings.

Nick surprised Oskar. In six months he doubled *Der Tag*'s circulation by featuring his own editorials on the front page and switching his allegiance from the Kaiser to a new democracy for Germany.

Some bought the paper because they believed as he did—others bought it out of sheer outrage. Oskar, true to his word, supported the marriage, and gave—even though the family was in official mourning—a reception in the Langheimer house on the Wilhelmstrasse. Despite the war there was French champagne and Strasbourg pâté. As a wedding present he gave Nick *Der Tag*. It wasn't that Langheimer was old: he was embittered. He had wanted his sons to run his newspaper, but now there were no sons.

He left Berlin for an estate he had bought on the banks of the Danube some thirty miles upriver from Vienna. He wanted to putter in his greenhouse, to eat five meals a day, to read half a dozen books a week, to forget about the Kaiser and the Kaiser's mismanaged war and the sons he had lost and couldn't bring himself to stop mourning. He blamed himself. He had been, he said, too good a German.

Der Tag flourished. Nick had Bauhaus's Gropius design him the much-talked-about glass and steel villa in the Lentzeallee in Dahlem. He hired a dozen servants, many of them Russian émigrés with titles, and surrounded his wife with the sort of luxuries she couldn't do without. Ermine bed jackets and sable booties. They were divinely happy. Or so it was said.

"Personally," Lillie declared, "I fancy Nick wasn't so happy. I know: the spurned woman talking. But still. Viktoria was too coddled and not bright enough to challenge him. What Nick liked about her most was that she looked right for the part she played.

"There's a famous Gebhardt photo of them entering the Staatsoper that's impossible to forget. He's in tails and white tie, smiling and dimpled, radiating charm and sexuality. She's in emeralds and Worth, exuding high birth and delicate sensitivity. Nick's frank and trustworthy. Viktoria's narrow-eyed and smoldering.

"He would have grown tired of her, given time. She was too fragile and too hard for him. If she had lived, it would have been better for everyone. Then he could have gone on and had affairs and a perfectly lovely life . . . well, until current times."

But Viktoria had died giving birth to Rennie. Nick blamed himself for his wife's death. There was some trouble, ill defined, about getting the doctor, but it wasn't Nick's fault. All the guilt was in his mind. Winterhagen, a novelist friend of Nick's, once said that all Nick needed to make his life complete was a major tragedy, and finally he had one.

Oskar Langheimer wanted to take his granddaughter Rennie to his Blue Danube estate, but Nick insisted she stay with him. He found an old family connection—"that kosher horror, Tante Lizbeth"—and hired tutors and nannies. He spoiled Rennie, Lillie said, for any other man.

For Rennie Jablonski lived every little girl's dream: to marry one's father. He took her everywhere. She was his official hostess at age nine. "It was an extraordinary sight, seeing the two of them at a performance of a *Ring* opera, hand in hand. He wore tails and had that exquisite pained look in his hand-painted gray-blue eyes, which only made him the more attractive. He had the good sense not to tart her up. She wore simple gray silk dresses, high stockings, patent leather shoes, all very *à l'anglaise*.

"Of course she had that hair and a delicious little pout to her upper lip. But she could sit perfectly still through almost any event—a dinner for forty or the opening night of a Brecht/Weill opus—as long as Nick held her hand. And he never let it go."

It became odd to see Nick Jablonski without his daughter. In the twenties there were far more peculiar sights to be seen in Berlin night life than a devoted father taking his daughter to a fancy dress ball given by the Greater German Association of Women Wrestlers.

It hadn't been what her grandfather Oskar called a normal childhood. During the summers she would go to Oskar's estate and ride about in her own blue pony cart, with two attendants. She went to tea parties with the local gentry, rose at appropriate hours, had breakfast in the morning rather than in the middle of the night, and went to bed at the hour when, in Berlin, she would be sitting down to supper.

"I adored Rennie," Lillie said, her eyes growing hazy at the memory of the child. "I suppose I'm as close to a mother

as she ever had." Lillie had been Nick's Berlin mistress long
before he had married Viktoria Langheimer. He used to
visit her even during that first final year of nuptial bliss.

"True, I was never a beauty, but I did have this delirious
red hair and I was always long and thin and evil in the way
Nick thought Viennese women of the demimonde should be.

"Of course he should have married me. Either before or
after Viktoria, but he never thought of it and I was too
something—proud or subtle or stupid—to bring it up. I
knew he would marry me if I asked, but I also guessed I
would lose him if he did.

"He was always kind and generous. He bought me the
Kleist Kasino as a kind of nonwedding settlement, with
money from Viktoria's *dot*. We fought constantly, but I
don't believe he has slept with another woman besides me
since Viktoria died."

She smiled, remembering. "Of course Rennie kept us together." Lillie adored Rennie; Rennie loved her. She began
calling Lillie *"Mutti"* early on, and it seemed appropriate to
almost everyone with the possible exception of Tante Lizbeth. Lillie chose her tutors, her clothing, her food. She had
never been able to have a child, and she gave Rennie all the
love a maternal but childless woman could give.

"I couldn't have asked for a better child," Lillie told
Butch. "Now I'm getting all soppy. Give me your handkerchief, will you?" She dried her eyes and blew her nose
noisily. "Cheap champagne always makes me unforgivably
sentimental."

"How did she come to go abroad?" Butch asked, giving
up all idea of lunch, smoking his cigar, watching the restaurant empty.

Late in 1935, immediately after the so-called Nuremberg
Race Laws and the *Erbgesundheitsgesetz* made anti-Semitism
official, Oskar demanded that Rennie join him in Austria.
But the Austrians were even more virulently anti-Semitic

than the Germans. Nick didn't want her to leave at all, but
there were too many incidents.

Lillie insisted Rennie go live with one of Nick's obscure
cousins in London. Rennie drew and painted with great
talent—and perhaps more—and there was every genuine
reason why she should study at the Slade. Besides, London
was safe, certainly safer than Vienna or Paris and not as
distant as New York. It had to be a city. A big city. That
was what Rennie demanded when she agreed to leave Nick
and Lillie.

She returned fairly often. The Nazis let up a bit on the
Jews for the Olympics, and Rennie managed to spend nearly
half of 1936 in Berlin. Nick and Lillie visited her in London
a few times before Nick's traveling privileges were revoked.

No one thought Rennie could live away from her father
for any length of time, but she proved more resilient than
expected. She left the cousins, having made friends with a
group of quirky upper-class English girls. "The ones with
bad teeth and worse pearls," Lillie commented. She took a
Marble Arch flat with one of them while she continued to
study at the Slade. Her professors—and two or three men
in Berlin to whom Nick showed her work—said she possessed, at the very least, great talent.

When the situation in Berlin grew worse, Rennie began
to insist Nick and Lillie join her in London. It was obvious
that if Hitler remained in power, Nick would have to leave
Germany. He had been one of the first and most ironic of
Nazi detractors. *Der Tag* had been shut down any number
of times, the SA stationing men by the entrance, telling
anyone who entered they were to be marked as Jew sym-
pathizers. This didn't stop the gentile printers from entering through the roof and getting the day's edition out
through the back doors.

After the Kleist Kasino was threatened with closing (a
good German cabaret owner wouldn't associate with a

filthy Jew like Nick Jablonski, Lillie was told), Nick and
Lillie staged a public falling-out at a gypsy restaurant in
the Keithstrasse frequented by Gestapo salon spies. She
called him a great many anti-Semitic names; he slapped
her face; and officially, she was a good person again.

They continued to see each other in secret. Eventually,
the big business interests backing Hitler began to be vocal
about the traitorous slant *Der Tag* presented. Krupp and
Farben were backing Hitler, and they didn't want a journalist named Nick Jablonski doing him in.

But there were many international admirers and sup-
porters of *Der Tag*. The Polish-Jewish roundup, however,
provided the perfect opportunity to get rid of Nick and his
Der Tag. Nick learned about his imminent arrest an hour
before it was to occur, and he went underground.

"Rennie has foolishly come back to find him," Lillie told
Butch.

"And has she?"

"That's one story I don't propose to tell. But needless to
say, she's found Berlin a far more dangerous place than she
had supposed. If the SS or the Gestapo knew she was here,
she wouldn't be in an enviable position, and that's putting
it mildly."

"Yet she's out driving with an SS general."

"Jealousy, Butch, doesn't suit you. You must learn to
give in graciously to the ironies of our times." She drained
the last of the champagne and looked at him. He realized,
almost at once, that he was far drunker than she. "I'm going
to ask you this just once. I will understand if you refuse. I
may not respect you if you do, but my respect has little
cash value these days."

She stopped as she fitted an oval cigarette into her jade
holder and waited for him to light it. She inhaled. And then
she said, "Will you take Rennie out of Germany when and
if she gets the necessary papers? I warn you that the neces-

sary papers may be forged and that you might get into trouble."

"Why me?" Butch asked, after a moment.

"You're an American in good odor with Dr. Goebbels. You are free, more or less, to come and go when you choose. You could easily set up an appointment with, say, Count Ciano, in Italy, to discuss the implications of the Axis, of the *Anschluss*, of Mussolini's pasta diet. Even if the 'worst' were to happen, nothing very serious would befall you. Will you do it, Butch?"

"Of course I will. You didn't have to get me tipsy on ersatz champagne, you know, to get me to say yes."

"Well, these days a girl can't be too certain when a man's going to say yes or no. Now let's get that bilious little waiter over here. I'm starving. We can work out the details over sauerbraten. I do think Italy, don't you? They'll be less likely to suspect Italy, and you could have a very good reason for going there. What about the Wiener schnitzel? Americans always order it, so you might as well. We have to have her out of Berlin and preferably Germany in three days' time."

8

"Say something," von Danzig told her. When she didn't, he glanced at her as he drove up the Martin-Luther-Strasse and then cut across to the Unter den Linden. "Please say something."

"Is that an order?"

"Not when I say please. Say something charming."

"Charm is not my long suit these days."

"Well, you look charming. What about a conventional conversation? How are you feeling today, Fräulein Nacht?"

"Tired. Overworked."

"If you'll pardon me for saying so, Fräulein, you don't seem so very overworked to me."

"I could say the same to you, General."

He laughed, and after a moment, so did Rennie. The Berlin air was as clear and invigorating as ever, but the November sun only shone sporadically on the embassies, government buildings, deluxe hotels, and showrooms lining Unter den Linden.

The Argentine consulate, she noticed, had a mile-long queue winding around it. There wasn't a hope, for most of them, of getting anywhere near the consulate doors. Well, there wasn't a hope of getting into Argentina, either. The Argentines were no longer accepting German rejects unless they were very, very wealthy. The men and women on that line weren't very, very wealthy. If they were, they would have been somewhere else by now. In America or Mexico. And if they weren't somewhere else, they would be in concentration camps, working for the Reich. And if they weren't in concentration camps, they would be dead, former enemies of the Reich.

There were very few places and very few things a German Jew could be these days.

"What shall we do?" the handsome young general driving her about Berlin asked, as if coming in stage left to the wrong play. "Drive along the Avus? Or down to Wannsee? I have a friend who has a villa on the Havel . . ."

She stared at him for a long moment as if she had forgotten her dialogue; as if she were waiting for her cue. He looked so young and carefree, his butter-blond hair blowing in the brisk fall wind, his blue eyes smiling at her.

This man, she thought, is the embodiment of all that's naïve and wrong in Germany. He is a follower, a great big gorgeous bumpkin, willing to believe everything he is told. He is the reason my father is in hiding. The reason that poor boy with his cap is forced to live in an airless attic. The reason that thousands are suddenly poor and homeless and "detained" in work camps. And here am I, riding with him in this car he is so proud of. What does he do when he's not taking girls for drives around Berlin? When he's not playing nursemaid to American correspondents? Is he in that cellar at Spandau, dismembering Jews and other *Untermenschen*?

"Or we could motor into the Grunewald. I know a restaurant . . ."

"The zoo," she said suddenly. "I'd like to go to the zoo," she said, surprising herself. That was the answer she had always given her father when she was a child and offered an afternoon of his time. She had a Berliner's passionate love for the zoo and thought, "This might be the last time I'll see it."

"You wouldn't rather go to someplace more . . ."

"I should love to go to the zoo," she said decisively.

He spun the car around and headed toward the zoo. She looked at him and thought that despite the fact he was an

SS general, she would like to get him down in paint. Most men she met and liked—Butch Jarman came to mind—she wanted to draw. But there was something about the man sitting next to her that made her want to turn to the medium she was least accomplished in—oils—and get him onto canvas, just as he was at that moment, apolitical, without angst, without any of the shadows and ghosts most men she knew carried with them.

"I love to watch you when you sing," he said, as he maneuvered the Mercedes into a parking space a few yards from the zoo's main entrance. "It's like the old days in Berlin, when cabarets like the Kleist Kasino were radiating glamorous decadence." He switched off the motor and turned to her. "I have a confession to make: I was once a *conférencier* in a Kurfürstendamm cabaret. A long time ago. It was called Der Tango. A very poor and sad cabaret."

"You? A master of ceremonies in a political cabaret? Hard to believe."

"Nonetheless true."

"I think of you as spending your youth in a rigid cadet school somewhere in East Prussia, getting up long before dawn, bathing in icy water, enduring ten-mile hikes on a tablespoon of gruel."

He laughed, making no move to get out of the auto. "If my father had had his way, that would have been an accurate picture of my early years." It was pleasant sitting in the car under the chestnut trees, chatting. He felt a need that was strange to him: to talk about himself. He wanted her to see him as he was.

"I'm not a pure Prussian, you know." She took a cigarette, a Nigeria, from her jacket pocket and lit it herself. She offered him one, but he refused. "My mother is Bavarian. She married my father early in the century and went to live, unwillingly, on his estates near Danzig. Most of the estates, not to mention Danzig, are in Polish hands, thanks to the Treaty of Versailles.

"My father was a general in the Kaiser's war and my grandfather was an aide to Bismarck. We were poor for a long time after the war, but with the National Socialist revolution we are rich again. My father disapproves of Hitler, nonetheless. He calls him the Bohemian Corporal. But he accepts the prosperity Hitler has brought. And when Hitler brings Danzig back into the Reich, my father will accept that, too."

"And does this accepting father of yours accept you, too?" she asked, impressed—despite herself—by his seriousness.

"Definitely not. Father doesn't believe in SS generals. He wants the Kaiser back. Or at the least, one of his sons. He claims I'm in Hitler's army. We barely speak. Mother says he likes to lock himself up in his study and blame himself.

"When I was eighteen and there was no money to educate me, when he was trooping friends in to drill my brothers in tight-formation marching, I ran away to Berlin to become an actor. I ended up at Der Tango as a *conférencier* but I assure you not a very good one." He smiled at her, and she found herself smiling back. "I was too anxious to please."

"I think you still are."

"Oh, I would do anything to please you."

"You would, would you? Someday I may put you to the test. In the meanwhile, tell me how you made the switch from Berlin lowlife in the Weimar Republic to *Oberstgruppenführer* under the National Socialists."

"My father refuses to talk to me, but that doesn't mean he has lost all interest." He laughed, his cheeks coloring, as he told her how his father persuaded Göring to send him to one of the illegal flying schools in Westphalia after he lost his job at Der Tango and arrived home without money or prospects.

"Father and Reichsmarschall Göring were great pals during the war." He didn't tell her that it was his mother who had pressured his father into taking the train into Berlin, into lunching with Göring at the Herrenklub, into asking Göring for the favor. Wolff's father was not a man who liked asking anyone for favors.

Wolff was considered foolishly brave at the flying school —formally outlawed by the Treaty of Versailles—and so they sent him to Spain with the Condor unit. His commanding officer, von Schwebble, predicted that he would either die early or become a national hero. He was shot down on his first mission and returned to Berlin on a day when the minister of propaganda, Herr Doktor Goebbels, particularly needed a hero. Sentiment against Germans fighting in Spain's civil war was high.

"I finally became an actor," Wolff told her.

He was featured in all the magazines for several weeks, and the newsreel that ran at the Gloria Palast showed the ceremony in which the Führer made him a general.

"Did you feel immortalized?" Rennie asked.

"I felt like a fool," he said. "I often still do." His father had been less than pleased, describing his generalship as that "colossal charade." Only Hugo von Niedermeyer, of all his former comrades in the Condors, still talked to him. There were too many others wounded, shot down in Spain, who deserved Wolff's honors. He hadn't been especially brave; only handsome. He knew he was a show soldier, fighting his battles in salons and embassy drawing rooms, on call at all times to cameramen and propaganda personnel.

There weren't many people on the paths leading through the zoo, the uncertain weather keeping them away. They crossed the ornamental bridge which led to the elaborate Egyptian-style ostrich cages. "Peculiar, aren't they?" he asked as they watched the ostriches moving clumsily about their gilt cages.

"The most peculiar," Rennie agreed. It was so quiet, so tranquil in the zoo. It seemed as if they were a million miles away from the Kleist Kasino's attic, from Kimmel.

"What do you suppose is going on in those little heads?" he asked, watching, fascinated, as the ostriches did their best to ignore the two observers.

"They're your typical Berliners," Rennie said. "Burying their heads in the sand, content to keep their eyes closed to what's going on around them." She looked away from the ostriches, who seemed, suddenly, less interesting. "What do *you* think is going on in those little heads?" she asked him, struck by his boyishness, his enthusiasm for the birds.

"They're wondering what's going on in ours and why on earth we're not hopping about on one leg, making high-pitched noises, flapping our wings, and looking feverish."

She smiled and let him lead her away, deeper into the zoo, past the antelopes surrounded by Moorish sculpture and over another, larger ornamental bridge that spanned the artificial swamp where the wild boars stared up at them thoughtfully.

"If I were a fanciful person," Rennie said, "I would say that the zoo is an allegory for contemporary German life."

"I know what will put a stop to all that fancifulness. Food." They stopped at the zoo café, where the only patrons were an old man in a beaver coat and two prostitutes wearing short imitation-leather boots and pinched expressions on their overly rouged faces.

Von Danzig ordered *Currywursts* and dark beer, which made her think of her father and the cold *Wursts* Pepsi served him in Lillie's attic.

"Let's go dine with the monkeys," he said, nearly but not quite taking her arm. "The monkeys are my favorites."

"I should have known," she told him, trying to match his bantering tone.

They ate their sausages and drank their good dark beer while sitting on the green wooden benches in front of the outsized gold-and-silver-barred monkey cages. The Vierwald-stätter See, the zoo garden's artificial lake, spread out behind them, reflecting the moving clouds and a sudden, direct ray of sunshine.

"What are you thinking about at this moment?" he asked.

"I was remembering a game I once played with a group of older, tougher girls, here in the zoo. For some reason they were to take care of me for an afternoon. The game was a team one, called war, though each player played for herself.

"The penalty was something dreadful—like getting spat on—and I've forgotten what the objective was. But the feature of the game which fascinated me was that you were safe if you could reach the monkey cages. One couldn't win, of course, if one spent all one's time being safe in the monkey house. But I was frightened, out of my depth among all those Amazons. I wasn't all that interested in winning."

The sun finally came out in earnest, and two tiny monkeys with white beards emerged from their house. They tested the water carefully, like two cautious old ladies, and then, giving whispered shrieks, dove in. Von Danzig laughed with delight.

"How old are you, General?" she asked, laughing with him.

"That's the first genuine personal question you've asked me."

"Don't consider it a sign of a monumental thaw. Just tell me your age."

"Yes, *gnädiges Fräulein*. I am twenty-eight years of age, in sound health and nearly sound mind, and you must stop calling me General. It makes me feel a thousand years old."

"Like the new Reich."

"Not exactly like the new Reich," he corrected her. "The new Reich is only a few years old. It is going to live for a thousand years."

"You believe in it totally, don't you?"

"It's the Fatherland's last chance to be great again. Look

at what Hitler has already done for Germany. Ten years
ago I couldn't get a job and I couldn't follow my father
into the army because there wasn't any army, thanks to
Versailles. Just a lot of outlaw bands of hoodlums, *Frei-
korps,* dressed up in mismatched uniforms, running around
the country stealing to eat.

"The middle class had been wiped out and the aristocracy
was starving. Yes, Art was being created in Berlin, but the
rest of Germany couldn't eat Art. Hitler came along and by
perfectly legal means—"

"Well, not perfectly—"

". . . he took over the government and then the country,
and today we're the greatest power in Europe, and the only
country in the world who can stop the Communists from
taking over the West.

"Today Germany has more economic and political might
than she ever did. Despite what the politicians and the
left-wingers predict, there is no war. And there won't be a
war. We're accomplishing our goals without arms."

"And the Jews," she asked, looking at him, wanting an
answer. "All those enemies of the state?"

"In every revolution, even as peaceful a one as ours, there
have to be victims. The Aryan nonsense will evaporate one
day, as soon as Hitler's goals are achieved. Now *Judenrein*
is a sop to Goebbels, Himmler, and Bormann. To the super-
stitious mobs who must have a victim, a scapegoat. Saner
minds, like Göring's, will prevail."

"But in the meanwhile, General—"

"In the meanwhile," he said, catching hold of her hands,
"call me Wolff. I beg you."

She disengaged herself. "It's far too soon. Prussians rarely
allow mere acquaintances to be so familiar. I shouldn't have
to tell *you* that. Before we call one another by our given
names, we must engage in the *Duz Freunde,* lock arms,
toast *Brüderschaft,* mix blood. And even then . . . we are
not of the same class, General."

"We live in a new world, *gnädiges Fräulein*. Old formalities are breaking down."

"I used to hate those formalities. Now I think I prefer them."

The sun disappeared, seemingly forever, as gray clouds hid the sky. The monkeys retired inside their gold and silver cages. Rennie slipped her arms into her fur jacket and stood up. "It's getting cold and late. And I have a song to sing tonight, General."

They heard other singing as they walked along the central path leading to the exit. It sounded as if a thousand men were chanting some ancient mystical prayer. And under the singing they could hear the sound of men marching.

"It's a parade of some sort," Wolff said, looking uneasy.

"Oh, we know what sort."

They saw them as they left the zoo. Not thousands but hundreds of them—a sea of men and boys in brown SA uniforms—marching east across the Budapester Strasse. They goose-stepped in tight, perfectly cadenced formations, carrying NSDAP banners rolled around wooden staves at the end of which were cast-iron swastikas.

Unconsciously, because she needed to, Rennie put her hand through von Danzig's arm as the marchers drew near. They were moving with a fanatical energy, their boots striking the pavement as if they would give off sparks.

And as they marched, they sang their song—the *Horst Wessel Lied:*

> The banner high, the unit in close order
>   The SA marches with quiet, solemn tred;
> With comrades killed by Red Front and reaction
>   We march in spirit with the honored dead.

The SA captain leading them called for a halt as they reached the zoo entrance where Rennie and von Danzig were standing. He ordered the men to split ranks.

They did so to reveal, standing in the center of the formation, a young woman. Rennie thought she couldn't have been more than twenty. She had long, curly brown hair and large, terrified black eyes. It was difficult to tell whether she was pretty or not. Her cheeks had been slashed with a razor and one of the wounds was still bleeding. The dress she had been wearing—a shoddy red and black low-cut dress—had been torn so completely that her breasts and buttocks were revealed. There were large black bruises on her body where she had been beaten and kicked. Hanging around her neck was a gray cardboard placard. On it was printed in muddy red ink:

I AM THE GREATEST SWINE, I OWN
I GIVE MYSELF TO JEWS ALONE.

The most terrible thing she wore, Rennie thought, was her smile. The blood from her cheek had mixed with her lipstick and yet she kept that forced, wide grin on her face, as if she had been shocked into an idiotic sociability.

Behind her, nude except for black ankle-length stockings and the sort of brown shoes clerks wore, stood a short, thin, middle-aged man. One lens of his eyeglasses had been broken. His white skin—soft, bluish, without definition—was a mass of overlapping black bruises. He held his long, surprisingly graceful white hands helplessly in front of him, as if to deny his manhood. He, too, smiled, as he looked down into the Budapester Strasse gutter, wanting—Rennie thought—to appease someone, anyone.

Two SA sergeants poked the girl in each breast with their halberds while a photographer snapped their picture. They are fixated, Rennie thought, on recording their crimes. The SA soldiers had begun to chant, over and over again with hypnotic intensity, the word *"Untermenschen."* The photographer was directing one of the sergeants to insert his halberd into the woman.

"There should be a sign," Rennie said, looking away, "telling us where the zoo begins and ends."

Moving quickly, von Danzig forced his way through the men to the place where the girl and the nude clerk stood, knocking down the photographer, pushing away the soldier attempting to penetrate the girl with his halberd.

Startled, the sergeant jabbed at Wolff as another SA man kicked him, aiming for the groin, connecting with Wolff's stomach. Wolff rolled off to the edge of the Budapester Strasse. The soldier who had kicked him bent down, his face nearly touching Wolff's. Wolff could smell the beer and tobacco and sweat as the SA man carefully spat in his face. "Next time, *mein Herr*, keep your sausage out of state business or we'll slice it off."

The photograph was taken, as planned, the *Horst Wessel Lied* was resumed, and the brownshirted SA men and boys —along with their victims—marched on.

Without thinking, she took charge. She managed, with some difficulty, to get Wolff into the two-seater. He had an inclination to fold up, automatically. She drove the Mercedes across Berlin refusing to allow it to bother her that she no longer had a legal license. She parked the Mercedes neatly in the alley running alongside the Kleist Kasino. She waited, coolly, for a moment or two to see if von Danzig could get out of the car on his own. When it was apparent he couldn't, she left him there and called Pepsi, and between them they got him up and into the bedroom she shared with Lillie.

"I'm all right," Wolff said, trying to stand, trying to focus on Pepsi with half-closed eyes. Pepsi helped him down onto the bed. "*Danke schön*," Wolff managed to say. "*Danke schön*." He closed his eyes.

"Pretty, ain't he?" Pepsi said, looking down at him. "I remember when he was a boy, passing himself off as a gigolo to get into the Kleist Kasino. Oh, those were the days, weren't they, honey?" He removed Wolff's jacket and shirt, gently, like a mother undressing a child. "It didn't matter what color you were, what sex you practiced, what planet you came from. Berlin was free."

He took off Wolff's shoes, stockings, and trousers. The wound from the swastika halberd wasn't deep, and the blood, what little there was, had dried. It was the kick, given full force, meant for the groin but connecting with Wolff's stomach, that had hurt the most. "I guess there's no reason to take off his shorts," Pepsi said, winking at Rennie.

"You are an animal, Pepsi," Rennie told him, removing Lillie's scanty first-aid kit from the dresser, applying antiseptic to the wound.

"You and der Führer say we're animals, Miss Rennie, and the Lord knows, I hope you're both right. I like to think of myself as an animal. A great big gorgeous Jesse Owens of an animal. When Owens did his stuff in the Olympics, that was the last laugh I had in this town. Only reason I'm still here—you'd best put some sticking plaster over that, girl—is my deep and lasting infatuation with La Froelich. My act went years ago. They declared it and me degenerate. Them Nazis only appreciate drag when they're wearing it, honey."

A thin bell rang somewhere in the building. Without one wasted motion, Pepsi was at the door. "I'm going to have to leave you two. I hope that man is safe with you, Rennie, honey." He closed the door after him.

Rennie watched von Danzig, as he lay, half unconscious, in Lillie's bed. She found herself no longer wanting to paint him. Well, yes, she would, given the opportunity. But what she wanted to do more than anything was to touch him. He opened his eyes and looked up at her.

"Are you all right?" he asked.

"I'm fine. It's you I'm concerned about."

He touched his solar plexus carefully. "A little sore but the worst is over."

She couldn't look at him. "I cleaned the wound but I think you should see a doctor. You might need a stitch or two."

"Very good, Nurse Nacht."

"Luckily, the swastika wasn't very sharp."

"Luckily." He stared up at her with his deep blue eyes and country-boy smile and she found herself staring back. He reached for her hand and then she found herself sitting next to him on the bed. "I want to make love to you, Rennie." The coverlet had fallen from him. His body was finely muscled. A thin line of blond hair began at his chest and ran down his torso.

"I thought the SA brute had rendered you *hors de combat,*" she said, with a confidence she didn't feel. She wanted to clear her throat, to swallow. She felt both cold and hot and wondered if he knew she was trembling.

"His aim was too high for permanent damage." He looked into her eyes for a long moment and she realized there wasn't anything he might ask her to do, then, that she wouldn't. She felt both weak and a little dazed, as if she had been woken too quickly from an afternoon nap. She knew, finally, what it meant when Lillie described a man as making her "drunk."

He pulled her to him and she could feel the heat from his body radiating through the sweater she wore. He kissed her and she kissed him back, her arms going around his muscular shoulders as she breathed in his clear, clean scent. She hoped that the kiss would never end, that they could stay that way, holding one another forever.

"I love you," he said, his lips still touching hers, his hands going under the black sweater, caressing her breasts. "I shouldn't. We're not going to do one another any good, that's certain. But I can't help myself. Neither can you."

He pressed his lips against hers, his mouth open as he began to undo her trousers when the door opened.

"My poor general," Lillie said, moving into the room like

an English nanny, removing her hat, switching on the light, taking over. "Pepsi told me what happened. Now, you mustn't move. Stay here and rest. Rennie can dress downstairs, in her dressing room. Come, *Schatzi.* You have your song to sing."

Later he stopped in the dressing room to say good-bye. "*Auf Wiedersehen,*" she said, not looking at him, wondering if she was blushing, wondering if Lillie—who stood next to him—could guess how she was feeling.

"*Wiedersehen,*" Wolff said, smiling at her.

Afterwards she told herself that he was, despite his bravery, an SS general, dedicated to *Judenrein.* And she was a Jewess whose father was wanted by the Gestapo. They were the most inconceivable couple.

Still, she couldn't get his touch, his smell, the heat of his body, out of her mind. Even the thought that Kimmel was waiting for her—that she had now but two days to get away from him—didn't erase the memory of Wolff from her consciousness.

Oddly enough, it was Lillie who didn't want to discuss finding Rennie and von Danzig in what might have been described as a compromising situation. When Rennie had attempted to bring it up, Lillie had laughed, embraced her, and sung a bar or two of one of her old songs: every lady needs a little comfort, now and then.

Rennie had sung her own song that night to a full house. Butch Jarman was at the center table, host to a group of foreign correspondents, properly appreciative of what she considered her own, limited talents.

There were fewer noncommissioned officers and enlisted men in the audience, now that her celebrity was growing. Officers and civilians in dinner jackets filled the tables while the "other" ranks stood two-deep at the bar. She looked for von Danzig, disappointed he hadn't turned up. She told herself again that he was an SS general, that she was a Jewess; that this was hardly a propitious moment for getting involved, much less falling in love. And even if it were, virtually any other German would be more suitable with the possible exception of Adolf Hitler.

As she stepped down into the audience to sell her silver roses, she thought, for a moment, that Kimmel had missed a night. But no, he was at his usual station, behind a Wehrmacht sergeant, at the far end of the bar, his feet planted solidly, his small yellow hands grasping a dark beer. He looked at her through his monocle but she pretended not to see him, finishing her act by disappearing through the leather curtain that was supposed to keep out drafts and didn't. It led backstage, to the stairs leading to Lillie's flat. Rennie raced up them, without pausing to remove her makeup. She wanted, she needed, the reassurance of her father's arms.

"What's the matter?" he asked, as he held her.

"The usual, *Vati*," she said, clinging to him.

"Oh, the usual. That's not so terrible. Now if it were the unusual, then we'd be in big trouble."

She laughed, allowing him to comfort her. They played rummy under Tante Lizbeth's watchful eye for a while and then, as had become her habit, Rennie went to sleep on the davenport in the far corner while Nick and Lizbeth argued in *shtetl* Yiddish.

He had learned it as a boy when his mother had sent him to the country for a summer. Spending a summer in Tante Lizbeth's *shtetl* was supposed to make him less sophisticated. If anything, it made him more, providing him with all the reasons he needed for never entering a synagogue again. He had thought—and worse, said—that Judaism was an old, tired religion, filled with empty traditions and rituals, designed to keep its followers enslaved.

"An opiate for the masses," he said, "to coin a phrase." He was fourteen and had somewhere found a pamphlet by Marx.

"You're not a Jew," Lizbeth opened, as usual. She sat in the straight-backed chair Rennie had occupied, on the far side of the folding table, knitting that eternal piece of worn gray wool. In the light from the green-visored lamp she looked like some ancient, vengeful deity.

"Tanti," Nick said, giving her his smile, dimpling. "Please. I beg you. Not the You're-Not-a-Jew lecture. Please."

His tired good humor, his charm, didn't work on her. She continued to knit, Madame de Farge-like, her face angry in the green light. "Your father wasn't a Jew either."

"He was a cosmopolitan Jew. He went to *shul* on high holidays."

"And you? You're only a cosmopolitan. No belief, no history, no nothing."

"I am not a religious Jew," Nick said, hurt again. Because despite the repetition of her arguments, she always found new ways to sting him. "But I am a Jew, Tanti." She sat silently, accusingly, knitting. "What did you want of me? To go around like the *Ostjuden,* your precious East Jews, dressed in old frock coats and skullcaps, a tattered prayer shawl around my shoulder, groveling, living in dirt and ignorance?" She wouldn't look at him, despite the urgency in his voice. "I wanted to see the world. I wanted to live in the world."

"And now that you've seen it? And now that you've lived in it?"

"I am still a Jew," he said, but quietly.

"No you're not. Neither, poor thing, is she," Lizbeth said, tossing her head in Rennie's direction. "If your daughter dies now, she'll die a nothing."

"If she dies now," Nick said, stung into retorting, "Rennie will die a German."

"A German?" Tante Lizbeth stood up and spat on the floor. "I give you that for your Germans. How can you be so ignorant after all this time? What have the Germans done for you? For us? What are they doing for our people now? The Germans, you poor fool, want to extinguish you and me and Rennie. You don't know yet? They want to *kill* us."

"All Germans are not Nazis."

Rennie turned on the davenport, looked at them through half-closed eyes, and went back to sleep.

"See a rabbi, Nick," Tante Lizbeth implored him, whispering, urgent. "I plead with you. Rabbi Levi is still in Berlin. Talk to him."

"And confess?"

"And become a Jew again."

"It's too late, Tante Lizbeth. It's too late."

"It's not too late for Rennie," Tante Lizbeth whispered to herself, suddenly giving up, gathering her gray wool, kissing Nick's forehead, then Rennie's, going to the door. "It's not too late for her."

Lillie came through the door before Tante Lizbeth could leave. "It's scheduled for tomorrow. I spoke to Kornwasser myself."

"Kornwasser," Tante Lizbeth said, shaking her head. He had been a friend of Nick's after the war, a rich doctor's son, a gentile, who had longed to be intellectual, like Nick and his friend, the novelist Winterhagen. They had let him sit at their table at the Romanische, but they put up with him rather than enjoyed him.

Kornwasser had become, by default, a successful doctor at an early age. The Jewish doctors had been forbidden to practice, and Kornwasser had inherited their patients. He had early on given up seeing Nick in public and later in private, though he had once, ruefully, offered to help when Lillie had called upon him. It was she who kept up the tenuous relationship between him and Nick.

"I do think you're taking a risk, Nick," Lillie said, sitting down in the chair Lizbeth had vacated. "We have a little time. Pepsi thinks he's traced a man we've used for papers once before. Why not wait . . ."

"You're going outside?" Tante Lizbeth asked. "Why?"

"He's going to Kornwasser's office to pressure him into getting Rennie proper papers. He may be able to do it. Odd as it may seem, Kornwasser has powerful friends now."

"He did it once before," Nick said. "He can do it again."

"Yes," Lillie sighed. "He got Winterhagen out. But it was a long time ago, and Winterhagen wasn't Jewish, only married to a Jew."

"He got her out, too."

"It's different now, Nick."

"So why shouldn't Kornwasser come to *you*?" Tante Lizbeth asked, looking at her nephew with concern. "Why do you have to go out, expose yourself to danger? Tell me, wouldn't it be safer for him to come here?"

"Safer for me. Not for him. Why should he?"

"Friendship," Tante Lizbeth said.

"One's career and perhaps one's life is rather a high price to pay for friendship," Nick told her, getting up, going to her, putting his arms around her.

"I still think," the old woman said, allowing herself to be kissed, "he should come to you. Have Lillie call him up on the telephone. Have him come to you, Nick. Please."

In the morning, when she found out about the excursion, Rennie insisted on going with Nick. "He's going for me, isn't he?" she asked, and that was an argument difficult to refute.

Pepsi pulled Lillie's old black-and-curtained Maybach sedan into the side alley. Nick stood just outside the Kleist Kasino's stage door for a moment, his eyes growing used to daylight. "At least I drew a sunny day," he said, looking up at the wedge of sky, taking a deep breath. *"Berliner Luft,"* he said. "Is there anything more palliative, more restorative, than Berlin's air?"

"Nick, darling," Lillie told him, taking his arm. "This is no time to go all rhapsodic over the air. This isn't a holiday outing. Do get into the car."

"Why shouldn't it be a holiday outing?" he asked, taking another deep breath, then doing as he was told, climbing into the back of the cavernous motorcar, sitting between Rennie and Lillie. He put his arms around them. "I am going on a holiday outing with my two favorite women. We are going for a motor ride around Berlin. Pepsi, my friend, drive down the Budapester Strasse. I want to see the Romanische."

"Nick, the longer we're out in the car, the more dangerous it will be," Lillie said. "Rennie," she appealed. "Tell him."

"It's true, Father. We can't . . ."

"I don't care. I am drunk on the air. I want to see my Berlin." He traded places with Rennie and peered out the side curtain as Pepsi expertly navigated the back streets of Berlin to emerge on the Budapester Strasse, near the location of the café where Nick had once held court.

To Rennie her father seemed more boyish than ever, a truant out on a forbidden trip. He held her hand as Pepsi stopped for a moment opposite the Romanische. Rennie remembered how they used to take second breakfast at the café: sweet tea with heavy milk, a Linzer Torte. She looked over her father's shoulder through the narrow space between the black curtains. The Romanische was nearly empty. Not so many years before, the cultural vanguard of Europe would gather at the outdoor Romanische tables to argue, fight, flirt, and drink. Usually, Nick Jablonski was in the center, at least a head taller than most of his antagonists.

Now there were only a few occupied tables. Those Jews and left-wing intellectuals still in Berlin and suicidal enough —or fatalistic enough—to be seen in public bent their heads together over the marble tabletops, conspiring in hoarse, frightened voices.

"Once Berlin was a city of shouts," Nick said, sitting back, letting the curtain close. "Now it's a city of whispers."

"Should I go on?" Pepsi asked.

Nick looked up at the clock on the Gedächtniskirche. It read quarter to eleven. "Yes. Go on," he answered. "I'll meet you all there. Forgive me. I need more air." He was out of the car and walking before they could stop him. "I'll meet you at Kornwasser's office," he said, putting his hands in his trouser pockets, moving jauntily away from them in the direction of the Kurfürstendamm.

"I'm going to join him," Rennie said, getting out of the car, too, running after him. "I need more air, too."

"Fools," Lillie said, watching Rennie catch up with her father and take his arm. "I love them but they shouldn't take such risks."

"You love them, baby, because they take such risks," Pepsi said, starting the car, driving slowly.

Lillie watched them as they strolled and thought that they looked so right, so unextraordinary. Nick wore a cap and the tweed suit he had been wearing when he had arrived at the stage door that frightening night.

Pepsi had brought him to the dressing room. She was just taking off her makeup. "Don't tell anyone I'm here, will you, Pepsi?" Nick had asked.

"You're not here," Pepsi said, leaving them alone.

"Nick, what is it?" Lillie had asked. She had never seen him so pale, so unnerved.

"You don't have anything to drink hidden down here, do you?" She had given him a glass of schnapps. He drank it down and asked for another. "It's finally happened," he said. "The Gestapo want me for questioning."

"*Lieber Gott!* Nick, you must get away."

"A little difficult now, dear Lillie. I wouldn't have come here but the truth is, I had nowhere else to go." She went to him and he put his arms around her. "I have a terrible confession to make, Lillie."

"You'll stay here. In the false attic. Just for a short time. Until we can get you papers, transport—"

"I'm frightened. I'm scared. I can't remember ever having been so frightened before. Look." He held his big, firm hands out in front of him and they trembled. "I wouldn't have come here for all the world, Lillie. I wouldn't have implicated you for anything. If I only knew where else to go."

"This is the only place to go, Nick." She had held him and fed him schnapps until everyone had left the cabaret and then had taken him up the back stairs.

"All I need," he had said, jaunty again in the morning, "is a stroll along the Ku-damm to chase the blues away."

He liked that phrase, "the blues." He had picked it up from Pepsi and used it a great deal. He was a brave man, and if he thought walking along the Ku-damm would chase away his blues, then she was all for it. She watched as Rennie held on to his arm. She wore her sad brown suit, the slouch hat.

And Lillie remembered the Gestapo coming, very polite, searching the cabaret and her flat and even the attic, missing, luckily, the false door which led to where Nick was hiding. And Tante Lizbeth appearing after they had left, saying she had spent the night "at home, where else? They didn't want me." No, they had only wanted Nick. They still did.

"*Lieber Gott,* don't let anything happen," she said, aloud.

"They're going to be all right," Pepsi reassured her as he drove past them.

Rennie was echoing his words. "We're going to be all right, aren't we, Papa?"

He patted her hand, but he wouldn't answer. He knew quite well that the chances were they wouldn't be all right. The Gestapo was too thorough. There were too many people working for it. They wanted him too badly. If there's any chance at all, he thought, Rennie might have it.

They strolled down the Kurfürstendamm like any middle-aged father and his young daughter. Respectable. Not too badly dressed. For all intents and purposes, solid Aryans. Just like everyone else on the Ku-damm on that bright early-November day in 1938.

Window-shopping. Reading political messages on posters plastered around the kiosks. Here, on Berlin's answer to the Rue de la Paix, there was nothing sinister, nothing out of the way. Nothing except perhaps the discreet signs forbidding Jews to enter the premises of virtually all of the shops.

But here on the Ku-damm in the fashionable West End of Berlin, money changed hands with agreeable regularity. Here, no one needed further proof of the economic miracle Hitler had wrought.

Once, Nick thought, it had taken a wheelbarrow filled with money to purchase a loaf of bread. Now one could have a loaf of bread for under a mark and that same wheelbarrow filled with marks could buy a small car. Money spoke to the German public infinitely more effectively than the posters on the kiosks or the *Judenrein* signs on the shop doors.

Suddenly there was the sound of metal hitting the pavement. It was his ring. The signet ring Viktoria had given him on the day before their marriage. His hands had grown too thin.

Rennie bent over, picked it up. He closed her palm over it. "You keep it, *Schatzi*. Hold it for me until I gain a little weight."

"I don't want to, Papa. I want you to wear it."

"But I want you to. This is my holiday. I get anything I want today." He took the ring and placed it on the middle finger of her right hand. Then he looked up and saw a kiosk selling *Wursts*. "Oh, *mein Gott*, a small miracle," Nick Jablonski said, forgetting about the ring. "Can I believe my tired eyes? I am going to have, at long last, a proper *Currywurst*, hot with the right sauce. Not like those gray cold ones Pepsi, bless his dark heart, brings me. Do you want one, Rennie?"

"No," she said, looking at the ring and then up at her tall, thin, handsome father. "No. I couldn't eat now. But you go ahead."

He bought two *Currywursts*. "Who knows when I'll have the opportunity again?" he asked, covering them with mustard. He ate as they walked, finishing them as they arrived at the corner entrance to his friend Kornwasser's office.

"Keep walking," he told her, suddenly serious. "Lillie and Pepsi are waiting in the Maybach at the far end of the street. I'll come out the side entrance and join you when I'm finished." He took her in his arms and held her tightly. "I love you, Rennie. I've always loved you in a special way . . . a way I've never been able to love anyone else. Not your mother. Not Lillie. I am so proud of you. I am proud that you came back for me. It was foolish but it was brave, and to be brave and beautiful and good and kind is very difficult in this world."

"I am not brave, Papa. I'm a terrible coward. I'm frightened all the time."

"That's a sign of bravery, believe me." He held her a little away from him and she saw that there were—once again—tears in his eyes. "No matter what happens to me, I want you to promise that you'll keep going on; that you won't give up. For me. Will you promise that, Rennie?"

"I promise, Father."

He kissed her, hugged her tightly, and went up the two marble stairs into Kornwasser's office. She wanted to follow him but she didn't. Instead, she walked around the block, found the Maybach at the end of the street, and got in.

"He's all right?" Lillie asked, breathless, as if it had been she who had been walking down the Ku-damm.

"He's fine."

She looked at the ring he had given her and tried to smile at Lillie. It was only later that she realized he must have had a fairly good idea, a solid premonition, of what was awaiting him.

Nurse Gruppe let Nick in. She was a new addition to Kornwasser's staff, taken on when he had joined the party and party members' wives had begun to come to him. Nurse Gruppe, who might have been any age between twenty and fifty, smiled. Her fat, red cheeks made her look like an NSDAP illustration entitled "The Happy Peasant."

"Herr Schmidt?" she asked in a high, singsong voice, as if she were talking to a child. "Herr Doktor will be with you in a moment." She stared at him for a time with her mock-friendly milky blue eyes, round and interrogative. "We have met before, Herr Schmidt?"

"Not that I know of," Nick said, sitting down in an over-upholstered sofa, picking up a pamphlet.

"You seem so familiar."

"I have an ordinary face."

"No. That's not true. You have a memorable face."

The pamphlet was an NSDAP tract. "If you need counsel or aid, turn to your party organization," the front page of the pamphlet cautioned. He did need counsel and aid, admittedly. But he thought his local party organization might not welcome him with open arms.

Nurse Gruppe was still filling up the doorway which led to Kornwasser's infirmary and offices when Nick Jablonski looked up. She was staring at him openly. He smiled, uncomfortable. She reminded him of a malevolent cat. He turned to look at the League of German Girls poster that took up most of the opposite wall. Two beautiful blond girls, on holiday, sat on a hill, sailboats in the background. Their heads were close together. One held a Nazi flag in her hand.

"Wonderful, is it not?" Nurse Gruppe asked, following his eyes. "Holidays for the *Jungvolk* and always amid their own kind. So comforting, so right to be among one's own kind, is it not, Herr Schmidt?"

Nurse Gruppe turned with some difficulty, her starched uniform and solid body making her movements slow and awkward. She went back through the door leading to the offices, leaving it open. Her desk, which was just outside Kornwasser's study, was a model of organization. She sat at it, sighing as she always did when she sat down, opened the bottom drawer to the left, and found, almost immediately, what she was searching for.

Nick had gotten up, ostensibly to examine the poster. Actually, he wanted to see what Nurse Gruppe was up to. He stood in front of the poster but looked in through the open door. She was only reading *Der Stürmer*, Julius Streicher's rabidly anti-Semitic weekly. She took it by sub-

scription, religiously preserving each copy, taking it with
her for her nephew's enlightenment when she visited her
sister on Sundays in the country.

Nick, reassured that she wasn't telephoning the Gestapo
—for she had seemed quite capable of that—moved back to
his seat. But Nurse Gruppe was not engaged in idle reading.
On the second page of the particular issue she had located
was a photograph she had remembered. "Enemy of the
State," the caption read. A Polish Jew masquerading as an
Aryan. All the worse because he appeared to be Aryan. He
was wanted, *Der Stürmer* said, for questioning. But there
was little doubt in Nurse Gruppe's mind that he was wanted
for more than questioning.

Kornwasser, a balding, tall man with narrow shoulders,
put his head over the half doors that separated Nurse
Gruppe's office from the infirmary and said that he would
see Herr Schmidt.

"Have you been treating him long?" she asked. "I have
not been able to locate his records."

"No," Kornwasser said, staring down at her. "This is his
first appointment." When she didn't avert her gaze, he went
on. "He was recommended by someone or other that I met
at lunch at the Kaiserhof."

"We must be careful about these recommendations, Herr
Doktor Kornwasser. You are too important to see just
anyone."

He polished his gold-framed pince-nez, avoiding Nurse
Gruppe's eyes. "Yes," he said, turning away from that milk
blue stare. "I suppose we must."

Nurse Gruppe smiled broadly to herself as she made the
telephone call. She didn't even have to look up the number.
She was proud of herself for keeping such details always at
hand in the file in her mind. She smiled even more broadly
after the call was completed. Life was good. Germany was
great. She, meaning herself, felt rewarded for doing her
duty.

Politely, scrupulously, she showed Herr Schmidt into the doctor's office. He barely glanced at the copy of *Der Stürmer,* now facedown on her desk. After all, it occurred to her. She might be wrong. She had told the voice on the other end of the wire that she might be wrong. But taking one last look at Herr Schmidt's handsome profile, she was quite certain she wasn't.

"I shall see what I can do, Nick," Kornwasser, again polishing his pince-nez, said. "It's more difficult now. Winterhagen chose to leave at the right time. Of course I still know people in the Records Section, but the document makers are being carefully scrutinized, especially now with the Polish roundup. In a week or two, perhaps."

"A week or two will be too late for my daughter, Helmut."

Kornwasser put on his pince-nez and looked at Nick with a quick flash of anger. Yes, Jablonski always addressed him in the familiar way of friends but he had never been a genuine friend. He had suffered Helmut Kornwasser but hadn't encouraged him. Kornwasser had been, in those days, not just a wealthy doctor's son. He had also been a poet.

He remembered a particularly hot Berlin day when just to move soaked one with perspiration. He had gotten up the courage, somehow, to submit a poem to Jablonski for publication in *Der Tag*. Nick had sat across from him as he did now, the same embarrassed half smile on his face. He said he had shown the poem to several people who "know a lot more about poetry than I do. It's not for us, Helmut," he had said, handing the poem back to him. "I'm sorry."

"It's no good, is that it? I should stop wasting my time trying to write poetry and apply myself to my studies, is that what you are telling me, Nick?"

"No. I am only telling you, Helmut, that the poem is not for us."

He had ripped up the poem, and though he had wanted to throw it in Nick's face, he had pitched it into the garbage can on the street. He knew the experts Nick had shown his poem to. They invariably patronized him. He hadn't been able to wisecrack like them. He hadn't been able to argue with their spirit or conviction. They had had vast dreams for themselves, the world. His dreams had all been second-hand, given to him by his father.

And then, one night, his fiancée had taken him to the Sportspalast to hear Adolf Hitler speak. Instantaneously, he had been given his own dream: a pure, all-Aryan German state without decadent intellectuals to make him feel like a fool; a pure all-Aryan German state where he could attain the sort of life his ancestors—pure, all-Aryan—had meant for him. He wanted a house in Dahlem, a smart car, the attendant at the Adlon to know his name. He wanted to be listened to by his colleagues, respected. Just as Nick Jablonski was.

Adolf Hitler had given Helmut Kornwasser his own dream. He smiled and said he would see what he could do. And he would. He didn't hate Nick Jablonski. He only wanted him and his corrupting influence out of his country. He had helped Winterhagen with money, with papers for his Jewess wife and children. It had been a thrill to see the fat, famous novelist groveling, not knowing what words to use—for the first time in his life—to thank Kornwasser. He certainly would do what he could for Nick. But he wanted his efforts to be appreciated.

"I shall be in touch, Nick," he said, feeling unaccountably jaunty. "But you do know what you're asking?"

"Yes, Helmut. I don't expect you to risk your neck. But if you could only do what you did for Winterhagen . . ."

"I *wouldn't* risk my neck, Nick. It's too valuable now." He stood up and held out his nicely manicured hand. "I'll let you know the results," he said, loudly, for Nurse Gruppe's benefit. "Though I'm certain there is nothing to worry about."

Nurse Gruppe watched as Herr Schmidt left by the infirmary door which led to the side street. Her apple cheeks went a shade redder as she stared up at Herr Doktor Kornwasser with her wide, motherly smile. She held open the copy of *Der Stürmer* for him to see. "You need someone to protect you, Herr Doktor Kornwasser, *nicht wahr?*"

Suddenly deflected, Kornwasser agreed, moving quickly back into his office, shutting the door, locking Nurse Gruppe out. He tried to keep from his mind the vision of one of the Gestapo victims he had been asked—well, ordered—to treat.

They had called him in the middle of the night, taken him to a building in the old Jewish quarter behind the Opera and told him he had to save what was left of the wretched man lying on a bloodied mattress. They hadn't gotten what they had wanted from him. They had gone too far, Kornwasser was obliged to tell them. He couldn't revive the dead.

How disappointed the SS captain had been.

Kornwasser sat at his desk and thought of the tortured body they had ordered him to revive. Since then, he had seen many tortured bodies, many of them a good deal worse. But that first one still held impact. Then he thought of Nurse Gruppe and his SS captain friend and of Nick's belief that he could help him.

But Kornwasser, sitting at his desk, polishing his gold pince-nez, didn't want to think of Nick Jablonski. "I know nothing about it," he said, when he heard the noises from the side street, a few moments later, already preparing his defense. "Nurse Gruppe did it."

Rennie kept her eyes at the space between the curtains, looking up the street—in reality, no more than an alley— down which her father would be coming.

"It seems ages, doesn't it?" she asked, twisting the signet ring he had given her round her finger.

"Perhaps Kornwasser is attempting to get in touch with someone on the telephone," Lillie said, resting her bright red hair against the musty faded purple plush of the upholstery. "Someone who can help."

Rennie remembered once coming from a visit to Oskar's. Oskar had insisted on sending a solid Austrian maid with her. She had been shorter than Rennie, who at twelve was already tall and reedy. She had been unaccountably ashamed of the maid. "Papa always meets me at the station." But Oskar had insisted and, that one time, Nick had been late, an incident at *Der Tag* holding him up. She had felt so abandoned and, at the same time, embarrassed. She had tried to explain to the maid that something awful must have happened as the crowd thinned out and only the two of them were left at the entrance to the waiting room. The maid had stood there with her solid peasant face red-cheeked and disapproving until Nick had arrived, tipped her, and sent her back to Oskar. The relief at seeing Nick had made her forget all about her embarrassment.

"There's *Vati* now," Rennie said, relieved. Lillie put her face next to Rennie's at the car window. They watched as Nick—smiling, insouciant, knowing they were watching but unable to see them—made his way down the side street.

It was like a motion picture. It was too real, Nick—larger than life—strolling down the cobbled street toward them in the steel blue shadows cast by the old buildings lining the pavement.

And suddenly, instantaneously, two men in gabardine rain-coats, anonymous slouch hats not all that dissimilar to the one Rennie wore, stepped out of doorways on either side of the street, cutting Nick off from the car.

She wanted to scream, but that paralyzing fear, a hundred times more intense than ever, hit her as she reached for the door handle. Lillie put her arms around her, keeping her in the car. Nick, still casual, though his eyes had narrowed, turned and headed back toward the Ku-damm. For a moment it looked as if he would reach it, but then another man stood at the far end of the cobbled side street, blocking Nick's way.

And suddenly, again with the cinema's curious heightened reality, the two men closest to the Maybach had revolvers in their hands. She tried to see what they looked like, these men with revolvers, but the blue shadows blunted their features. Only the reflective metal of their guns could be seen in sharp detail.

Like someone totally caught up in the film she was watching, she sat still, held in Lillie's firm grip. Everything stopped for just a moment as if the film had broken down. And then it all started up again. Too quickly; she couldn't keep up with the action.

She heard the shots, closed her eyes for a moment, and then saw her father's body being spun around as if by supernatural force. He fell with his arms stretching out toward the car, toward Rennie. Blood immediately soaked his coat, the brown tweed cap which lay beside him.

"I've got to go to him," Rennie whispered. *"Mutti,* please. Let me go."

Lillie turned her face away from the narrow side street, burying her head in Rennie's neck, holding on to her. But Rennie couldn't turn away. She watched as a black Mercedes backed into the alley, as her father's bloodied body was thrown unceremoniously into the trunk, like an unwieldy, not very important parcel. They wouldn't see Nick's body again. Like so many others, it would simply disappear.

"There won't be a funeral, will there?" Rennie said, thinking of Tante Lizbeth. "We won't be able to mourn."

Lillie began to cry hot, steamy tears as the third man moved away from the Ku-damm and toward the official Mercedes. He wore a leather trench coat. The monocle in his eye wavered—transparent, opaque.

Rennie screamed then, but only once.

Pepsi waited for the Mercedes to leave the alley, to pass their car. He knew, with its black curtains drawn, the

Maybach looked like just another unoccupied auto. He waited until he was quite certain they were off before he started the car and began the drive home.

He couldn't stand the sound of Lillie's sobs. "They must have picked him up the moment he stepped onto the Kudamm," Pepsi said, because he didn't know what else to say. He looked in the rearview mirror. Lillie's red head was cradled in Rennie's arms. She was crying uncontrollably. The girl simply stared ahead, dry-eyed, lost.

Rennie knew she was in some sort of shock. She was aware of that. She felt as if some essential part of her had been amputated, cut off in a freak accident. She was still too numb to realize its importance. Later, when she wanted to use it, when she needed it, when she found it was gone . . . well, later she would grieve. Now all she felt was numb. But in the theater in her mind, she kept seeing her father's body being spun around as if by supernatural force. She kept seeing the man with the monocle tossing Nick's body into the trunk of the official Mercedes. It was as if the projector had gotten out of hand and could only play this one piece of film, over and over again.

Lillie, attempting to recover, had Pepsi stop the car at the top of the Kleiststrasse. She took her mascara from her purse and began to work on her eyes in the mirror of a gold compact Nick had given her. "I'm finished with crying," Lillie said. "But there'll be plenty of time for *you* to cry later. You can't let those damned Goose Girls see you've been crying. You'll make your eyes red so everyone in the audience will know."

Rennie looked at Lillie. "The audience? Lillie, I can't sing tonight. I can't . . ."

"Oh, yes, you can, *Schatzi*. You must. We have to convince them that nothing is wrong. That the Kleist Kasino is open, business as usual."

"But Lillie . . ."

She closed the compact and dropped it and the mascara into her purse. She put her arms around Rennie and held her close. "We can't have them searching the house, *Schatzi,*" she whispered. "There's you and your dubious status. And if you don't care what happens to you, there's me and Lizbeth and Pepsi. And my guests in the attic." She kissed her. "You *have* to sing tonight, *Schatzi.*"

And then Lillie began to cry again, the newly applied mascara running down her ruined cheeks. "Oh, *Schatzi,* what will I do without him?"

"What we all shall do," Rennie said with a strength she didn't feel. "We'll go on."

But she didn't want to go on. She wanted to stay in the back of the limousine, embracing Lillie, keeping her eyes wide open so she wouldn't have to see that terrible sight. When she closed her eyes, she could see the glint of the eyeglass, hear the trunk of the official Mercedes slam shut, the clamor of the men getting into the car. Out of sequence, she could see her father's body ricocheting from side to side of that Ku-damm side street.

She wondered, as she watched Lillie reapply her mascara with an increasingly shaky hand, if she would ever close her eyes again without seeing her father being murdered.

She wondered if she were going to be able to cry.

10

Lillie had forced her to drink two shots of French brandy, and that had helped. It had helped her to stop remembering.

She had gone down to the sad dressing room a quarter of an hour before she was supposed to sing, just as she always did. Pepsi had come in and stayed with her for a moment. She took his hand and then she put her arms up and around him, holding his cool face close to hers. "No tears," Pepsi said. "No tears, honey. That's the word from the boss." She held him close. She needed physical comfort. She needed someone to hold her close.

They weren't going to tell Tante Lizbeth, but she read the grief in their faces when they returned. She ran into her room, screamed, and ripped the collar on her black dress. Sobbing, she took her ancient prayer book from its place under her pillow, placed a handkerchief on her head, and got down on her knees to pray.

Rennie didn't have that consolation. She needed people. "No tears, honey," Pepsi said again.

"I'm not crying, Pepsi," she told him, stepping back, looking up into his round, brown, inconsolable eyes, realizing that he was crying, that tears were running down his smooth, black cheeks.

She took a handkerchief from her dressing table and blotted his eyes, his cheeks for him. He held her hand for a moment. "You don't get to meet too many men like Nick Jablonski. I'm going to miss him, too, you know?"

"I know, Pepsi."

He left her alone. The dressing room was filled, as usual, with flowers—mostly tinted silver roses—and chocolates. Usually, Rennie gave the flowers to the Goose Girls and the chocolates to the forlorn trio to take home to their wives. Tonight the overarranged bouquets, the too-thoughtfully-worked-out arrangements—the inevitable swastika motif dominated—seemed demoniacally suitable. They would be the only funeral flowers Nick Jablonski was going to get.

"I think I'm beginning to hate flowers," Rennie said as Lillie, head-to-toe in red bugle beads, came in.

"Not silver roses, *Schatzi*."

"Especially silver roses."

"Are you all right? Yes, of course you are. Stand in the light. I want to see your makeup. It is important that tonight everything be quite perfect." Rennie had known that. She had put her hair up into the silver lamé turban and had applied the silver half moons above her eyes in exactly the way Pepsi had taught her. The silver lamé dress clung to her, its neckline only just concealing her breasts. "You really are very beautiful, *Schatzi*."

"That doesn't help, Lillie."

"Not now. But it will." She went to the door. "Your father would be proud of you, darling. I'm proud of you, for what that's worth."

"A great deal," Rennie told her, and then Lillie was gone, out into the Kleist Kasino to greet her guests. Just as if nothing had happened. Rennie sat in her dressing room and waited while the trio made its way through its Hawaiian number. She felt hollow, still numb, a recent amputee. She felt as if she didn't much care what would happen to her now. For the moment, she wasn't even afraid of Kimmel. She went into the wings as the trio finished and stepped out onto the stage when Pepsi played the opening bars of her song.

She lit the brown stump of a cigarette, removed the turban with a theatrical, weary gesture, and moved downstage to strike the Friedrichstrasse prostitute's pose. Slowly, she ground out the cigarette with the toe of her silver sandal and then stowed it in the top of her stocking, giving the audience a view of her legs. Then she faced them and began to sing.

> I am the Silver Rose of Berlin.
> A flower a trifle past first bloom.

She saw von Danzig standing at one end of the bamboo bar, Kimmel at the other. And suddenly her voice caught. She turned away. She didn't want all those fine examples of German manhood who came every night to hunger after her to know something was wrong. Pepsi segued neatly into the bridge, waiting until she was able to sing again. It seemed to everyone that the pause was part of her act, a singularly effective one.

> I meet a man,
> We make a deal.
> I take him to the bed
> In my cellar room.

She stepped off the stage, taking the basket of silver roses with her. As she sang, as she sold the flowers, she finally thought of her father. Not the way he was the last time she had seen him, his body spun around by the force of the bullets in the alley off the Ku-damm. But laughing, playing rummy, wearing his old gray sweater with the oversized wooden buttons.

He hadn't been able to see her sing her song. How he would have enjoyed its theatricality, its cheap pathos. She touched the signet ring. Tonight she sang her song for him.

I am the Silver Rose of Berlin.
Someday I'll take a stroll
Into the Tiergarten, where it's dark.
I'll use a pistol (don't worry,
I shan't miss my mark).
And that will be the finale for
The Silver Rose of Berlin.

She finished at the end of the bar where Kimmel stood, holding his dark beer in his small hands. "Bravo, Fräulein Nacht," he said, as the audience stood and applauded. "You sang better tonight than you ever have. And I am something of an authority." He released the beer and put his hand into his trench coat pocket, searching for money. "I shall buy all the flowers."

"They are not for sale, Herr Kimmel." She handed the basket to Gunther, the barman, removing one, going to von Danzig, inserting it in the lapel of his jacket. "On the house," she said, looking back at Kimmel for a moment.

Then she disappeared through the leather curtain at the back of the bar which was designed to keep out drafts and didn't.

The lights darkened, the trio took their place while Kimmel tapped a coin on the edge of the bar's chromium surface. "I think it's time," he said to Gunther, looking at von Danzig, "that I settled my bill."

Rennie removed her makeup and went upstairs to the bedroom she shared with Lillie, changing into the white satin Russian dressing gown. She sat on the bed and listened to the terrible sound of Lizbeth chanting the Jewish prayer for the dead. It came through the thin walls as a kind of deafening whisper. For a moment Rennie thought of going to her, but Lizbeth, she realized, had her own solace, one Rennie couldn't share.

Instead, she went into the closet and through the secret

door up to the hidden attic. She heard the muted sounds of a radio broadcast in English coming from the room at the far end of the corridor. Miraculously, Lillie had found a nearly new Telefunken for the displaced family. "They'll go mad without some diversion," Lillie had explained away her generosity.

They spent most of their time listening to it. The father thought they might learn English from it. He had been told, originally, that they were going to be taken to England. It was why the boy, Lillie said, was so attached to his cap. He thought it was quintessentially British, what every London boy wore.

"Are you going to tell them about Father?" Rennie had asked.

"No. They have little enough hope as it is."

Rennie opened the door into the room where her father had spent the last weeks of his life. She wondered how much hope he had had. The green glass reading lamp had been left on, spreading a circle on the folding table. His playing cards were there, neatly stacked. The gray cashmere sweater hung from the chair. It seemed as if he had only stepped away for a moment.

And then she heard a muffled sob coming from the davenport in the far corner. Lillie sat there, her long legs crossed, her head in her hands, the geranium red hair more unkempt than ever. Rennie went to her, sitting next to her, putting her arms around Lillie, drawing the older woman close. "I thought you had finished with crying, *Mutti*," she whispered.

"I'll never be finished," Lillie said. "Oh, *Schatzi*, what am I going to do without him? He was everything to me. He was my courage, my warmth, my life. *Schatzi*," she said, burying her face in Rennie's neck, sobbing uncontrollably. "I need him so much."

Rennie looked at his sweater, thinking her father had been the most comforting person she had ever known. She remembered the first time she had menstruated. She had been crampy all through the night, and when she woke up, she first felt and then saw the blood. Quite matter-of-factly she had rung for the maid and the maid had gone for Tante Lizbeth, who hadn't been so matter-of-fact—"My God, oh, my God," she had said, over and over again—but at last Rennie had been cleaned and made comfortable. She had known what was happening; it had come as no surprise. She lay in bed all day, on Tante Lizbeth's orders, drinking hot chocolate, attempting to treat the incident as one of scientific interest. She had been detached.

And then Nick had come in and kissed her and looked at her for a long time and beamed. "I can see it," he said, as she blushed. "You're no longer a girl. You're a woman."

"But I don't want to be a woman," she had cried out, still very much a little girl, no longer detached. She had been, under the scientific interest, frightened at her body's betrayal. She wanted to stay as she was. "I'll have to wear high heels and corsets and forever be slimming."

Nick had laughed. "But you'll also get to drink champagne." The door had opened and a servant had brought in a magnum of French champagne and a silver tray of caviar and the tiny buttered crackers she adored. She hadn't much liked the caviar but she finished at least her share of the champagne. And when he kissed her good night, she had looked up at him in that golden haze the champagne had created and said, "Perhaps I won't mind being a woman so much after all."

"I think, *Schatzi*, that you're going to love it."

Well, she wasn't at all certain she loved being a woman, but Nick had always been there for her, to help her not be frightened. She wondered now if she was going to be frightened all the time.

The two women sat there on the davenport, holding on to one another, remembering, until Pepsi came into the room.

"Sorry to disturb you," he said, looking not at all like

himself but serious and sad. "However, Hitler's twin brother is downstairs, demanding to see Rennie."

"But we have another day," Lillie said, standing up, dabbing ineffectually at her hair.

"He said, in not so many words, that time's up. Herr Kimmel said this time it's official business."

"*Lieber Gott*," Lillie said, looking at Rennie. "I'll go down first. I'll see how serious he is. I'll tell him you're sleeping. That you thought you had another day to make your decision. That you're mulling it over. I'll tell him something." She left the door open as she moved into the corridor, followed by Pepsi looking like a serious scarecrow in his white dinner jacket. "You go down to the club, Pepsi. See if von Danzig is still there. . . ."

And then Rennie heard the door to the stairwell shut. She went out into the corridor. Kimmel was going to demand to see her. She wasn't frightened. At least she didn't think she was. She would be later, of course. When she couldn't produce papers, when Kimmel took her off to some airless room in the subcellars of Spandau. As in a nightmare, the terror was too real. She could see the room. She had visualized it for a long time now. It was always white, antiseptic as a room in a hospital. And as in a hospital, there were instruments. But these instruments weren't used for saving people's lives. . . .

"*Guten Tag, Fräulein*," the boy said, and she nearly screamed. He stood in front of her with his brown and white checked cap in his hand, smiling tentatively.

"*Guten Tag*," she said, reaching down, touching his black hair.

"*Guten Tag*," he said again, still smiling.

"What is your name?" she asked, in one of the few Yiddish phrases she knew.

His face lit up. "Ruben," he told her. And then a stout woman in an old-fashioned print dress appeared in the doorway at the far end of the musty corridor, holding her hands together, calling softly to the boy not to disturb the young lady. The man standing behind her wore a worn blue suit and a careful expression. He looked like a provincial school-master. Concern was in both their faces, making them seem more like brother and sister than husband and wife. A terrible, deep, and all-consuming concern.

"Ruben, come here," the wife said, and the boy, after a moment's hesitation, turned and ran to her on his thin, sad legs.

"*Gute Nacht, Fräulein,*" he called after her, waving the racy checked cap, his prize possession. "*Gute Nacht.*" His mother looked at him with a mixture of affection and re-proval, as if he had committed some mischievous act.

"*Gute Nacht,* Ruben," Rennie said, as she made her way down the stairs. It wasn't fair to let Lillie face Kimmel by herself.

Lillie stood in front of the oversized, romanticized portrait of herself holding her fine, large hands, looking—in the light from the candles she insisted upon—not unlike a Toulouse-Lautrec dance hall belle with too-red hair, kohled eyes.

Kimmel stood in the exact center of the room, his leather coat open, his small square feet wide apart, as if he were taking part in some military action. And perhaps, Rennie thought, he was.

"Then Fräulein Nacht has no papers, no identification of any sort?" Kimmel was saying as Rennie stepped through the beaded curtains. "Is that correct?" He turned and smiled. "*Gnädiges Fräulein.* I was told you were sleeping, but I am happy to see I am misinformed. Perhaps you can clear up what surely must be a minor misunderstanding." He bowed, his eyeglass catching the candlelight. "I must trouble you to show me your papers."

"I don't have any papers."

"Yes, she does," Lillie said, before Rennie could go on.

"Of course she has papers. Do you think I'd let her work in my club if she didn't have papers?"

Lillie fit a cigarette into her holder while Rennie walked across the room and stood in front of the window overlooking the Kleiststrasse. A staff car and two men in gabardine raincoats and slouch hats stood in front of the entrance to the Kasino.

"Then may I see them, Fräulein Froelich."

"She can't get them now. Rennie's ill. You can't ask her to go out into the streets at this hour, across half Berlin, to the friend's flat where she left them. It would be indiscreet, given the friend and his standing in the party. But she has papers," Lillie went on, pausing to inhale, to let the smoke drift out of her mouth. "Believe me, Herr Kimmel, she has papers."

He turned and looked at Rennie, who was looking down into the street, her arms folded. Unaware that he was watching her, she reached across a little table and took a cigarette from a lacquered box. She could have been in a drawing room or a theater lobby or an extravagant night club. She could have been anywhere but in that room being asked for papers by an official of the Third Reich.

"Now," Kimmel shouted, and Lillie's drawing room reverberated with the word. "I want to see them now," he said, in a lower but no less forceful tone. "Her time is up."

"Herr Kimmel." Von Danzig came into the room and stood next to Kimmel, taller, more handsome, and for the moment, more controlled. "Surely, Herr Kimmel, this can wait until the morning."

"Now," Kimmel said. "Right this moment." He was shouting again. His hand found its way into his trench coat pocket, locating the tin of *Lutschbonbons*, hesitating, not bringing the candies out.

For a moment he seemed to be in another place. He was thinking of Rennie, so cool and assured on the stage. He was thinking of her rejecting his offer to buy her flowers, of her flaunting her affection for von Danzig by placing a silver rose in his buttonhole. He squeezed the tin of *Lutschbonbons* in his pocket until his hand hurt, until the tin was crushed.

"Fräulein Nacht and I have an important engagement," von Danzig said, giving him time to control his fury. "I assure you it would be embarrassing to the Reich—which, I remind you, we both serve—were she forced to produce her papers now. They're difficult to get at, at this moment." Von Danzig put his arm through Kimmel's and led him to the door, talking to him as if they were friends, one good fellow to another. "I'll be responsible for her," he said, in a confidential whisper, winking. "Just until morning, Kimmel."

Kimmel stood at the door. His neck was pink but his round face was its usual gray. He looked up at von Danzig through his rimless monocle and, under control, smiled his damp, thin-lipped grimace.

"I am not ungenerous, Herr General. I merely have a job to do. You must understand that, just as I understand you and Fräulein Nacht have an important engagement." His eyeglass caught the light from one of the candles again, making him seem—for just that second—blind. "Certainly I shall give Fräulein Nacht until the morning to produce her credentials. Surely, under your protection, she will be secure. But I must ask you to have her appear at my office tomorrow morning at ten o'clock. That is not too early, is it? No? Good. I am at the Präsidium for the moment."

He turned slowly, retreating. "Naturally, Herr General, I shall have to report to my superiors. As I say, I am willing to wait and I am certain, once they know of your involvement, they will be, too. *Heil Hitler!*"

As the door shut after him, Rennie put out her cigarette. "I think," she said, speaking in a low voice, avoiding von Danzig's eyes, "that I'll lie down for a bit. I'm not feeling as well as I might." She put a reassuring hand on Lillie's arm and went through the beaded curtains.

"Let her go," Lillie said when von Danzig began to go

after her. "She really does have to rest, at least for a while, and you and I will have a chance to talk."

"You'd better tell me who she is," von Danzig said, looking at Lillie, who had no intention of telling him who Rennie Nacht was. She poured them both brandies. Von Danzig sipped at his, but she knocked hers off and poured another, lying down full length on the Napoleonic couch.

"You're an awfully attractive man, *mein Generälchen,*" she said.

"We don't have time for a flirtation, *gnädiges Fräulein.*"

"All right. She really is an Austrian," Lillie said, mentally crossing her fingers. "Viennese. I know. She sounds as Viennese as Emmy Göring, but she spent a great deal of time in Berlin in her youth. Her father was an aide to the Austrian ambassador to Germany for years, and more recently, he assisted Dollfuss. That was, of course, while Dollfuss was still the Austrian chancellor, before the Nazis murdered him."

She fitted another cigarette into her holder and lit it, waving away von Danzig's offer of a light, wondering what would happen if she told him the truth about Rennie, wondering if von Danzig could do anything else but turn her in.

"Of course she has no papers," she went on with her lie. "If she did, Rennie would be in a work camp by now. Or dead. It was fortuitous she happened to be in Berlin when Hitler made his *Anschluss* with Austria. I knew her father rather well—if I make my meaning clear—and of course took her in. She had some theatrical training and it occurred to me to put her in the cabaret. I didn't know what else to do with her."

Von Danzig smiled at her and she wondered if he were being taken in. "You could have had her as a guest," he said.

"That's all I would've needed: an unaccounted member of my household. Someone—the waiters or one of those damn

Goose Girls—would have been running to the Gestapo minutes after she moved in, reporting that I had Winston
Churchill's daughter here. Besides, no one ever asks to see
a cabaret girl's papers. The problem is, she's too good. The
Gestapo workingman's dream: sullied innocence. Kimmel
was onto her the moment he saw her.

"But the truth is she doesn't have any papers, she can't
get any papers, and she hasn't got a chance in hell of
getting any." She stood up and began to pace up and down
the room, moving without thinking between the unlikely
marriage of bizarre furniture. Moving quickly, but with
grace, as if she were afraid to stop, afraid of von Danzig's
smile.

"I don't know what to do. Rennie can't stay here tonight.
Not without papers. Perhaps you've put Kimmel off and
perhaps you haven't. The Gestapo might come calling any
moment. They've broken promises before. And though
you're an SS general, darling, I know SS generals who take
orders from Gestapo sergeants." She sat down, closing her
eyes. "I need help, Wolff."

"I might be more ready to give it to you, Lillie, if I
thought you were telling me the truth." He stood up and
crossed the room, picking up a framed photograph of
Rennie, balancing it in his palm as if he were weighing both
it and his decision. "All right," he said, after a moment.
"Have her downstairs in fifteen minutes." He slipped the
photograph into his jacket pocket. "We don't have much
time. She should be dressed as if she's going to spend whatever's left of this evening with a lover. She should be
dressed as if she's not expecting to wake up in her own bed."

"She has to be in Kimmel's office tomorrow morning at
ten."

"I'm aware of that, Lillie. Please go get her ready."

Some moments later, a chauffeur named Willie pulled his
general's official Mercedes to a stop in front of the Kleist
Kasino as Rennie Nacht met Baron General Wolfgang

Konstantin von Danzig in the foyer where he had been waiting for her. He took her arm in a proprietary way, helping her to the car. She was dressed in a black gown that fit her like a slip. There was a long, silver blue fox jacket on her shoulders, hiding the places were Lillie had pinned the gown to make it fit. A white rose, tinged with silver paint, was in her silver blond hair, which continually fell across one of her huge, silver blue eyes. She pushed it away, impatiently, only to have it fall again the next moment.

Halfway to the car she put one hand on von Danzig's shoulder and laughed her husky boy's laugh as she stopped to fix a strap on her silver sandal.

It was convincing. Kimmel, sitting in the back of his brown staff car, several yards away, watched them through the scrupulously clean windscreen. He didn't like to think of himself as an imaginative man. But watching the beautiful girl and the handsome general, he had a sudden and complete vision of the two of them making love.

Kimmel was angry. Perhaps angrier than he had ever been. He knew he would have to have his revenge. But for the moment Fräulein Nacht and her general were out of his reach.

He was a patient man. He would enjoy playing a waiting game. The longer he waited, the more pleasurable would be the punishment. And he knew that he would win.

11

They rode in silence through the Tiergarten. Von Danzig was, if not totally remote, at the least thinking of other things. Rennie still felt numb, but the shock of the day was beginning to wear off, slowly, in the way a powerful drug might. Just as after a severe operation, the pain was beginning to make itself felt. It was slow, sharp, and throbbing.

She tried not to think of Kimmel, of that unclean, animal-like aura he carried around with him. It was as if he were a predator and she were his prey. Once he trapped her, he would devour her. He made her feel nauseated, claustrophobic. Each time she saw him, she felt a great need to bathe.

But it was comparatively easy not to think of Kimmel. With far less success, she tried to erase the image of her father's body being spun around as if by supernatural force in the cobblestoned alley. She tried not to see, in her mind's eye, his body being hoisted and dropped into the trunk of the official Mercedes. As the shock wore off, the fear, the horror, the ineffable loss, began to make themselves felt.

She glanced at von Danzig as if he were a stranger. After all, the Mercedes her father's body had been taken away in wasn't all that unlike the car in which they were riding. She wondered how she had ever felt close to von Danzig, where that irresistible physical attraction had disappeared to. She had never felt more alone than at that moment. It was true von Danzig was rescuing her. But for what?

"I always used to think the heart of Berlin was in the

Alexanderplatz," she said, because she had to say something. She couldn't be left alone with her thoughts and her images any longer. "When I was a girl I used to go with Lillie and we'd watch the rich and the poor Berliners eating *Bratwurst* jammed up next to one another, cheek by jowl. It was all so lively, so full of camaraderie."

She stopped for a moment and looked past her reflection in the car window, out into the blue-black Tiergarten shadows. "Now I think the real heart of Berlin is here. In this small, damp, dark ancient forest."

He turned to her and looked at her as if he hadn't been listening. "Is this the only photo of you?" he asked, holding out the one he had taken from Lillie.

"There are some publicity ones of me in costume."

"No," he said, returning to his private thoughts. "This will have to do."

A few minutes later Willie stopped the car in front of an enormous fin-de-siècle apartment building on the Matthäikirchstrasse. Even in the dim streetlight, Rennie could see that it was a solid, tasteless mess, monumental gray marble faced with ornamental columns.

Willie held the rear door open as von Danzig helped her out. He had a whispered conference with von Danzig and then Willie and the Mercedes were gone, leaving them alone on that quiet, eerie street.

Von Danzig pulled on an old rope hanging by the rarely used front gates. "It doesn't look as if we've been followed," Rennie said, her voice louder, more forlorn than she had intended.

"No, it doesn't, does it?" He gave the rope another tug. "But they wouldn't have needed to. Kimmel knows where to find you. That was the idea, after all." A light went on at their feet, curtains were thrust aside, a shade went up. That invariably surprising sight—the Berlin *Hausmeister's* face —round and moon-colored and timeless—glared up at them. After a moment the lock on the outer gates was released.

The inner courtyard was a relentlessly well-lit circular place, paved with aged cobblestones. A small conical building made of brick stood in the center, the *Hausmeister's* daytime headquarters.

A wide set of marble stairs led to a dark red mahogany door, the entrance to Wolff's apartment. The first room was a large anteroom covered in red and faded damask. A middle-aged man wearing a dark jacket and pale trousers came to meet them. "This is Walter. Walter, Fräulein Nacht."

Walter, with ramrod posture and a dead left eye, looked past Rennie noncommittally as he took her fox jacket and moved off down a long, wide corridor.

"I suppose he improves upon acquaintance," Rennie said, wondering if it were possible to return to Lillie's flat. She felt so alone and von Danzig seemed more a jailer than a rescuer, cold and removed like this oversized old court apartment.

"Not at all. I've known Walter all my life and he's always been exactly as you see him." He led the way into a cavernous drawing room. "I inherited him from my father."

"I thought you and your father were at odds," Rennie said, going to the fire burning in the grate. The carved stone mantel featured what she presumed was the von Danzig coat of arms. Above it was a six-foot-square painting of the Battle of Mars La Tour, from the war of 1870.

"We are. But I am a general, even if I'm a general in what my father persists in calling 'the house painter's army.' Also, I am the youngest son." He smiled but not at her. "Youngest sons in families like mine are supposed to come to no good. My father wants me to ruin myself in the discomfort of his Berlin flat."

It was difficult to believe he was the same man who had held her close to him the day before. She looked up at the painting because she didn't know where else to look.

"Grandfather is the man in the center," von Danzig said.

"The one who has so picturesquely lost his horse and helmet. He was a staunch believer in the ancient German code of chivalry. Had he been born in the fourteenth century, he would have organized crusades. My father is much like him. War—and, as preparation, hunting—is supposed to be the von Danzigs' only occupation. Everything else is for lesser beings."

"*Untermenschen?*"

"That is not my code of chivalry, you understand. It is my father's."

She moved about the room as Walter brought brandy on a tray. She felt trapped and angry and sad, all at once. She forced herself to see the room, the nineteenth-century wildlife studies, the crossed swords, the medals mounted on purple velvet backgrounds. Two Iron Crosses had been given places of honor opposite the fireplace. Over them hung a framed and autographed photograph of Hitler.

In another place she might have finally allowed herself to cry. But she wouldn't cry here, not in this armed camp, so carefully decorated by the enemy. She turned away from the photograph of Hitler, accepted a glass of brandy, and sat on one of the honey-colored leather sofas flanking the fireplace. Von Danzig sat opposite, his long, muscular legs crossed, very much the professional host.

"You seem unhappy," he said, after a moment.

"No more so than usual." She drank the rest of the dark, bitter brandy and held out her glass for more. She wanted, she realized, her father's shoulder to cry on; not shoulders wearing silver swastikas. It had become a point of honor for her not to let him guess what she was going through.

"You're so very gorgeous, General," she said, after a moment. "But I suppose you know that. Even in your SS uniform you look fresh and young and innocent. Untouched." She felt out of control, a little drunk. But it wasn't the brandy. She didn't want to break down, so she went on speaking, not caring what she said. "Even in this mausoleum, you seem so very alive." She put the brandy down and took a cigarette from a Limoges box. He lit it for her with steady hands. Her own trembled slightly.

"I saw you once, years ago," she said, to distract him from her hands, her pallor.

"Really? Where?" It seemed no more than polite interest, as if he were talking to a stranger encountered in a business office.

She hadn't planned on telling him, but now, after all, it didn't matter. "Onstage. My father ..."

She stopped for a moment, seeing Nick again as he strode down the Ku-damm alley, his eyes slightly narrowed, his dimpled smile only a touch less ebullient than usual. "My father also suffered from knightly notions." She touched the signet ring.

"Who was he?" Wolff asked, trying not to let her see he was aware of her distress.

"An Austrian diplomat, stationed here in Berlin." She repeated Lillie's lie tonelessly. "He used to take me everywhere. He was interested in German culture. He had taken a subscription to the avant-garde versions of the classics Reinhardt was putting on at the Grosse Schauspielhaus and he took me to the matinee of *Hamlet*."

"Oh, no," Wolff said, with mock distress. He knew the scene with Kimmel had frightened her terribly. He didn't want to invade her privacy, her need to be brave. He thought if he were remote, a touch formal, she would have time to recover.

"Such a modern Hamlet. He was supposed to be angry, nonverbal, perpetrator as well as victim. There was no curtain. The play started when a very young man in a dapper suit strolled onto the stage in the then fashionable chimpanzee strut affected by the youths of the Hallesches Tor. My father and I were amused."

"No one else was," von Danzig said, smiling, hating the pain he saw in her eyes. "What excruciating reviews I got.

The critics predicted to a man that I'd never work in the theater again." He took up the decanter. "More brandy?" She held out her glass. He filled it and his own, moving to the seat next to her.

"They were wrong. You are in the theater again," Rennie said, unnerved by his closeness. "Only the 1938 version of your dapper suit is sleeker, more menacing; but still, costume."

He bent over and kissed her. It wasn't a long or passionate kiss. But the touch of his lips forced her to close her eyes. She wanted him to kiss her again.

Instead, he sat back, taking her hand. "You're scared and a little hysterical and no one can blame you. But you must believe that I am going to protect you. Not because I'm such a good fellow or, like my forebears, a chivalrous *Junker* knight, but because from the moment I saw you on the Kleist Kasino stage, I wanted you. Not only in bed. But everywhere. Across from me at the breakfast table and next to me in the cinema and holding my arm as we do the receiving line at a Chancellery reception.

"I know, Rennie. You are experienced, a world-traveled cosmopolite, a cabaret singer, light years ahead of me in sophistication. It doesn't matter. I want you. I want to own you. There isn't a particle of you I don't want to know, explore, touch.

"I haven't always gotten what I've wanted in my life, Fräulein Nacht. But I am going to get you. And you're going to come willingly. I knew that, too, that first night. I knew it yesterday in Lillie Froelich's bedroom."

She stood up and stepped away, deliberately misunderstanding him. "Of course I'll come willingly, Herr General. It's what is called a *quid pro quo*, is it not? You save me from being disfigured by Kimmel and Company, and I go to bed with you. Little enough to ask. Little enough to give. But I think we should adjourn to the bedroom now, Herr General. I'm dead tired. I'd just like to get it over with."

He went to her, took her hand, held it for a moment, kissed it, and then pulled on a faded blue satin sash. Walter appeared almost simultaneously.

"Please take Fräulein Nacht to the guest suite, Walter. Provide her with anything she might need." He turned to her. "Try to sleep," he said. "Try not to worry. I am going to take care of everything." He turned and left the room, and she found herself allowing Walter to guide her down the long corridor. She felt like a sleepwalker, relieved of all responsibility. Under the shock and the pain, she quite firmly believed that Wolff would take care of her.

In the book-lined room he called his office, von Danzig studied the photograph he had taken from Lillie's flat. It had evidently been shot in a passport studio, probably in London, but when it was reduced, it wouldn't be so obvious that it was taken outside of Germany. She had had her glamorous look on for the photographer: silver hair falling over one eye, a little pout to her lips.

He laughed, amused by her affected, stagy sultriness. She certainly was as glamorous as any German cinema star, but even in the semiamateur photo she possessed a New World innocence. It was as if the cinematographers in Hollywood and Berlin had discovered how to crossbreed European sexuality with American naïveté.

He stared at the photograph for some time, eventually telling himself that he had work to do, that he couldn't moon about like a schoolboy with his first crush. But that is exactly how he felt, like a teen-ager, hopelessly gauche, hopelessly in love. He stared at the photograph one last time and wondered what—if anything—she thought of him. Then, resolutely, he put it aside and placed a call to his friend in the official section of the S.D. Referat. It was an unseemly hour, but he knew it was the only time he might find von Niedermeyer at his desk. Hugo was constitutionally incapable of work during the day.

"Von Niedermeyer," a familiar voice said.

"It's Wolff, Hugo. Do you think you could have a drink with me in a quarter of an hour or so?"

"What sort of a drink?"

"An emergency drink. I'm having trouble with a certain young lady and I need your expert advice."

"In that case, of course. Pick me up here, Wolff. Soon as you can."

"*Danke schön,* Hugo."

Von Danzig took Rennie's photograph, had a few words with Walter, and went to meet the one person in Berlin who could help him. It wasn't fair, he thought. He was going to ask Hugo to become involved in what was patently a dangerous situation. But it was exactly the sort of situation, the kind of challenge, Hugo von Niedermeyer couldn't turn down.

She felt so cold. Despite the brandy and the heat radiating from the old-fashioned black and white stove in the sitting room adjoining the bedroom Walter had wordlessly taken her to. Despite the double windows which had been put up for the winter. It was the sort of cold that came from inside. She thought she would have been cold at high noon in Tierra del Fuego.

Walter had placed a soft cotton chemise on the wide, thick bed. Next to it, expertly folded like a military flag, was a Wehrmacht-issue robe, gray and stiff. She wondered, as she put them on, if the chemise belonged to Wolff's mother, the robe to his father. Or perhaps the robe was his grandfather's. There was an ancient quality to the rough gray wool.

She lay awake under the yellowed satin comforter, trying not to think of how cold she was. Trying to think of subjects, images, that would keep the other subjects, images—the horrifying ones—at bay.

She thought of the boy, Ruben, running up and down the musty corridor in Lillie's attic, grasping his checked cap for the time he went to England. *"Guten Tag, Fräulein."*

She thought, for no reason at all, of Pepsi and his dinner jacket. Of Lillie's warm, expensive perfume. And then, because she couldn't help herself, she thought of Kimmel's small, fat yellow hands.

And of her father, smiling as he strode down the alley off the Kurfürstendamm. It was his dimpled, reassuring smile, the one he wore when events were not going as they should have and he didn't want her to know. It was his it's-all-going-to-be-all-right smile. But of course nothing was ever going to be all right again.

She opened her eyes and sat up quickly, before she saw again, in that theater in her mind, her father's body being spun around as if by supernatural force. Before she saw those anonymous men throw his body in the trunk of the official Mercedes.

This was to be a quiet murder, she thought. Nikolaus Jablonski's fellow journalists in the non-Nazi world had admired him too much. His murder would give the NSDAP a bad world press. His body would never lie next to Viktoria's in the Jewish cemetery in the Grosse Hamburger Strasse.

Rennie wondered where it would lie. She thought of how alone he was. She wished she could be with him.

And then, because she had to stop thinking, because she felt so thoroughly cold, inside and out, she got out of the thick bed in Wolff von Danzig's guest room. The cold marble tiles of the corridor floor seemed nearly warm to her. She ran past the narrow hall which led to Walter's quarters and found, after a few uncertain moments, the room she had been searching for.

Wolff removed his tunic—he had put on his SS dress uniform for his journey to the Wilhelmstrasse—and placed the packet von Niedermeyer had so gleefully arranged for him on the mahogany bureau. Even as a child, Hugo had delighted in outwitting authority.

He didn't bother to switch on the light or to alert Walter that he was home. The less Walter knew—the less anyone knew—the better. Hugo might think it was all a lark, but Wolff knew just how dangerous it would be for both of them if someone who didn't like them found out.

Niedermeyer had been extraordinarily fast, but still it had taken hours, the details requiring great thought and attention. "We must be certain we have a *Gymnasium* record and a baptismal certificate. . . ." Hugo had enjoyed it all. He and Wolff had grown up together and had been in the Condor unit together. Then Hugo had been transferred to Paris, in charge of government agents. He had a firm groundwork in providing documents for people who had no genuine claim to them.

Hugo had taken on the job of supplying false papers to Wolff's poor Viennese girl as if it were a particularly challenging game. Wolff hadn't enjoyed the experience nearly as much as Hugo. Detail work always exhausted him.

He removed his boots now with some trouble, wishing for once that Walter was there to help him. He had begun to take off his trousers when she spoke. "I think you should know, General, that there's a lady present."

He continued to take off his trousers before he went to her. She was propped up on one elbow in the far corner of his oversized four-poster, the covers up around her so that only her face could be seen in the dim light from his sitting room.

She looked up at him as he stood over her and he could see violet shadows under her half-closed silver blue eyes. "I felt lonely," she whispered. "Bereft. I need to be held, to be made warm." It had occurred to her as she lay in his bed waiting for him that she was an orphan. She had always thought of orphans as characters in children's books, cliché figures to be treated with superficial pity. She knew, finally, what being an orphan felt like. It was as if she were going to be hungry for love, for affection, forever, as if that hunger were never to be satisfied.

But as she lay in Wolff's bed, she thought of his smile, of that firm chin and the yellow, unruly hair. She thought that he was the one person she knew who could make her feel whole again. "Will you hold me, Wolff?" she asked.

The bedclothes fell away and he could see her body in the thin cotton shift. In the half-light, with her silver blond hair pulled back from her face, she seemed no longer glamorous and self-assured. In that half-light she looked like a waif, a child who needed comforting. She seemed so impossibly vulnerable at that moment.

She put her arms around his shoulders and her face in his neck and closed her eyes. "You smell delicious," she told him. "You're so warm. You make me feel safe and secure and so warm, too." She sat up suddenly. "You're not ill, are you?"

He kissed her cheek, reassuring her that he wasn't ill. "I want to make love to you more than anything in the world, Rennie," he said, hesitating, feeling the excitement in his body. "But not tonight, Rennie. Tonight I only want to hold you." He felt her cool, sad tears running down her cheeks onto his shoulders.

"You're safe now," he said, misinterpreting her tears. "I have your papers. You can go anywhere you want with them. You're free again. In the morning, Kimmel won't be able to say a word against them." He spoke to her as he would to a child. "After tomorrow morning, after you meet with Kimmel, you won't have to be afraid again." He held her to him as if she were made of some fragile material, as if she might break. "You mustn't be frightened, Rennie."

"I'm not crying because I'm frightened," she whispered. "I've learned to live with fear. I'm crying because I'm sad, Wolff." He started to move away, to look at her, but she held on to him tightly, not letting him go. "Please, just keep on holding me, Wolff. I need you so very badly."

He was fully dressed, SS tunic perfectly pressed, silver swastikas firmly in place, when he woke her, early in the morning. "I have to leave you now," he told her, sitting on the bed, taking her hand. He had to place copies of her records in all the appropriate files. He had to meet Hugo, who as an SS colonel in charge of Reich documents on the civic level had the right and the duty to inspect any records he chose at any time. Even on a Sunday morning.

Especially on a Sunday morning, since there would only be sleepy caretakers to order about, to hoodwink (and how Hugo loved to hoodwink minor bureaucrats) while he and Wolff made additions to their files. It was exactly the sort of adventure Hugo relished. He had been abroad too long. He still hadn't realized the severity with which his Reich dealt with its servants who didn't obey its laws.

"You must return to your room, Rennie," Wolff told her. "If only to save face for Walter." He gave her a leather envelope—the sort women in business carried in lieu of a briefcase—and bent down to kiss her. She held on to him for a long moment.

"You're so warm," she said.

"My temperature is always a degree higher than everyone else's. It nearly kept me out of the SS."

"You've been wonderful to me," Rennie said, suddenly shy. "I don't know how I would've gotten through the night without you. I'm not very good at thanking people."

"I don't want you to thank me," Wolff said, a little angry. "I want you to love me."

She put her face next to his. "Oh, I love you, Wolff. There's no doubt about that. Perhaps I love you too much." She stepped back and looked at him. "It's odd. Last night, when you held me, I felt as if you were the parent and I the child. This morning it's the reverse. You're such a big, beautiful boy in your soldier suit. How do you keep all those swastikas polished?"

"Walter does it."

"I should have known." He pulled her to him and kissed her, at first gently and then with more force. "It's funny. I always thought I'd be deliriously happy when I finally fell in love. Happiness, it turns out, has nothing to do with it."

He kissed her hand. "After this morning, after Kimmel, you'll be happy again. I promise, Rennie. I'm going to make you happy."

After he left, she forced herself to return to the guest

suite bed. She lay in it for a time, thinking of Wolff, of his
clean, barbered scent; of the heat of his body. He was both
a boy and a man and she found she liked that. A father and
a son in one fell swoop. She remembered the way he had
kissed her before he left. As if they were both thirteen and
it was their first kiss.

And then Walter knocked and entered with a breakfast
tray. A pot of coffee, toast, jam, juice, a folded napkin,
silver cutlery, a slim Lalique vase with a blessedly normal
red rose. It was better service, she thought, than she would
get at the Adlon.

Walter cleared his throat and announced, in slow formal
German, that there would be a taxi waiting for her in a
half hour's time; that suitable clothing had been retrieved
from her aunt's flat; that a bath had been drawn for her.

She drank the coffee as she examined the contents of the
leather envelope. There was a birth certificate, a passport
with her photo, a diploma from a Charlottenburg *Gymnasium*, a baptismal certificate, an identity card, ration
books. All attested that the spinster Rennie Nacht had
been born in Berlin on September 4, 1918, to Eva and
Gustaf Nacht (Academician), both deceased. A union mem-
bership card identified her as an actress. The passport was
stamped with entry and exit visas to France.

She would be able to leave Germany now. It was too late
for Nick but not for her. She took her bath in the huge
marble tub. The idea of returning to London, to that Marble
Arch flat and those damp, rainy days, made her feel melancholy. Still, she had to get on with it. She touched the ring
her father had given her and knew that she had to get on
with it.

She also had to face Kimmel. Like an ogre in a childhood
nightmare, he waited for her at the end of every passage.
Wolff thought that the papers would make her free. Nothing would free her until she left Germany. She wondered if
she was going to cry again as she got out of the bath and

realized that she wouldn't cry again while she was in Germany. She wouldn't give Kimmel that satisfaction.

That settled, she felt better. She found the "suitable" clothing Walter had mentioned laid out for her in the bedroom. Her dark brown suit, that traveling "costume" she had bought in London and immediately regretted, lay beside fresh lingerie and what she thought of as her Girl Guide shoes. There was a tired silk blouse, her purse, daytime makeup, and the slouch hat.

She dressed, realizing that she was now cast in the role of Rennie Nacht, Daytime. Not nearly so glamorous as the Kleist Kasino's Silver Rose. Only a brown Berlin bird attempting to make ends meet, worried about her lovers, her lack of money, the run that had begun in her cotton stockings.

She poured herself a half cup of the cooled coffee, drinking it as she stood at the windows overlooking the Tiergarten. She pulled back the heavy draperies and the lace undercurtains. It was another gray, cold day. Soldiers were goose-stepping up the Bellevuestrasse. Field officers in Wehrmacht gray followed them in open staff cars. Rennie allowed the undercurtains and the heavy draperies to fall back over the window and was finishing the last of the coffee when Walter knocked on the door to tell her the taxi had arrived.

Formally, Walter escorted her down to the courtyard, where the moonfaced *Hausmeister* stood, not talking to the taxi driver.

"Where, *meine Dame,* shall I instruct the driver to take you?" Walter asked, bowing slightly.

"I am very sorry to tell you, Walter, that he is to take me to the Polizeipräsidium in the Alexanderplatz." Walter, unmoved, gave the driver directions, bowed again, and waited for the car to drive off.

The driver, pulling out of the courtyard onto the Matthäikirchstrasse, sensed a kindred spirit. "Trouble?" he asked.

"What's it to you?" Rennie answered, not wanting to admit that she no longer felt numbed by her father's death or comforted by her night in Wolff's arms. That despite the properly aged papers in the dark leather envelope, she was desperately frightened again.

"*Mir ist alles Wurst*," the driver, pulling down the peak of his cap, said. It's all sausage to me. When he let her off in front of the immense drab mass of greenish stone that filled one entire corner of the Alexanderplatz, he turned down the tip she offered him. "You need it more than I do," he said, not unkindly. "Good luck, sister."

Quickly, because she wanted to get it over with, she climbed the marble steps leading to the main entrance of the Polizeipräsidium. A man in a green uniform gave her directions. "Herr Kimmel is expecting you, *Fräulein*," he said, smiling.

She walked up several flights of gray-green stone steps as anxious officials passed her in both directions. Those in uniform lugged bulging dossiers while those in street clothes carried leather briefcases. White porcelain washbasins stood at each landing, glossy, recently installed. The Nazis were nothing if not clean.

When Rennie reached the fourth floor, she wondered if she was going to be ill. She had an urge to throw the dark leather envelope into the glossy white washbasin and to run down the steps.

She forced herself to go on, turning down a windowless corridor, suddenly stopping. Kimmel stood, framed in a doorway, several feet away, waiting for her.

"*Guten Tag*," she said, advancing, smiling.

"*Heil Hitler!*" he returned, stepping back into the office, forcing her to pass by him. She gave an involuntary shiver as she did. He waited for her to be seated in the red leather visitor's chair before he sat behind the heavy wooden desk. He stared at her for several moments before he said, "And now, shall we begin, Fräulein Nacht?"

13

Sitting in the red leather visitor's armchair in the office Kimmel had borrowed—for the occasion, he said—she felt an overwhelming fear. It was the unreasonable, unnatural sort of fear that made her feel all hollow and her mouth dry. She folded her hands in front of her, waiting for it to fade, hoping it wouldn't make her say something she would regret, something that would give her away.

Kimmel sat behind his desk, smiling. There was nothing on its surface except a black telephone and a metal reading lamp. No blotter; no ink well; none of the usual signs of low-level bureaucracy.

"I have my papers," she said, after a moment, smiling, reaching for authority, achieving only an ill-at-ease hostess tone, as if an important guest had finally turned up long after everyone else.

His small, pale, hairless, and well-padded hands touched hers, deliberately, as she handed him the dark leather envelope. She had meant to place it on the empty desk but he had been too quick, half standing, reaching with a speed that suggested a younger, better-conditioned man. She remembered that first night in the Kleist Kasino when the Luftwaffe cadet put his arms around her. Kimmel had touched her then and she had felt nothing. Now it was as if her hand had been grazed by something unspeakable, obscene.

She wished she had kept her gloves on. They were brown, like her suit and her shoes and her hat. She was brown all over. Brown was a favorite German color. Brown and black. The colors of feces, of death.

She tried to remember all the brown things she owned. She tried to think little thoughts, but that was impossible while Kimmel, his eyeglass flashing about like a small, intense torch, carefully read and touched each of the papers, each page of the passport. She felt like a student waiting for a particularly feared teacher to critique an examination she knew she had failed. She hadn't studied hard enough. She was ill prepared.

She tried to fill her mind with pleasant moments in her life. A picnic with her father and grandparents in Austria on her sixteenth birthday, white-coated servants in attendance. A man she had thought she could love who taught perspective at the Slade. Her first fur coat. Her first glass of champagne. That visit to New York with Nick and the marvelous, magical skyscraper hotel they had stayed in. The touch of Wolff's lips.

A thin spotlight of sunshine began to creep into the narrow, high-ceilinged room through the one high official window. Rennie concentrated on it, shifting her attention when Kimmel looked up, his pencil-line mouth smiling. She knew he had found a flaw, that oversight that should have been detected. Again she found herself wanting to run, out of the room, out of the greenish mass of the Präsidium.

"Very much in order," Kimmel said in his one-note voice, looking directly at her, waiting for a sign of relief. "Very much in order. Your papers couldn't be more in order, Fräulein."

"May I have them back?" She put on her gloves, as if to leave, extending her hand. But Kimmel spread the papers and the passport across the surface of the desk in a kind of fan, as if he were going to perform card tricks.

"Where were they?" he asked, looking down at them.

"In a friend's flat."

"A friend's flat in the Matthäikirchstrasse?"

She waited for a second or two, hoping to get the timing right. "Well, yes."

His thumb and forefinger caressed the passport cover. "How long have you known the general?"

"Not so very long."

"But you know him well, *nicht wahr*?"

"Tolerably well."

He gathered up the passport and the papers and carefully placed them in the leather envelope. Then he closed the envelope and moved it closer to him, as if he thought she might snatch it from him. He folded his small, fat hands across his paunch. He looked at her, settling back ·in his borrowed chair. He rummaged around in a drawer and found a box of his *Lutschbonbons*, offered her one, which she refused, and put a red one in his mouth, sucking on it with gusto. It was as if he were saying, We are in no hurry. Let us have a little conversation now that the annoying, official business is out of the way. We, too, know one another tolerably well. There's no reason on earth why we shouldn't spend a few moments chatting.

He continued to smile as he moved his candy from one side of his mouth to the other, his shallow, faded brown eyes staring, registering a dull, persevering intelligence.

Rennie sat back as well, though she didn't remove her gloves. Of course there would be time for a chat. Though she refused his offer of coffee. He had a boy bring him a cup.

"I am addicted," he admitted, crunching away the last of his candy. "What can I do? It's a small vice." He put three teaspoons of sugar into the cup and added cream. Then, without drinking, he pushed the cup away, ready for a gossip.

"The von Danzigs are a fine old *Junker* family," he said, stirring the sugar about in his coffee cup. "They are of the *Uradel*, you know. The *Uradel* is our most ancient aristocracy. To belong, a family's rank and title must predate the thirteenth century. Imagine, Fräulein Nacht. The thirteenth century! And the von Danzigs have been barons since even before that.

"Do you know the proverb that goes, Humanity only begins with the rank of baron? General von Danzig is a most humane man, *nicht wahr*?"

His fingers, short and wide with pared-down nails, reached for the envelope again, opening the flap, removing the passport, riffling through it; an unconscious gesture. "I don't know about the Nachts," he said, smiling again. "But there have been no barons and little humanity in the Kimmel family since at least the thirteenth century. We have always been poor. Working class. I grew up hungry, my belly never full. Like our Führer, I was a mere *Oberschaftsführer* in the war. No one wanted to make me a general because of my exalted family or my beautiful face, you understand?"

He waited for her to nod, to agree. And when she didn't, when she continued to look at him, he smiled even more good-naturedly, and went on. "We never got enough to eat, not even during the war. I admit I was surprised—I thought the Kaiser would feed his soldiers. But it seems he was too busy feeding his Jews.

"Of course now I get too much to eat. That's obvious, no?" He put the passport down and patted his stomach affectionately, as if it were a badge of some honor. "When I was a lad, Fräulein Nacht, I used to walk all the way out to the Grunewald every Sunday like clockwork. I would get up at dawn and slip out of the house and walk. It was warmer walking than sitting still, and how I enjoyed going out past the old hunting castle to look at millionaires' houses.

"Sometimes I'd wander into Dahlem, where the men had fur coats and fleece-lined gloves and motorcars, and the plump maids were busy cooking Sunday goose and potato dumplings.

"Do you happen to know the Lentzeallee in Dahlem?

Rich, fashionable, exclusive Jewish families built their villas there with the proceeds they made from betraying Germany. I would get as close as I could to those villas so I could savor the smell of the goose and the dumplings. Sometimes I would hear a telephone ring and I would wonder what those rich Jews had to talk about on the telephone. If I had been one of those Jews, I would have sat very quietly in the paneled dining room in my warm villa, eating my goose and dumplings.

"Imagine. I was dreaming of other men's food. Of Jews' food. Of their conversations. I was fighting the war while the Jews were handing the Fatherland over to the enemy, eating their goose and dumplings on the Lentzeallee in Dahlem. There aren't many Jews left in the Lentzeallee in Dahlem now. They've either left Germany or are in work camps. Or they're otherwise disposed of. Der Führer tells us we have a new aristocracy. An Aryan aristocracy based on good German blood and accomplishment. Even your baron, General Wolfgang Konstantin von Danzig, must remain pure in the new Reich."

He picked up his coffee cup and drank from it slowly, glancing down at her passport over its rim.

"Herr Kimmel," Rennie managed to ask, after some moments of watching him apparently lost in thought. "Are my papers in order?"

"Most assuredly, Fräulein Nacht. Have I been keeping you, while I chattered away? I am sorry. I know you have a living to make so I shall not detain you." He stood up, with his hand held out, waiting for her to remove her glove. It would be too rude, his manner implied, for her to offer him a gloved hand. Quickly, she took off the glove and extended her hand. He grasped it, and then he raised it to his thin, humid lips, slowly kissing it.

After a long moment he released it and handed her the leather envelope.

"They're all right?" she asked again, putting on her glove. "My papers are all right?"

"Obersturmbannführer Eichmann might not be impressed, but I am, Fräulein Nacht. I am. I am extremely impressed." He stood close to her, looking at her as if she were a Sunday dinner in Dahlem's Lentzeallee, as if she were warm and comfortable and secure and he were still cold and hungry, leading a hard and tenuous sort of life.

He wanted her. That was clear. But he hated her at the same time. "You are free to go, Fräulein Nacht," he said. "We shall meet again, of that I am certain." He reached behind her and grasped the door handle, holding it closed. "*Heil Hitler!*" he said and waited.

She could smell the sticky sweet odor of the *Lutschbonbons* under the heavier odor of the milky coffee. "*Heil Hitler!*" Rennie managed to say. He smiled at her, taking his hand from the door handle, stepping back, allowing her to leave. She opened the door and moved off down the wide, pale, windowless corridor as quickly as she could.

But when she had turned the corner and was out of his sight, she had to stop and stand for a moment by the white porcelain water basin.

"Are you ill, Fräulein?" a young man in a dark blue uniform asked.

"Yes. But I'll get over it."

She walked down the seemingly endless steps of the Polizeipräsidium feeling oddly invisible. None of the clerks or soldiers took any notice of her. She emerged onto the Alexanderplatz and shivered, the north wind cutting through the brown gabardine traveling suit as if it were paper.

She began to walk, without deciding on a destination. Men as well as women often said they felt raped after an interrogation by the Gestapo. Rennie thought that she didn't feel so much raped as seduced.

She should, she knew, have thrown the passport into Kimmel's potato-gray face. She should have told him she was a Jewess, Nick Jablonski's daughter. She should never have allowed him to touch her, to press those damp, thin, colorless lips against her hand. She should never have said those two final words . . . those two terrible debasing words.

But she wasn't a heroine. She knew herself well enough to know she would have *Heil Hitler*ed herself up and down the Präsidium steps a thousand times if it meant not being tortured. Her worst fear—the one that caused her stomach to seem bottomless, the fear that paralyzed her—was of being tortured. The rumors that came out of the Gestapo cellars had a permanent place in her memory. Pried-off fingernails; gouged-out eyes; dismemberments, amputations; electrical prods. The entire catalogue was always there now, in her mind.

Without knowing it, she found herself on the tram that rode up and down the Kleiststrasse, the tea cozy dome of the Nollendorfplatz in the background, the bas-relief goddesses of Erwin Piscator's theater voluptuously supporting their marquee as the tram circled round for its return trip.

No, Kimmel hadn't tortured her in his borrowed office. But something equally filthy had occurred during that interview, and she felt horribly unclean.

The female tram conductor—stern, marcelled, uniformed —didn't question the fact that Rennie remained on the tram for trip after trip.

Perhaps, Rennie decided, she *was* invisible. In her brown suit with her hair hidden by the odious slouch hat, with her faded makeup and her laddered stockings, she looked like any other desperate Berliner, outside the Nazi pale, keeping warm on the Kleiststrasse tram.

"Sunday is a hard day, *nicht wahr?*" the marcelled conductor said, as she collected Rennie's fare for the sixth time.

She realized then why Kimmel had been reminiscing about

the Sundays of his youth. It was Sunday. Sunday in Berlin. She felt for the signet ring through her glove. Sundays, Nick used to say, are nearly insupportable. Especially in Berlin.

On Sundays, he would bundle her up, much to Lizbeth's annoyance, and take her for long rides in one of his elaborate autos. They would drive to the Havel and sit in the car, holding hands, staring at the frozen river. "Have you ever in your life, *Schatzi*, seen a more depressing sight than the Havel on a cold, gray Berlin Sunday? Good thing it's frozen or the entire population would jump in."

She had been born on a Sunday in Berlin and her mother had died on that Sunday in Berlin and her father, Nick, who had everything—honor and good looks and intelligence and money—couldn't get through a Sunday without some mention of his wife, her mother, Viktoria.

When she thought of Viktoria, she thought of some distant, angelic being, far too beautiful and good to be real. She had known, of course, that she was supposed to take her mother's place. Especially on Sundays. He would take her with him to restaurants, gaming clubs, East End *Lokals* and West End cabarets. She had seen and heard things children never saw or heard.

Everyone had predicted ruin for her.

And when Nick traveled—to Paris, Cairo, London—she would go with him, accompanied by a succession of governesses, maids, tutors, and always that *kvetch*ing, *yiddling* Lizbeth, the only other relative Nick said he owned.

In every new city, the first item on Lizbeth's agenda was the location of a synagogue, preferably an Eastern-oriented *shul* with an orthodox rabbi, bearded, shawled, smelling of old books and tobacco. "She is my conscience," Nick liked to say. "Tante Lizbeth prays for me."

"I don't pray for you, *shmigege*," Lizbeth told him, in that annoying singsong Yiddish of hers, redolent of Polish *shtetls*, of dreary, sandy backward country towns. "I pray for her. You, you *yonkle,* you had a choice. She, that poor little thing, you ain't giving her one. You're making her a *shiksa.* God's going to punish you, sure as I'm standing here."

"There is no God," Nick would say, and that would set Tante Lizbeth off on a long stream of invective and prayers, of spitting on the ground to ward off evil.

Well, it was Sunday in Berlin again and Nick Jablonski had been punished but not by Tante Lizbeth's God and there were no amusing cabarets to go to. Only the tram that rode up and down the Kleiststrasse.

Rennie knew that when she went back to Lillie's flat it would be only to say good-bye. It was that knowledge that kept her from getting off the tram. With the passport and her papers, she had to try to leave.

She thought of Wolff, of his body that ran a temperature a degree too high, and was relieved that they hadn't made love. The idea that she loved him was one that she didn't want to face. She told herself for the tenth time that day that she was a terrible coward. More than anything else, she wanted to feel safe again.

She cleaned off the window that had steamed up a bit, using her gloved hand. The East Enders were moving up and down the Kleiststrasse with great purpose. It was a street-collecting Sunday. Mounted SS and SA cavalry trotted up and down on muscular chestnut-colored horses, reassuring and out of reach, threatening only to those who didn't, who couldn't, belong to this miraculous new Thousand Year Reich.

Lesser soldiers walked along the sidewalk in pairs, clattering their boxes, collecting for the *Winterhilfe,* for Strength-Through-Joy, for rearmament. At the Wittenbergplatz, the Salvation Army had set up a tall, illuminated tree. It was surrounded by middle-aged women with innocent faces, wearing shabby blue uniforms, singing *"O Tannenbaum"* in thin, reedy voices.

It's only early November, Rennie thought. Far too early for Christmas.

Boys in knickerbockers or Hitler Youth uniforms hawked postcards featuring their Führer beaming at a blond child wearing lederhosen, staring up, adoringly, at him. Others sold copies of *Mein Kampf;* hair oils with likenesses of Hitler or Göring on their labels; ceramic mugs with decals of godlike German warriors pasted on their covers. Shoes, shirts, tea cozies, all featuring Nazi motifs, were being sold to aid what was being billed as a great and noble cause.

Even silver roses, the paper sort, could be had with tiny bloodred swastikas imprinted on their rice paper leaves.

Rennie wished she were walking up the Kleiststrasse, searching for a Christmas present for her *Mutter*. She wished she were Aryan, a shopgirl with genuine papers and a solid, gentile ancestry. She wished she were a proper German girl, with nothing to fear, nothing to think about but Wolff's arms around her.

And then the radio horns began to crackle. They had been set up at every corner, quite high so the *Eckenstehers*—the corner boys—couldn't get at them. The shrill, unmistakable voice of Joseph Goebbels cut through the clean, damp air.

A German diplomat had been assassinated by a Jewish boy in Paris. The German people, Goebbels quite reasonably thought, are entitled to identify all the Jews in Germany with this crime. The German people—and here his voice rose—are entitled to punish the Jews in Germany for this murder. Jewish shops, Jewish houses, Jewish bodies—he shouted, seeming to lose control—would no longer be protected against true German citizens taking revenge for this cowardly blot on the Reich's honor.

We are working—his voice reached a higher, hysterical pitch—to rid Germany of these *Untermenschen,* of these cowards who would destroy all German youth in their prime.

The German people, he screamed, seeming to lose all control, are entitled to revenge.

The radio horns went dead, and the tram conductor clicked her tongue. "I wouldn't want to be a Jew in Germany tonight," she said.

It seemed obvious to Rennie that she had to leave, as soon as she could. She couldn't be a Jew in Germany on this or any other night. But the thought of Wolff made her wonder if there weren't some way she could stay, to be near him. She had a split-second fantasy in which he hid her in his flat and took care of her until the horror was over. But perhaps the horror would never be over.

She left the tram and pushed her way past two good-humored gray-uniformed SA men, rattling their collection boxes at her. "You don't want Jewish money," she told them. But either they didn't hear or they didn't care, because they continued to rattle their collection boxes as the Salvation Army women once again began to sing *"O Tannenbaum."*

As she crossed the street, an official Mercedes with a silver swastika on its hood blocked the way for a moment. As it drove off and she ran into the Kleist Kasino, she wondered if she would ever see Wolff again.

14

"Where have you been?" Lillie asked, pulling Rennie into the drawing room, embracing her, releasing her, embracing her again.

"With the *sheygets*," Tante Lizbeth said, before leaving them alone. She touched the ripped collar of her ancient black dress, the traditional sign of Jewish mourning. "Where else on the night of her father's death?"

"Tante," Rennie began, but the old woman had already disappeared through the black beaded curtains.

"You're too pale," Lillie said, ignoring Lizbeth's departure, looking at Rennie with concern. She was wearing a black imitation silk wrapper trimmed with red feathers and appeared, if anything, more disheveled than ever, her frizzed red hair limp and undone, her penciled eyebrows characteristically arched and surprised. "Did it all go all right? Kimmel? The papers?"

"Yes. It went extremely well," Rennie said, removing the brown coat, moving to her place at the window. "Extraordinarily well." She gave Lillie the leather envelope.

"*Mein Gott im Himmel*, he's been thorough," Lillie said, going through the papers.

"I've just heard Herr Doktor Goebbels's latest pronouncement on the radio," Rennie said.

"Yes. Well, I knew this morning what was coming as soon as I heard that vom Rath was killed in Paris. That stupid boy. Vom Rath was anti-Nazi. Well, we mustn't cry over spilled blood. Though I do wonder what will happen to that boy Greenspan." She fitted a cigarette into her holder, inhaled, and said, "I've made preparations for tonight. Goebbels has just given the man in the streets a free hunting license to kill Jews. Now that you've got your papers, you must leave. There's nothing holding you back now."

"No," Rennie said, thinking of the bed in the apartment in the Matthäikirchstrasse. "Nothing at all."

Lillie looked at her with her heavy-lidded big brown eyes. "Wolff? You'll get over him, believe me." She took Rennie by the arm into the bedroom they both shared. "You must change quickly. I've packed a small case for you, hoping it only looks like an oversized purse. Actually, it looks like an undersized suitcase, but that can't be helped. Now don't argue. Wear the black sweater and those trousers and the fox jacket, naturally."

"I'm not arguing," Rennie said, getting out of the brown suit. She looked at Lillie in the dressing-table mirror. "So I'm going motoring again. Who with this time?"

"The American. He's driving to Italy this morning, unescorted, to meet with Count Galeazzo Ciano, Mussolini's son-in-law and foreign minister. In reality Butch is going to Italy to take you over the border and deliver you to an American boat that's headed for New York and your grandfather."

"Why?"

"Why what?"

"Why is Butch risking his position in Germany for me?"

Lillie laughed. "*Schatzi!* He's head over heels in love with you. You must have realized that? And also, his heart is in the right place. Two very good reasons."

"And what about your safety tonight?"

"I am covered, as they say in the American films. I'm a pure Aryan, God help me, and Pepsi is both smart and strong. He's boarding up the windows at this very moment, putting a CLOSED sign across the door and making the house seem as impregnable and deserted as possible. They'll have more attractive game than me tonight, I'm afraid."

"And Tante Lizbeth? The boy and his parents upstairs?"

"Pray no one remembers her and knows about them." Lillie closed the fox jacket, readjusted the angle of Rennie's hat. "There's no urgent reason for me to leave, just yet. And a few good ones to stay. I'm safe for the moment. It's you, *Schatzi*, who must leave. He's waiting for you now, downstairs."

"You'll say good-bye, *Mutti*, to Wolff for me? You'll explain. That I'm not Austrian but a Jewess. You'll tell him why I left, won't you, *Mutti*?"

"Yes. But I don't know if he'll thank me for it. He's committed a treasonable crime," Lillie said, putting the leather envelope into the oversized purse she had packed for Rennie. "Oh, I know, *Schatzi*. Wolfgang von Danzig is different. I'll talk to him. I promise. But go. Please go, now, *Schatzi*."

She handed Rennie the purse, and the two women kissed. Then Rennie ran halfway down the steps, came back, ran through the drawing room's black beaded curtains to the tiny back bedroom, and kissed Lizbeth, who grudgingly kissed her back and began saying a prayer in Hebrew for her.

Rennie kissed Lillie again, embraced Pepsi, who was waiting, downstairs at the door, and finally was gone.

It was a dark blue Packard saloon with black leather upholstery and seats for children built into the rear doors. It came equipped with a picnic hamper, a black-dyed rabbit car rug, and a number of what the manual described as "important" accessories. It was solid, hard-driving, and luxurious.

"One could live in it," Rennie said.

Butch glanced at her occasionally as he drove. She seemed

tired. But still glamorous, ready to face anything. Lillie had told him that Nick had been killed. He had thought Rennie would be teary-eyed, a little broken. He had thought that she would need comforting. He said as much.

"I took a vow," she said. "Never to cry in Germany again. I plan to keep it." She found one of her fragrant Nigerias in the purse Lillie had packed for her and lit it with the Packard's chromium lighter. She exhaled slowly as Butch drove past the *Rundfunkhaus* where he made his broadcasts, turning out of the Masurenallee into the Messedamm, putting on speed, taking the Avus west and then moving onto the Autobahn. "Tell me about this motorcar," Rennie said, because the silence in the big car made her nervous. Because she knew that if she didn't speak, he wouldn't. He was almost too considerate.

Butch explained that a friend of his, a fellow correspondent named Bones Marrow, had put him onto it. A millionaire manufacturer of pots and pans had died the day the Packard was to be delivered to his mistress. It had been ordered months before, completely paid for. His wife sold it sight unseen.

"It had but fifty kilometers on it when I got it," Butch said. "Only the mechanic had driven in it."

"The poor mistress. I don't suppose she ever saw it."

He couldn't tell if she was being serious or not. Her eyes seemed more silver than blue in the grim gray daylight, but there were faint shadows under them. Her skin was finer, more translucent than it appeared on the Kleist Kasino stage. He felt uncomfortable, uncertain of himself. Not a usual sensation for him. He had the thought that though he was ostensibly rescuing the girl, she was in charge of the operation. It amazed and confused him, her being so strong, so poised. He had never known another woman like her. He had no idea what she was thinking of; what she was feeling; even what she would say next.

"I suppose she had other compensation," Rennie said.

"Who?"

"The mistress who didn't get the Packard."

He didn't know how to respond; how to talk to her. Which was ridiculous because he had learned how to talk to everyone from John L. Lewis to Myrna Loy. His hands felt clammy in their mocha driving gloves. He was glad to be driving, to be performing some act that called for at least minimum attention. He felt as if he were fifteen years old. He tried to think of all the women he had met, of past love affairs with women who had made it all so easy for him. And still he felt gauche, callow.

She asked if he minded the radio. They listened to a drama, a story about a young party worker who fell in love with a married man. Rennie seemed to take it seriously, laughing only during the confrontation between the wife and the home wrecker.

"You're far more interesting than any German broadcast," she told him.

"You've heard my broadcasts?"

"Two or three times. Illegally, of course. You have a good voice. Strong, with conviction. Though I can't always tell what you're convinced about. I suppose that's why Goebbels allows you to broadcast. You present the facts and then allow your listeners to make their own judgments. Very wise."

She slipped out of the fox jacket, asking him to turn down the heater. The gray countryside was depressing. There were few autos on Hitler's newest road. Mercedeses, trucks, vans making record time traveling from one end of Germany to the other.

They stopped for lunch at a roadside picnic area. An elaborate bronze marker explained that it had been constructed by members of the Young Folks Leaders' School, Department of Roadside Conditions. The names of the participants had been inscribed below an eagle sitting atop a swastika.

Rennie stood under the marker, reading it, as she made short work of a smoked turkey leg. "There are a great many young *Völker* named Adolf," she concluded, joining Butch at the table, sitting on it rather than on the seat. "Either their mothers were supernaturally prescient or their names have been changed." She knew she wasn't behaving well, that the cosmopolitan chitchat she was indulging in was a shield she had learned to use as a child to deflect sad feelings, unhappy thoughts.

"Do you ever wish you were someone else?" she asked Butch. "No, I don't suppose you do," she said, before he could answer. "You're so complete."

"Do you?" he asked, looking at her with his green eyes.

"All the time. I'm so tired of being me."

When they were back in the Packard, she began to speak in English. She had an Anglo accent with only a hint of German background. "I had best practice my English, hadn't I? Actually, I had better practice my American. You must teach me to speak American, Butch."

He looked at her and realized, suddenly, that she wasn't being hard and modern because she was superficial. She was being hard and modern because she was frightened.

They spoke in English for a time, Butch telling her about his youth, his father, New York. Much later, after Munich, they lapsed back into German.

"I've always loathed and despised Bavaria," she told him. "Kitsch. Lederhosen, dirndls, cuckoo clocks. Passion plays laced with anti-Semitism. They live in the past in Bavaria, but such an uninteresting past. It's the past of one hundred years ago. It's no wonder the Nazis began here. The Bavarian peasants are all like Hitler: naïve, single-minded, cruel. I'll be happy to reach Italy, where they're only naïve and single-minded."

He put his hand on hers. She didn't withdraw her hand; not immediately. "We'll be in Italy soon enough," he told her.

* * *

The series of signs leading up to the border control unit all began with *Achtung* and ended with *Heil Hitler.*

It was late at night and considered the optimum time to approach the border control, when even the most dedicated German soldier might be understandably sleepy, not at his most alert.

The soldier who very nearly goose-stepped out of the concrete and brick border control building was not, however, sleepy. His cap was set firmly on his head; his hard black Bavarian eyes read duty-at-any-cost.

Butch gave him his passport, his documents, an official letter from Count Ciano confirming the appointment, countersigned by a Goebbels aide.

"And your documents, Fräulein?" Rennie gave the leather envelope to the *Oberleutnant,* who about-faced and walked stiffly back into the control unit.

"It's going to be fine," Butch told her. "They're never that officious when they're going to do you in."

"Of course it's going to be fine."

He wondered who was reassuring whom while they waited for the *Oberleutnant's* return. It took an hour. A very long hour. And finally they heard the doors of the concrete building swing open and close. But their *Oberleutnant* had been replaced by an SS captain. He wore blue-black boots, dark brown jodhpurs, and a tan shirt with silver swastikas on his epaulettes. The red, black, and white party armband was old and faded but no less malignant because it had been aged.

The *Hauptsturmführer* approached them. He had a lantern jaw, hunter's eyes, and a death's head cap. He clicked his heels, *heil*ed Hitler, and handed Butch his documents. Silently, he moved around the car and waited while Rennie rolled down her window. He handed her the leather envelope. As she took it, he opened the car door.

"You are free to go on, Herr Jarman," he said, bending

down, leaning into the car. "Have a safe journey." He spoke in English, carefully. "Return to us soon. Fräulein Nacht's passport, unfortunately, does not qualify her for international travel. She will be taken back to Berlin immediately. At the Reich's expense, of course."

Butch got out of the car. "I insist that Fräulein Nacht accompany me. I have a letter signed by . . ."

"Yes, Herr Jarman. I have seen your letter." The SS captain smiled, placing his gloved hand on his holster. "I am sorry. But you must understand, Herr Jarman, I have spoken to my superiors in Berlin. I have my orders." Two men took up positions in front of the steel barrier gate.

Rennie put out the last of her fragrant Nigerias in the Packard's no longer pristine ashtray. "You'd better give it up, Butch. It's no use." She began to get out of the car.

"We will take care of Fräulein Nacht," the captain said. "You are free to go on, Herr Jarman."

"I've changed my mind." Butch got into the car. "Rennie, get back in. I've decided not to meet with Count Ciano after all. I'll see that Fräulein Nacht gets back to Berlin."

He backed the car up and spun it around, driving back toward Munich. As the Packard's balloon tires spun, as the dirt from the shoulder of the road flew from under the car, Rennie looked into the lit concrete border patrol building through a door that had been left ajar. Back-lit as if he were onstage, astride a painted wooden stool—the sort clerks in illustrated stories perch upon—was Kimmel, his leather trench coat open, his rimless eyeglass reflecting the Packard's headlights, his thin, damp lips stretched into a smile.

Of course he had flown from Berlin's Tempelhof Airport, but there was something mystical about his being there, as if he could be anywhere he wanted; as if he could get anything he desired. She realized then that the interview in the morning had been not the final one but the first in a series of inquisitions. He was playing a waiting game. She bit her lips so as not to scream.

* * *

Butch drove the Packard for several miles with his foot pressed down on the accelerator and then, suddenly, pulled off the road. "I'm sorry," he said, not looking at her.

"There wasn't anything you could do, Butch."

"I suppose that's why I'm sorry." He turned to her. "I've never been in a spot like this, where I feel so paralyzed. I'd like to smash something, someone, but I don't know who. I feel caught, trapped inside myself. Nothing seems fair or right."

"Nothing is."

He wanted to drive into Munich, to take rooms at the Vierjahreszeiten, to have a deluxe meal. She pointed out it was the middle of the morning. That she was in trousers and a fox jacket and that they hadn't any luggage to speak of. That the Vierjahreszeiten was a very proper hotel. The concierge would be polite but as adamant as the border patrol.

Besides, Goebbels's free hunting license affected not only Berlin but all Germany. A big American car riding through the streets of Munich wouldn't be particularly safe. Instead, she suggested an inn—a fake chalet sort of place where van drivers put up—just off the highway.

They took the only available rooms, waking up the owner to get them. Butch asked if it was possible to get something to eat at that hour.

"I wouldn't go into the village tonight, Herr Jarman," the little man told him. "We're paying back the Jews tonight. I wanted to go, but the wife wouldn't allow it. They say the sight of the synagogue in flames was something to see, but the wife . . ." He held out his hands in a gesture meant to be comical.

Butch asked if sandwiches and beer could be sent up, but Rennie said she wasn't hungry. "I just want to sleep, Butch."

The chalet owner watched carefully as Rennie made her way up the stairs which led to the bedrooms. He thought

she must be famous and almost risked waking his wife.
She knew all the movie stars. She would certainly recognize
whoever that woman was with that silver hair and those
furs, with the man with the big foreign motorcar.

Rennie and Butch stopped at the top of the stairs. "Good
night, Rennie," he said, looking at her with longing, wishing
she would make some gesture, some indication that he might
spend the night with her.

"*Gute Nacht,*" she said, kissing him on the cheek.
"*Gute Nacht,* my American." She went to her room and
lay down on the too-soft bed under the eiderdown, fully
clothed, and shut her eyes without switching off the overhead light. She fell asleep almost immediately, dreaming of
her father. In the dream he was standing at the top of Lillie's
stairs, holding his arms open to her. She began to run up
the stairs into them when her father turned into Wolff. As
she began to kiss him, Wolff turned into Kimmel and she
screamed.

She woke, got out of the sweater and trousers, washed.
She lay down again, but sleep was harder now. She was as
afraid of Kimmel in her dreams as she was of Kimmel in
real life.

She lit a cigarette, realized that she hadn't ever really
believed she was going to get away so easily. She didn't
really believe she was ever going to get out. Her luck didn't
run that way.

She put the cigarette out and consoled herself with the
thought that though she was going back to Berlin and
Kimmel, she was also going back to Wolff.

By the time Butch and Rennie arrived back in Berlin,
Dr. Goebbels's devastation of the previous night already
had a name, inspired by the value of broken glass, esti-
mated to be nearly twenty-four million marks: *Kristallnacht.*
But the Berlin streets were deserted now. Radio Berlin was
soft-pedaling what had been a night of horror.

Butch switched off the radio. The Packard was the only auto moving up the Kurfürstendamm at an hour when that busy street was usually crowded with cars, picking up and discharging shoppers.

In the clear, cool November early-evening air, the Ku-damm—for once without people—had an obscene look to it as if the German obsession with *Scheisse*, with feces, had exploded on Berlin's most exclusive shopping street.

All the shops and showrooms were covered with anti-Semitic graffiti. They had been smeared over the doors, windows, walls, and sidewalks in dark red, nearly brown, waterproof paint. Cartoons on the walls depicted the classic Jew caricature—banana nose, elephant ears, sprigs of black hair, a tiny, misshapen body. He was being beheaded, hanged, castrated, tortured, dismembered.

The smashed windows had not yet been boarded up. Discarded loot from the shops was strewn over the sidewalks, mixing with paint, shards of glass, burnt merchandise floating in the gutter.

They saw but one person on the entire Kurfürstendamm, the owner of the exclusive stationery store at the Uhland-strasse intersection. He was a nice-looking, neat, bald man, his coatless arms behind his back. He stood in front of what was left of his shop, rocking back and forth on the tips of his toes, as if he were praying. He had been ruined. The glass windows had been smashed, his fine Egyptian paper and rare French linen stationery tramped into the gutter.

As Butch stopped the Packard for a traffic light—the only lights still working on the Ku-damm—two SA soldiers came down the street. They were young, still in their teens, working-class youths. Casually, the older of the two forced the stationery owner down on his knees. The boys, without any real enthusiasm, began to kick him as they barked orders.

Rennie realized, as he tried to comply, how old the man —now down on all fours—was. The SA boys were forcing him to pick up shards of glass with his hands, which quickly became covered with blood. They seemed bored, sated with violence but unable to stop.

Rennie reached for the door handle as Butch accelerated, driving on, picking up speed.

"You should have let me help him," she said, when they stopped for yet another traffic light. The irony of the traffic lights didn't escape her. There was some glass—Reich glass —the crowds wouldn't break.

"To be used by those SA hoodlums? You couldn't have helped, Rennie."

She knew he was right. It would have been a futile gesture, theatrical heroism. Still, she wished she had gotten out of the Packard, gone across the Ku-damm, and slapped and kicked and punched at those animals. She wished she weren't so helpless. She wished she could make a futile gesture and not care how it would end. Someone had to start being heroic if they were ever going to be stopped. She understood, suddenly, why Nick hadn't left Berlin, why he had continued to do what he could as long as he could.

And then she smashed her fist against the Packard's window. Though she used all her strength—though she knew her hand would be badly bruised—the window didn't break. Unlike the stationer's, it was shatterproof.

15

She hadn't been able, quite legitimately, to sing the night she returned from her abortive attempt to leave Germany.

She had been exhausted, her nerves betraying her. Lillie had sent Marlene on in her place while Rennie waited upstairs for Wolff to come.

He hadn't come by the time the second cabaret was over. Lillie sat on her bed, smoking. "Poor Marlene. She tried 'Silver Rose,' which was, of course, a mistake. When they began walking out, she took off her blouse, and then, when they started to show a little interest, she took off her skirt. An obliging girl, Marlene."

"Wolff didn't turn up, did he?"

"No."

"Kimmel?" Rennie asked, to stop Lillie from going into any of the possible reasons why Wolff might not have turned up.

"That one's always here. But he won't do anything now. You have your papers. Besides, they'll all be quiet for a little while. At least until the world forgets *Kristallnacht*."

Rennie waited until Lillie had gone upstairs to see her "family," while Pepsi made absolutely certain that every waiter, chorus girl, and bartender had left the Kleist Kasino —he didn't want any middle-of-the-morning explorers. Then she put on the fox jacket and found a taxi that would take her to the Matthäikirchstrasse.

The block of old flats looked more formidable than it had when Wolff had taken her there. She didn't care. Her anxiety, her need to know how he felt, made her brave. She tugged the old bell rope until she woke the *Hausmeister* and gave him the note she had prepared while waiting in Lillie's bedroom. He said he couldn't deliver a note at such an hour.

She insisted that it be delivered immediately, giving him a far too generous tip to persuade him.

Grumbling, struggling into his overcoat, he allowed her to wait in the courtyard while he made his way to Wolff's flat. She circled the *Hausmeister*'s conical daytime head-quarters while she wondered at her need to see von Danzig. Need. That was, of course, the key word. She felt needy. And guilty. She should have said good-bye, she knew that. But suppose she hadn't come back. Suppose it had worked and she was in Italy now, just getting on a ship for New York? It would have been far better had he thought she had simply deserted him.

She looked up at the stars, which seemed especially close and bright, and touching her father's ring, tried unsuccess-fully to identify Pegasus. It had been Nick's favorite con-stellation, mostly because, he had admitted, he enjoyed the idea of a winged horse hovering above them.

She realized, suddenly, that it was cold. She had for-gotten gloves, a scarf. She pulled the fox jacket around her and wondered what she was doing: attempting to explain to an SS general that she hadn't been able to say a proper good-bye because she had been too busy attempting to save her life.

Just as she decided he wasn't coming, he came out through the *Gartenhaus* door. He was in dress uniform, which didn't help, the black of his tunic fading into the dark, the silver braid and swastikas standing out like tiny warning beacons. *"Guten Abend, gnädiges Fräulein,"* he said, stopping several feet away from her, bowing his head slightly, formally. His face looked hard and remote, his body rigid. "In what way may I help you, Fräulein?"

"I came to explain, Wolff."

"Ah, but you have nothing to explain to me, Fräulein. You are a free agent." He smiled. It was a smile she hadn't seen before, aristocratic, filled with condescension and dismissal. "You owe me nothing, Fräulein."

He stopped smiling that terrible smile and stepped back a foot or two, into the shadows. She tried to see his face, but all she could make out were the swastikas, the rigid, parade ground posture.

"And now it is late, Fräulein . . ."

"But not too late for me to apologize, Wolff."

"As I have tried to make clear, Fräulein, you do not owe me . . ."

"I only apologize for disturbing you at such an hour. No, you are perfectly correct, as always, General. I have made a mistake, but I shan't make it again."

She turned and crossed the courtyard, the heels on her silver sandals unpleasantly echoing on the cobblestones, her hands clenched in the pockets of her jacket. The *Hausmeister* must have been listening, for the outer door opened the moment she reached it.

Outside, she began to run, as quickly as she could in those silver sandals, one size too large, into the great darkness of the Tiergarten. It was dark and solitary, but for once she wasn't frightened. Only angry and embarrassed. And then a hand gripped her arm, spinning her around.

Now she could see his face, just, in the lights from the Bellevuestrasse. His expression wasn't cold and formal like his words. It was furious. He looked as if he wanted to kill her.

"Did you creep into Herr Jarman's bed and tell him you were cold and ask him to hold you all night? Americans will do anything for a woman, they say. Did you kiss him with your mouth half open and tell him . . ."

She slapped him as hard as she could, but it was as if she had slapped thin air. He didn't move but continued to grasp her arms. "Or did you go further with him? After all,

I only secured documents for you. He was getting you into Italy."

She tried to pull away, but he held her in his grip. "How did you find out? Your spies? One of the girls at the Kasino? The border patrol?"

"Your little friend in the Gestapo, Kimmel, provided me with a complete report. He took great pleasure in doing so."

"It wasn't what you think, Wolff."

"No? Perhaps not. But was it a good experience, *gnädiges Fräulein*? That is what I am curious to know. Was he loving, tender? Or was he brutal? They say American men don't know how to make love. Perhaps you taught him?"

"Damn you." She pulled free and began to run again, but he caught her easily, spinning her around, putting his face close to hers. "Is he going to provide you with American documents, also?" he asked, hurting her as he grasped her. "Is that why you did it? Or was it the money? His father is as rich as Krupp and far more powerful."

"You're hurting me."

"I don't care. I want to hurt you. I am not acting like a German gentleman, I know, Fräulein. I am acting like an American gangster, but that is reputed to be a successful tactic to use on you. Besides, I have been asking myself these questions for two days now. I have a great need to know the answers."

"Will you please let me go?"

"No. I want to hear what you wanted to tell me. What your excuse is. Please. I want to know."

"For personal or political reasons?"

"Oh, personal. Your case doesn't fall within my departmental guidelines, Fräulein."

"All right. I confess. I was trying to escape from Nazi Germany. Yes, *Nazi* Germany, not NSDAP Germany. Not the Third Reich. But Nazi Germany. I have false papers, General. I should be in the basement at Spandau having my teeth knocked out of my head at this very moment. Then I

should be locked up in a camp, working for the good of your
Reich. Yes, work makes you free, isn't that the motto? I
thought that I could perhaps be free without work, but I am
wrong. I confess all, General. Arrest me. I give up."

"Your papers are fine," he said, letting her go.

"They're not fine," she said in a low voice. "Don't you
think Kimmel knows they are fake?"

"You don't understand. No one can prove they are false.
You have a complete set of records, going back to your
birth, filed in all the appropriate sections and ministries.
Your papers are fine."

"They didn't get me out of Germany."

He looked at her. "*I* didn't want you out of Germany."
He took a cigarette from his case, offering her one, lighting
them both. "Did he want to sleep with you?"

"The subject was never discussed."

"Very noble, our American friend."

She tried to slap him again, but he caught her arm.

"I hate you," she said.

"I hate you, too," he told her, and then he pulled her to
him, and though she could feel his medals and his swastikas
pressing against her skin, through the thin silver dress,
hurting her, she returned his kiss with more passion than
she had ever felt before.

"I want to go home," she said, when he released her.

He took her arm and led her out of the Tiergarten. She
looked up at him and saw, in the light from the streetlamp,
that he had forgotten his general's cap. His butter-yellow
hair was in disarray, and despite his uniform, he looked
young and vulnerable.

"Yes," he said. "You had better come home."

He had taken her to his bedroom and kissed her as he
undid the zipper on the silver dress. The dress fell away
and she stepped out of it as if it were the most natural act
in the world. As if she had performed it every night of her

life. He looked at her for what seemed a very long time and then he took off his uniform and, taking her hand, led her to the oversized four-poster bed.

"I want to make love to you more than anything else in the world, Rennie. I don't care who or what you are. I need you." His hands touched her slender breasts.

"And I want you to make love to me more than anything else in the world, General," she said, stepping back, taking his muscular hands in hers, looking at him as if she were afraid of the effect her next words would have on him. "But ..."

"But what?" he asked, taking her hands away, pulling her closer to him.

The heat of his body, the magnetic force, almost made her lose her resolution. But she felt that she had to tell him, now.

"I've never been made love to by anyone before. I thought you had better know that, General."

His expression would have made her laugh if he hadn't been so obviously, seriously unnerved. "I am a virgin," she said, to make absolutely certain he understood. "You'll have to be patient with me."

"But that's not possible. When you stand on that stage at the Kleist Kasino and sing that song . . . no woman could move the way you do—could be so sophisticated—and still be a virgin."

"You're the consummate German male. You always believe what's onstage, General."

"But look at you. Men must have wanted you. Men must have ..."

"But I didn't want any of the men. Not until I met you."

He took her in his arms again and the touch of his hard, ungiving body made her feel defenseless. "I am no virgin, Rennie. I have been with other women." He held her close, looking into her eyes. "Tell me what you want, Rennie."

"I want you to make love to me, General."

"Then you must call me Wolff. You must say 'I want you to make love to me, Wolff. I want you to be my first man.' Say it."

"Make love to me, Wolff. Be my first man."

And at first, tenderly, he made love to her. And then, when they both forgot themselves, he was not so tender, not so gentle. And the harder he thrust himself into her, the more passionate she became, the more ready she was to receive him.

She succeeded, at least for that night, in forgetting the horrors of her day.

16

Both Wolff and Lillie insisted, and finally Rennie gave in. Some ten days after her return from Italy, she retired officially, giving up her career as a cabaret entertainer. She moved into Wolff's flat.

It had been more difficult than she thought. She knew she would miss the Kleist Kasino, the Goose Girls, and the forlorn trio. But not as much as she did. Leaving had been, for her, as difficult as it had been that first time when she had been sent off to London. Once again she was leaving her family. She felt very adult, moving in with her lover. But there was a part of her that wanted to stay with Lillie and Pepsi and even Tante Lizbeth, who had only grudgingly kissed her good-bye when she left. There was a piece of her that wanted to continue to sleep in Lillie's big feather bed, to be coddled by Pepsi and chastised by Tante Lizbeth. She wasn't so very sure she wanted to be an adult.

"At least," she said to Lillie, "I'm spared seeing Kimmel's eyes following me at every turn, night after night."

"You should have been flattered. It was obvious that he didn't want to come, to stand by the bar and be spurned by you every night. But you had become a sort of obsession to him. The best move you could have made was to retire."

"I still get the feeling he's watching me. And it's not flattering. He doesn't see me. He's seeing some private fantasy of his."

"And your fantasy?"

Rennie refused to admit .either to Lillie or herself how much she needed to be held by Wolff each night. How much

she needed their lovemaking. She only owned up to it when
he began to make love to her. The bed—that bed—had
acquired a magical life unto itself; it was a place where she
didn't feel frightened; a place where nothing bad could
happen.

"I was going to warn you, *Schatzi*, not to get in too deep
with von Danzig. Now I suppose it's too late." A tradition
had begun soon after she had left Lillie's flat. Several mornings a week, they had breakfast together in Lillie's tiny
kitchen.

"No, you're not too late, *Mutti*," Rennie said, reaching
across the enameled table for one of the tiny, poppy-seeded
cakes she liked. "I know exactly what Wolff is: handsome
beyond belief; romantic in the grand old style; kind as a
child; loving as a parent; and a Nazi."

"You don't talk about his politics, do you?"

"Not for an instant. He believes the entire NSDAP mythology. Swallowed it all, hook, line, and sinker, as Pepsi would
say. There's an autographed snapshot of Hitler in the drawing room, party-approved tooth powder in the medicine
cabinet. I won't deny I'm enjoying my new life, Lillie. It's
marvelous to be so pampered, so protected. But I'm biding
my time, Lillie. Until Kimmel forgets. Than I'll slip out. I
still have my papers. Kimmel can't dog me for the rest of
my life, can he?"

Lillie reached across the table and took Rennie's hand.
"You're as transparent as your father, *Schatzi*. You care
about Wolff, it's obvious. But you must promise me that
when you can leave, you will leave."

"As soon as the opportunity presents itself. Don't worry.
I'll take it. I'm far more frightened of Kimmel than I am
enamored of Wolff."

"I don't believe you for an instant, *Schatzi*." She looked at
Rennie carefully. "You almost look like your old self. Radi-
ant. You couldn't be pregnant?"

"In such a short time? I doubt it. Besides," she said,

looking away, "Wolff can't have children. It nearly cost him his commission when they found out. Hitler's own doctor, Morell, performed the tests. SS officers are supposed to be potent and perfect, it seems."

"It's just as well, isn't it? You wouldn't want children now, would you? In times like these? Being who you are and who he is?"

"I don't suppose so," Rennie said, still looking off, as if she weren't quite certain. It seemed terrible to her that Wolff would never have a child, someone like him. It seemed even worse that she would never have his child.

"Do you really think, *Schatzi*, you may be able to get out soon?" Lillie asked, pouring coffee, following her own thoughts.

"I might even be able to take Tante Lizbeth with me."

"*Lieber Gott,* what a blessing that would be."

"Does she have papers?"

"She's had them for months. But she wouldn't leave without your father, and now I can't very well put her on a train by herself and tell her to keep her mouth shut. She'd be in a camp before the train left the station. Your grandfather sent word that he is willing to vouch for her, to get her from Paris to New York. But one has to get her to Paris."

"I'll get her to Paris. Now, don't ask questions, Lillie. Something's up, and if it becomes a reality, I'll let you know." She left her then, to forestall any questions, to go up to the secret attic to say *Guten Tag* to Ruben.

He stood in the dark, none-too-fragrant corridor, twirling his checked cap, looking up at her with awe. He never quite believed she was real, that she hadn't stepped out of the pages of one of the books he had been forced to leave behind.

She went into the room her father had hidden in. Ruben stood in the doorway, watching. She could hear the sounds of the Kleiststrasse and, above that, the Telefunken. Ruben's parents listened to it night and day. She wondered what they were listening for. Some magic decree, setting them free, allowing them to go home again.

She wished she could take them with her when she left, but they so obviously didn't have papers, passports, friends to get them from one country to another. All Ruben had was that terrible, poignant hat. It was his talisman, his passport to British boyhood. She didn't want to think what the British boys she knew would make of Ruben and his brown and white checkered cap.

She touched the signet ring her father had given her, which was her own talisman. Then she left her father's hiding place, kissed Ruben on the cheek, and went down the secret stairs. He stood twirling his cap on one finger, watching her go. "*Gute Nacht*," he called out. "*Gute Nacht, Fräulein.*"

"*Gute Nacht*, Ruben."

In the kitchen she found Pepsi and Tante Lizbeth, both sipping tea as if they were engaged in some contest to see who could make the most noise. Pepsi stood up, bowed, smiled, showed a keyboard of white teeth. "You sure are a sight for sore eyes, baby," he said.

Lizbeth allowed herself to be kissed. In between sips of tea she knitted that gray, shroudlike garment she never seemed to finish. She looked older, meaner, paler, in her black dress with the torn collar.

"Just your ordinary Berlin tea party," Lillie said later, as she walked Rennie to the door. "Two Jewesses, a *Schwartzer* from New Orleans, and an aging Viennese vamp." She put her arms around Rennie. "You will take care, won't you?"

"I promise."

"And Rennie," Lillie said, before she left, "I'll tell you this. Someday you're going to realize that you're far braver than you think you are."

"Promise?"

"I promise, *Schatzi*."

* * *

She had found the gown hidden in Lillie's closet. Lillie had worn it once, a decade before, to a great formal ball at the Egyptian embassy and then had decided it wasn't her color, there wasn't enough dress for her.

It was silver, made of some smooth, silky, clingy material neither Rennie nor Lillie could identify. It fit more like an undergarment than a dress, held up by two thin silver straps, cut low in the back.

"You don't think it's a bit too much—or too little—for the Nazis?" Lillie had asked as Rennie modeled it. "Their public women—their wives and such—always wear yards of material." Lillie had stepped back and shaken her head. "It's a very suggestive gown, *Schatzi*."

"I'm a former night club entertainer, aren't I? I mean to be suggestive." She had borrowed Lillie's paste diamond earrings and had piled her hair on top of her head. She wore her silver sandals, the fox jacket over her shoulders, and minimal makeup, just a hint of silver over her eyes.

Wolff had been on duty all day taking visiting Japanese generals about, not having time to stop off at the flat and change. She was to meet him at the Adlon, where the Japanese were staying.

At the last moment, as she caught a glimpse of herself in the full-length mirror in Wolff's dressing room, she almost lost her nerve. In that startling silver gown, with the paste diamonds shimmering in her ears, her silver hair making her seem adult and sophisticated piled like that on her head, she looked exactly as she had set out to look: glamorous, cinematic, a little dangerous.

She wondered if she was up to the part. She wondered if she, Rennie Nacht, née Jablonski, a Jewess, could really get through an evening at Hitler's Chancellery without giving herself away. She was, she realized, both frightened and exhilarated. She was walking into the lion's den on silver high-heeled sandals.

"The limousine is here, Fräulein," Walter said, looking somewhere to the right of her bare shoulder.

"Here goes nothing," she whispered to herself, repeating one of Pepsi's phrases.

Willie, the chauffeur, couldn't find a parking place in the Adlon's circular driveway, so she got out and went into the Adlon to find Wolff.

Wolff was standing at the end of the long, carpeted entry hall when he saw her. He caught his breath. Her beauty never failed to nonplus him. Tonight she seemed more desirable than ever.

He went to her, aware that all the men in the Adlon lobby had turned to stare. One of the qualities he liked most about her was that she seemed totally unaware of the desire she provoked. She waited for him, smiling. Even in the Adlon's wonderfully vulgar entry hall, filled with Chippendale chests, gold-capped marble pillars, Chinese tapestries—with every eye on her—she managed to appear both poised and vulnerable.

"You look wonderful," he told her as they got into the Mercedes.

"At the last moment I didn't want to come," she said, kissing him, taking his arm.

"It will be an enjoyable evening, I promise."

"I thought you said all Chancellery functions are inherently boring."

"Not with you there." He held her close to him. "Don't you understand? I want to show you off."

Willie maneuvered the car into place at the end of the long line of Horchs, Maybachs, and Mercedeses waiting to discharge passengers onto the Vossstrasse. Men with decorations on their chests and women in dark furs made their way up the steep Chancellery steps with difficulty, the November wind doing its best to blow them down. The OKW staff, resplendent uniforms perfectly pressed, moved up the monumental staircase with stiff-backed dignity.

"It's like an opera, isn't it?" Rennie asked. "All those costumes and that stage set of a Chancellery. There should be, at the least, a clap of thunder."

He took her hand and held it, attempting to reassure her. He knew she was far more ill at ease than she pretended to be.

A matched pair of enlisted men, wearing black and gold cuff titles signifying they were entrusted with Hitler's personal safety, met them at the top of the stairs, saluting Wolff, bowing to Rennie.

As they led Rennie and Wolff through the high, formal rooms that made up the Chancellery, she whispered, "I feel like a little girl playing dress-up."

He took her arm, supportively, as they entered the *Ehrenhof*, Hitler's Court of Honor, and found themselves at the top of yet another flight of marble steps. Several hundred people barely managed to fill the enormous space, drinking champagne, dancing to music supplied by an orchestra situated directly in front of the oversized windows overlooking the Wilhelmstrasse.

SA soldiers, dressed as footmen, circulated around a white-linen-covered buffet, a series of tables banked with masses of purple and white orchids.

A receiving line waited at the bottom of the stairs for them. As she and Wolff hesitated at the top of the steps, they all looked up and Rennie had the distinct feeling they knew who and what she was, that when she reached the bottom of the stairs they would gather around her and take to the cellars for what had ironically become known as routine questioning.

She wondered, literally, if she was going to be able to get down those steps, but suddenly she was at the foot of the steps and Wolff was introducing her to Reichsminister Göring, who wore a personalized version of the Death Head Hussars' uniform—scarlet and blue—and carried a gold baton. "Lovely," he said to Wolff. "Absolutely lovely, von

Danzig." As if she were a new motorcar or a well-trained hunting dog. His wife, Emmy, took her hand and pressed it while Joachim von Ribbentrop—Hitler's foreign minister— kissed her hand and held it a moment too long. He wore diplomat's white tie and tails, a monocle, a diamond-encrusted swastika in his lapel.

"They seem like dangerous children," Rennie said, after the ordeal of the receiving line was over, "dressing up."

"They are children," Wolff said, getting them champagne. "But not so dangerous." He touched his glass to hers. "To us," he said and they drank.

"But where's der Führer?" she asked, as he found them seats at a table and waiters offered her caviar, smoked meats.

"He'll be here soon enough," Wolff said. "Drink more champagne. There's nothing to be nervous about." He introduced her to Hugo von Niedermeyer, to the Turkish ambassador and his wife, to the Japanese generals.

But still she had that empty feeling in her stomach, that overpowering indication of fear, of the hunted outsider suddenly, irrevocably in the midst of the hunters. Von Niedermeyer, who was short and thick and dark, asked her to dance. The music, a Strauss waltz, sounded off-key. As he propelled her around the room with more style than grace, the other dancers took on a sinister, unreal quality: ghouls embracing one another in a final, fey dance.

"You're far more fortunate than you deserve, Wolff," von Niedermeyer said, returning her to the table. Wolff stood up, and she put her hand on his arm to tell him she was ill, to ask him to take her home. But just then the floor-to-ceiling doors at the far end of the *Ehrenhof* opened and a team of Waffen-SS blonds, each carrying a pistol in his holster, entered the court. The orchestra stopped playing in midsong, everyone in the room stood, their hands flying upward as they shouted, as they screamed in spontaneous hysteria, *"Heil Hitler!"*

He stepped into his Court of Honor, looked about him, and casually raised his hand. It was his ordinariness that shocked her. Rennie had expected, if not bolts of fire, at least that extraordinary magnetism he had become known for. His cutaway fit him less than well. His salute would have cashiered him from any respectable military unit.

After a long moment he lowered his arm, signaling to an SS captain that the orchestra could resume. He stood there for a time, his hands in front of his genitals, as if he were protecting himself, looking about the room. Next to him stood Goebbels and his wife Magda, and behind him, as always, was his deputy, Rudolf Hess, in uniform.

Rennie watched Wolff as he smiled at his Führer. He seemed—he was—perfectly comfortable while she felt paralyzed, incapable of movement. Magda Goebbels was beckoning to him. She was a large statuesque blonde with iridescent eyes and an ill-conceived orchid pinned to her frilly gown.

"Frau Goebbels wants to meet you," Wolff said, taking her hand.

"I don't suppose we could avoid it."

"I'm afraid it wouldn't be politic."

He put her hand in his arm and led her to where Magda Goebbels stood. "The famous Silver Rose," the older woman said, offering her hand. There was something both sad and coarse about Goebbels's wife. "Berlin salons have talked of no one else for months. You're quite as lovely as your admirers would have you and far more aristocratic than I pictured you. And now you've snagged young Danzig. We must have tea. I long to know all about you." She seemed genuine enough, but her eyes couldn't meet Rennie's and she appeared to be relieved when Hitler suddenly joined them.

"Might I have the pleasure of bidding you good evening, *gnädiges Fräulein?*" he inquired, bending over her hand, pressing it to his lips. He straightened up and looked at her with his famous hypnotic stare. For just a moment Rennie stared back, attempting to see what lay at the bottom of those cobalt blue eyes.

"Our Wolff is lucky," he said, in an undistinguished voice. "You must bring the Fräulein to us more often, Wolff," he went on, smiling. Then he allowed Goebbels to take him off to meet the immensely rich Prince Ratibor-Covey and his two daughters.

As the young princesses reacted with proper awe to their Führer's hand-kissing, Rennie stood perfectly still for a moment. "The Führer has hypnotized you?" Wolff asked, amused.

But it wasn't Hitler's stare that had incapacitated her. Over his shoulder, standing half-hidden behind a column, was Kimmel, his eyeglass reflecting the enormous chandelier, his mouth stretched in that familiar thin and damp smile. It was as if the man in the ill-fitting diplomat's suit were an impostor . . . as if Kimmel were the real despot.

Rennie turned and asked Wolff if he would take her home. "I'm not feeling as well as I might."

"One dance," he said, taking her hand.

"One dance," she agreed.

It was another Strauss waltz. She closed her eyes as he spun her around. He was so proud and happy, like a country boy showing off his new wife. His butter-blond hair fell across his forehead; his blue eyes were bright with happiness. Rennie held on to him tightly, afraid to let go.

"At first I thought he was funny," Rennie said, the following morning, having coffee with Lillie in her kitchen. "Hitler, I mean. Funny odd. Not funny amusing. Like a lucky actor who landed the starring role only because he was first in line when the casting call went out. Like someone hired for the night.

"But then I looked into his eyes and I thought I was going to be ill all over the *Ehrenhof*'s inlaid floor, if not all over Herr Hitler. The thought that kept running through my mind was that he was supposed to be able to smell a Jew a mile away."

"Perhaps he had a cold. *Gott im Himmel,* I wish you could get out. I wish ..."

"I am getting out, Lillie," Rennie said, drinking her coffee, looking away. "Wolff is taking me to Paris. He received final confirmation of his trip last night from von Ribbentrop. It seems there are some points to be worked out about the French-German nonaggression pact. He'll only be there a few days, but he thought it would be nice if I came along."

She took her cup and moved into the drawing room, to her favorite place, the window overlooking the Kleiststrasse.

"I'm so relieved," Lillie said, following her, lying down on the Napoleonic sofa, fitting a cigarette into her jade holder. "So relieved."

Rennie rested her head against the cold glass of the window and looked down to see a plain brown staff car parked across the street. She closed her eyes. "I've asked if I could take a maid. I said I knew a woman who was old and ill and wanted to see Paris. He said of course. He not only believes everything the Nazis say; he believes everything I say."

She turned and looked at Lillie. "You'll make arrangements for Lizbeth, once she's in Paris?"

"I'll get Butch Jarman to make arrangements."

"Not Butch."

"Why not? He's willing to help, and God knows we can trust him. He'll make arrangements for you and for Lizbeth." She tapped the edge of her cigarette against an ashtray in the shape of a pelican. "You love Wolff very much, don't you?"

Rennie looked out the window once more, down at Kimmel's staff car. "Yes. But not enough. I shan't come back from France, *Mutti.*"

17

She had always, as long as she remembered, adored the golden eagle which sat over the arched entrance to the Friedrichstrasse Station. When she was very young it had meant the beginning of adventure, a trip abroad with her father, and occasionally Lillie, and always Tante Lizbeth.

Her father always traveled with excess baggage: dozens of matched sets of luggage and trunks filled with items he considered essential to his well-being. Portable electric steamers; complicated coffee-making systems. Shoes and boots of every description could be found in elaborate trunks created especially for them.

There would usually be a male servant, hired at the last moment, whose job it was to look after the baggage. Usually these valets were young, and often they were not to be trusted. One had left them in Moscow, taking with him a ledger of useless checks. Another had disappeared in Biarritz with a pair of gold cuff links and a platinum cigarette case.

The actual journeys had been nearly anticlimactic after the preparations, the weeks of buying linens (Nick hadn't trusted hotel sheets) and scented shaving soaps and all the other necessities—tobacco, chocolate, tea—he felt one could only purchase in Berlin.

They would arrive at Friedrichstrasse Station only moments before departure time. Nick would sit Rennie in the first-class private compartment he had reserved and then would disappear, arriving back at the compartment only at the very last moment. He had gone to the *Wurst* kiosk and purchased half a dozen *Currywursts*. Because, as he liked to explain, of all the luxury items they wouldn't be able to purchase abroad, *Currywurst* would be the most dearly missed.

Rennie thought of her father as she passed under the golden eagle some half-hour early, Wolff following, a little diminished by the thought of the trip. He had explained he didn't like to travel. She touched her father's ring, the heavy gold giving her reassurance. She was thankful that of all her favorite public Berlin places, Friedrichstrasse Station had changed the least.

Yes, there were too many men in uniform. But the shops selling candies and periodicals were the same, as was the noise and the great leaded paned ceiling, through which the gray winter sky could be seen.

"I'd like chocolates—not the dark kind but milky—and a magazine. I don't care which, but it has to contain stories about film stars' secret lives." She felt giddy, nearly hysterical. She was leaving Berlin. Wolff had gotten her seated in their first-class compartment, which was upholstered in green felt and leather and exactly like the compartments she used to share with her father. She couldn't decide if she was happy or sad or both. She couldn't quite believe she was actually leaving. Wasn't there going to be some last-minute move by Kimmel?

She had just had time to make one telephone call before leaving for the station. *"Auf Wiedersehen,"* she had said, softly, to Lillie. *"Auf Wiedersehen, Mutti."*

"Here is your friend," Wolff said, breaking in on her thoughts, his arms filled with magazines, chocolates, mineral water. Lizbeth, in a too-long old black coat, a hand-me-down of Lillie's, stepped into the compartment and stood in the center, managing to look simultaneously forlorn and cantankerous.

"Lizbeth," Rennie said, forgoing the *Tante* to keep up the pretense of the old woman being a maid. "How are you?"

But she wouldn't answer. "I'll show her to her seat," Wolff said, setting down the magazines and candy. He wore a casual dark blue cashmere suit and seemed, like Rennie, in the middle of two moods; both buoyant and nervous. "She'll be in the first of the second-class cars." He took Lizbeth's arm, she pulled it away, gave one last reproachful stare at Rennie, and then followed him into the corridor that led to the other coaches.

Left alone in the compartment, she knew that she was once again frightened. She wondered why fear seemed to strip her of all the more decent virtues. Truth and bravery, the ability to speak one's mind. She liked it best when she wasn't thinking. When she was in bed with Wolff. When they were making love.

"Quite a girl," Wolff said, referring to Lizbeth, bending over, kissing Rennie. "Are you all right? You seem suddenly pale."

"I'm worried." She tried to make her voice light, to pass it off as a joke. "The Gestapo. If they wouldn't let me into Italy, it suddenly occurs to me that they won't let me into France."

"Ah, but you are going into France with an SS *Oberstgruppenführer,* a personal friend of the Führer's. It would take Rudolf Hess and Heinrich Himmler combined to stop you."

He kissed her again, on the tip of her nose. She was frightened. He could see her small, upturned breasts under the silk blouse. He felt paternal and amorous. "I'm responsible for you."

He sat next to her on the green plush bench and put his arm around her. "What if," she asked, "I should take it into my head not to return from Paris?"

"You wouldn't do that."

"But suppose I did."

He sighed. "There would be an investigation to determine

if I had any knowledge of your plans. If I had helped you. I would be found innocent, which has always been my problem. I am innocent."

"What if you were found not innocent?"

"Rennie, darling, this is the most unpleasant conversation to be having just when we . . ."

"What if you were found guilty?"

"There is an unspeakable punishment for members of Hitler's inner circle who are found guilty of treason, which is what the charge would be."

"What is it?"

He inhaled through his mouth, making his cheeks round, and then blew out the air, deflating them, like a boy imitating a frog. "In the cellar under the Chancellery there is a room lined with meat hooks, the sort butchers hang sides of beef from in slaughterhouses. Hitler has his traitors hung on the meat hooks. They struggle to get off until they're dead. My friend Hugo says it's a reflex action. The more they struggle, the deeper the hook goes into their bodies. Hugo says it can take a long time to die that way. Days."

At that moment the last boarding call was sounded. Rennie found a Nigeria, Wolff lit it for her, and she stood at the windows, watching other people's friends and relatives calling out their good-byes. Some were laughing, others were crying, but most seemed merely impatient.

She wasn't at all surprised to see Kimmel cut through the crowd at the last possible moment and look up at her with that terrifyingly bland smile of his.

"They probably won't let me into France after all, so we shan't have to worry." She wondered if Kimmel had managed to get on the last car; if he'd be waiting for her at the border.

"I'm not worried," Wolff said, slipping his hand around her waist, pulling her to him.

* * *

At the frontier, the French and German inspectors were scrupulously polite. To one another. To Rennie and Wolff. Their luggage was not searched, their passports and exit cards were given but cursory attention.

The German officer, an *Oberleutnant*, was intent on getting his form correct, clicking his heels with noiseless precision, *heil*ing in a hoarse voice, his eyes focused on the decorative milk glass roof of the compartment's ceiling. It was evident that he had been alerted, that he was well aware of Wolff's rank.

There was to be no getting out of the train, no queueing up. It was all so civilized, a mere formality. And all the while Rennie waited, clenching her fist, feeling her father's ring. She waited for Kimmel.

Miraculously, he never appeared. As the train crossed the border into France, she found another of her fragrant Nigerias. She felt, for the first time in a long time, free. As Wolff lit the cigarette, she noticed that his hands weren't as steady as they usually were.

"And what are you so nervous about, General?" It was difficult to believe that anyone who looked like Wolff—that perfect physical specimen—could have nerves. But his usual high color, she saw, had deserted him. Those nearly red cheeks were suddenly pale.

He smiled, but it wasn't his self-assured smile. "It's this journey. Traveling makes me edgy. I've never really been out of Germany before. Yes, I was in Spain, but I was with my comrades and we ate German food, went about in German transport, spoke German all the time. I might as well have been in Berlin."

"But you speak perfect Parisian French."

"My mother has a French cousin, Herbert. My father loathes and despises him because he is French, one, and two, he likes men. Mother adores him and she used to have him visit as often as she could. She'd make him speak French to us when all he wanted to do was go to Berlin to find boys. Then Mother, who has several languages, always spoke French to us at evening meals. Even during the war. Once, when father was home on leave, I thought he was going to strike her."

He took her hand and held it in his. "But we never traveled, not abroad. There was no money. Now that I am finally going to Paris, I am anxious. And surprised."

She laughed, putting her arms around him, drawing his blond head to her breast. She kissed his neck. He smelled of bay rum. His skin was hot. "*Mutti* will take care of you, my little Wolfgang. *Mutti* is responsible for you now."

He buried his head in her lap and laughed. "I feel as if I'm six years old." He looked up, giving her his delightful smile. "Little *Mutti*," he said, reaching up, kissing her.

A half-dozen diplomats in morning jackets and striped trousers were waiting to greet them. They looked, to a man, long-faced and displeased as only French gentlemen can look. They had had to interrupt their afternoon to greet a German. They turned noticeably less sour when introduced to Rennie.

"*Très chic*," the Comte de Chevilliot said later, when discussing her with his aide, Vincent. "Not quite Parisian but still . . ." He kissed his forefinger and thumb and made a smacking noise in appreciation.

The French diplomats had certain questions about the rearmament clause of the recent nonaggression pact that had been signed with Germany. Von Ribbentrop had given them one figure as to the number of planes in Göring's Luftwaffe, their spies had given them another. The French knew enough to believe their spies. They also knew they weren't going to do anything about it. But they did feel a need to make a small, token stand.

To allow them to salvage what dignity they could, von Ribbentrop had sent the personable, French-speaking, and

noble baron, General von Danzig, to talk to them, to—as
Rib put it—"hold their hands while I deal with Beck and
Poland."

After appropriate salutations Rennie, Wolff, and a more
silent than ever Lizbeth were driven to the Ritz. Lizbeth
was let off at the Rue Cambon entrance, Rennie and Wolff
at the Place Vendôme. The Comte bid them adieu under
the porte cochere while the *porteurs* saw to their luggage.
Wolff was to have supper with the Comte and a group of
other dignitaries and their wives. It was unfortunate, the
Comte said in an aside, but Madame was not invited.
"French wives are so stuffy, don't you know?" he said,
leaving them.

"It doesn't look at all like the Adlon," Wolff said as he
took Rennie's arm and they went into the Ritz.

"All superior hotels don't look alike, General." She was
amused and pleased by this recently discovered lack of
sophistication.

"Ah, mademoiselle!" Marcel, the little *sous-directeur*
came tripping out of the small writing room on the left of
the entrance, clasping his hands together, and then pressing
her hand between his. He smiled volubly, his absurdly long
cutaway again reminding her of an extra in a Marx Brothers
film. "And your father? He is well?"

"Oh, not so very well, Marcel. But you, how are you?"

"*Très bien.* In the pink, as the Englishmen like to say."
He escorted them through the main lobby, waving away
the need to register, to fill out forms. The lobby was filled
with those blond ladies holding lapdogs, wearing tea gowns
under Russian sables, trying to make up their minds to
leave Paris once and for all. Usually, at this time of the
year, they were in Egypt or Mexico, but they had stayed
on in Paris, despite the weather, to see what would happen.
The nonaggression pact hadn't soothed them. Unused to the
temperature, many of these women, who had learned the
secret of looking forever middle-aged, had developed hot-

house colds. They carried snippets of silk and lace tucked into their expensive sleeves. If the Duchess of Windsor hadn't left, they weren't going to either.

"I hope," Marcel went on, "that rooms over the garden will again do." He escorted them into a gilded birdcage of an elevator, grabbing a set of keys, nodding to the elevator boy. "The house has never been so occupied. Madame Ritz is distraught. Refugees—but only the right sort, *assuré-ment*—are still pouring in from Eastern Europe on their way west."

The rooms over the gardens did nicely, as usual. Marcel, a master of tact, had known exactly what the situation called for. Two bedrooms, each with its own bath, shared a common sitting room. Daisies from the Mediterranean lightened the formal Louis XVI furniture César Ritz had chosen to fill this particular suite with. Lizbeth had been put in one of the gabled attic rooms, reserved for better servants.

The flowers, Wolff learned from a card, came from Butch Jarman. "The American follows you everywhere."

"Not at all. He's here for a conference with his chief."

He kissed her, and then went back to adjusting his white tie in the sitting-room mirror. "I wish you were coming with me tonight, Rennie. You don't mind being by yourself, do you?"

"Not in the least. Even though I know all those wives are going to make a dead set at you. But you mustn't think of me curled up here all alone, eating chocolates, listening to the sounds of happy couples in the corridor while I search for fresh handkerchiefs to dry my tears, a stranger in an alien world and culture . . ."

He pulled her to him and kissed her again, for a longer moment. When his hand began to search under her blouse, she pushed him away.

"Now, now," she said, pretending to dust off his jacket. "None of that. You're going to mess up that suit Walter so beautifully overpressed for you, and you must look your very best for the Reich's sake."

"I should have told them you were my wife."

"They would have known that I wasn't. The French have noses for that very reason."

He kissed her once more, and for a moment she clung to him. He was so strong. She wished she could stay exactly where she was, in his arms, the moment never ending. "Go," she said, breaking away. "Have a perfectly marvelous time. You mustn't worry about me. I'll order myself an omelet and a glass of wine. Or perhaps I shan't eat." She made her eyes big and sorrowful.

He laughed, kissed her a last time, and was gone.

Butch called her from the lobby a few moments later. He had been waiting for von Danzig to leave. He asked if he could come up. After a moment's hesitation, she said yes. She was betraying Wolff, though not in the way one might expect. Butch Jarman must have felt something of the same, because he was all business as he sat on a fragile chair, his kitchen green eyes serious and downcast.

With the help of his father's Paris staff he had worked out the details. On the following night Rennie would go to Lizbeth's room and find her feverish and ill. She would call the house doctor, who was being replaced for the night by a German Jew named Diehl. Dr. Diehl would diagnose typhoid.

Both Lizbeth and Rennie would be immediately removed to the American Hospital, where they would be put under quarantine. Papers would be sent to the appropriate section in Berlin stating that neither of them could be moved; that both were in critical condition. "In a month, death certificates will be sent to the appropriate Berlin authorities. Von Danzig himself will be convinced, and certainly, despite anything Kimmel might try, free from any suspicion.

"By that time, you and Lizbeth will be safe in America with your grandparents."

"Poor Oskar. He's always loathed Lizbeth. He used to call her The Professional Jew. He must've been relieved that he would never have to see her again, and now she's following him into exile. He'll be depressed."

Butch lit one of his Balkan cigars and, smoking intently, went over the plan again, reassuring her. "You will have contracted typhoid from Lizbeth. You will have to be quarantined. No one, not even von Danzig, will be allowed to see you. He'll be told the prognosis is good but that it will take months to effect a cure.

"He'll have no choice but to go back without you. The hospital personnel will believe you are, in reality, suffering from typhoid. Nothing scares the French medical fraternity more. The Germans will eventually attempt to send one of their own men in, but by that time you will be declared irrevocably and officially dead."

She looked at him and he looked away, stubbing out most of his cigar in a porcelain ashtray. "They won't believe the typhoid story, will they?"

"Probably not," he admitted. "But—if you don't mind my saying so—you're not important enough to cause a major ruckus. Not now. Hitler only has eyes for Poland at the moment and he's softening up the French to let him have her. There'll be a certain to-do about you, but nothing that will go down in history."

"And Wolff?"

"They'll believe he was taken in by you, that you used him for your own ends."

"And so I have."

"His career won't suffer overly much. They don't think of him as a heavyweight. Der Führer likes him and Göring has backed him and Goebbels thinks he makes for good public relations. He has no real enemies. He's their glamour boy. Their very own *Junker*, their tie to the imperial past.

He looks great in uniform, being photographed standing in open cars. He's strong and innocent and nice. He'll be all right."

"You can't be absolutely certain." She thought of Kimmel sitting in the borrowed office in the Polizeipräsidium, detailing the von Danzig family history. She thought of Kimmel in the Friedrichstrasse Station. "He has enemies." She thought of the meat hooks in the cellar under the Chancellery. She wondered why they always committed their most atrocious crimes in cellars. There was no one to stop them. They should have placed their meat hooks in the more public places: the *Ehrenhof* or the Pariser Platz or under the golden eagle at Friedrichstrasse Station.

"You can't go back, Rennie. If there's war over Poland, you won't have another chance to get out."

"I might have. They might trust me more. They might think, Well, if she came back this time, we can drop our surveillance. The dope's to be trusted."

"They don't think like that, Rennie."

"No, they don't, do they?"

She stood at the door, watching him walk along the elegant, carpeted, muraled, friezed corridor to the gilt elevator. When he reached it, he turned and called to her, "I have this terrible feeling you would go with him to the bottom of hell, if he asked you."

"Hell, perhaps. Germany, no." But she said it without conviction.

Rennie went back into the sitting room and opened one of the windows overlooking the Ritz gardens, letting the misty Parisian air clean the room of the smell of Butch's Balkan cigar. She leaned out the window for a moment, remembering the window in Lillie's flat, remembering the traffic on the Kleiststrasse. She felt as if she had left there years before.

She switched off all the lights but one in her bedroom and got into the bed that was nominally hers. She pictured Wolff coming to her, smelling of champagne, of bay rum, his body heat at its usual high. She thought of holding him all night, of the indescribable feeling his finely muscled body gave her.

And then she thought of the American Hospital, of the long, dreary trip to America.

She left the bed and quickly, decisively turned the key in the connecting door to the shared sitting room. She lay awake until she saw the knob turn and felt his hesitation, his disappointment, when the door wouldn't open.

She didn't bother to turn off the night lamp but fell asleep regretting that locked connecting door. She knew that she had willingly punished herself, denying herself the consolation of one last night of making love with Wolff. She knew that would be a punishment she would have to live with every night of her life.

She tried to convince herself that he wouldn't be blamed for her escape. She tried to get herself to believe that Kimmel wouldn't persevere, when all the time she knew that perseverance was Kimmel's stock-in-trade.

She dreamed of Hitler again, of his moustache, of the sinister way he had looked at her in the Chancellery Court of Honor, as if he knew who she was.

She dreamed he kissed her hand and when she looked down, it was gone.

18

"You locked your door last night," Wolff said, when he called her from the lobby in the morning.

"Did I? I was so tired."

He hesitated, suddenly unsure. "Will you take lunch with me today?"

"Of course."

"I have a brief meeting and then some arrangements to make. I shall meet you here at noon."

"I must be back by six. I've promised to have cocktails with Butch and some of his compatriots."

"You're certain I shouldn't be jealous of your American?"

"Quite certain."

She put on the brown traveling suit and had breakfast and more magazines sent up from the kiosk in the lobby. She thought of going to see Lizbeth but decided she was melancholy enough. There would be plenty of Lizbeth on the ship going to America.

She ate her brioche while she thumbed through a copy of American *Vogue*. The models wore mink coats, high heels, corsages on their lapels, hats with tiny veils, gloves of unexpected colors. They seemed frail, strong, and asexual.

Butch spoke to her on the phone, briefly. He wanted to be certain she understood that the rendezvous was for six P.M. sharp. When Wolff called for lunch, she deliberated for a moment and then changed into her dark trousers, the black turtleneck sweater, the blue fox jacket with the rakish hat. Lillie would've approved, she thought, looking at herself in a full-length mirror. And she didn't care what the blond and pink ladies in the Ritz lobby thought of her trousers. She wanted this last afternoon to be a happy one, and she couldn't be happy in her brown traveling suit.

An enormous ancient and scarlet Rolls-Royce waited for them under the Place Vendôme porte cochere. A driver in elaborate livery sat behind the steering wheel, which was on the right-hand side of the car in the British manner. He had ivory-colored skin, faded blue eyes, and a perfectly serene manner. He sat quietly as the doorman helped the mademoiselle in trousers into the cavernous passenger compartment of the Rolls.

Wolff got in after her, and as the car pulled away from the Ritz at a majestic crawl, he wrapped an oversized mink blanket around them both.

It was a cloudless, cold Parisian day, the sun oddly moonlike, ornamental. The Parisians, sharp-nosed and pale, hurried about their business, which seemed—when Rennie looked at their half-closed eyes—certain to be nefarious, illegal, or unpleasant.

"My father used to say," she told Wolff, taking his arm, "that Frenchmen only laugh at the end of an important meal. Do you suppose that's true?" She was determined this was going to be a delightful afternoon. No memory of the past or thoughts of the future were going to mar it.

"No," Wolff answered. "Frenchmen also laugh when somebody falls down. The French music hall comedians who played in Berlin were always falling down, wondering where the laughs were."

They rode in silence through the narrow streets of Paris. Rennie felt secure and a little happy in the back of the Rolls. "The chauffeur is a kilometer away," she said, as they left Paris.

"As he should be." Wolff put his arm around her. He wore his soft blue cashmere suit. Rennie put her hand inside the jacket pocket.

"I thought you were supposed to be working on this trip," she said.

"I'm taking a short holiday." He pulled her closer to him, kissing her. "You always kiss me as if we're never going to see one another again," he said, looking into her silver blue eyes. "I love you so much, Rennie."

"The chauffeur," she whispered, clinging to him.

"He's deaf and dumb and blind." Wolff kissed her again. "I can't believe my good luck. I thought, that first night in Lillie's flat, that I would never be able to know you, to kiss you, to make love to you. You were so distant."

"I was afraid I was going to make a fool of myself and jump into your arms."

"I think about you all the time, Rennie, even when my mind should be on other things. There are moments when I wish you'd go away—when I have work to do—but your presence is always with me." He found her hand in his pocket and held it. "I'd like to keep you in this pocket, Rennie, and only take you out when times are good."

They held on to one another as the Rolls drove west, moving onto Route N 13 as it began to snow. Families in their best clothes walked in close groups along the side of the highway. It was Sunday again, Rennie realized. The families were coming from church, going home for their Sunday afternoon meal.

"What would your family be doing today, on Sunday?" she asked, thinking of Lillie, of Pepsi and Ruben, of Lizbeth waiting for her. She freed her hand for a moment, to touch her father's signet ring. "Will they miss you?"

"Not my father. He barely can bring himself to talk to me. He was, is, a *Generaloberst*—a general in the army— while I, I am a mere *Oberstgruppenführer*, a general in the SS. He thinks the SS is a joke, a piece of cheap theater, like Ribbentrop adding a von to his name. I suppose he's right. I'm a general with no men to command, no war to fight.

The truth is I'm a second-string actor in the diplomatic corps. I don't mind, but Father thinks the honor of the von Danzigs is being soiled. He blames Göring. When he meets him at the Herrenklub, he cuts him dead.

"At this very moment Father is in the old church in the Grunewald, praying for me and the return of the monarchy. Yet once again, because of Hitler, we have our Grunewald villa and can afford to occupy it. We're rich thanks to Hitler. Our I. G. Farben shares rise daily, the produce from our farms is earning more than it ever has. The von Danzigs are back in business, as they say.

"After church, Father will eat an enormous breakfast. Sausage and eggs and liver and steak and a loaf of bread, heavily buttered, with marmalade heaped on top of the butter."

"And what does he have for lunch?" Rennie asked, teasing.

"On Sunday," Wolff replied, consciously deadpan, "breakfast is his only meal of the day. Afterwards, he'll go into his library to refight the war."

"Who wins this time?"

"We do, of course."

"And where is your mother?"

"Walking her dachshunds, refighting her own, social wars. While my brothers and their wives squabble over missed chances for gain in the Gartenhaus."

"They adore you?"

"They're furious with me because I am the youngest yet I am able to get their children into special schools. And it is to me they must come when they want an invitation to some tea or reception or when they need money for their private enterprises. You see, I was the one who was supposed to fail. I am my mother's son."

"She's pleased with you?"

"Ecstatic. She keeps a scrapbook with my photos clipped from the newspapers." He laughed, ruefully. "I am Mother's

Bavarian revenge on the von Danzigs and all the Prussian *Junkers* she's despised since she married Father.

"Now she has me and the glory of my uniform, my high connections to throw in their faces. I never take her to tea at the Eden without wearing my medals." He took Rennie's hand from his pocket and kissed it. "I have yet to introduce you to my family because, unlike my father and my brothers and, yes, even Mother, I dislike dissension."

"They wouldn't approve?"

"My brothers would approve too much, so their wives wouldn't. Father would dismiss you because you don't come from high middle Prussia and there's no von to your name. Mother would be unalterably opposed because you have no fortune and are more beautiful than she—and a good deal more sophisticated."

The Rolls abruptly turned, driving under an ancient brick arch, manned by two men in the same scarlet livery as the chauffeur was wearing.

"Where are we?" she asked, not much caring. She wished that the ride would go on forever. She didn't want to think about her appointment at six P.M. "sharp."

"We are five miles east of Saint-Germain-en-Laye, a town inordinately proud that it was built around a chateau originally constructed by King Louis the Fat. Louis XIV, the Sun King, was born here and kept his mistress, Mme. de Maintenon, in a house on the Rue du Vieil Abreuvoir."

"You've been memorizing a guidebook."

"Nothing of the sort. When Mother's French cousin—the pederast, as Father calls him—came to visit, he would tell us stories about King Louis the Fat. He used to promise me that I would one day visit him, but now that I'm in France, he isn't. Herbert is the last of his line, the only Frenchman I know who chooses to live in Italy. He's very rich and keeps his chateau permanently in readiness for what he is always threatening as his immediate return. He hasn't returned in ten years."

The Rolls pulled up at the drawbridge, under which was a dry moat and over which was the entrance to the sixteenth-century chateau. Wolff explained, in his guidebook voice, that it had been built by one of Herbert's ancestors who had the confidence of François I. As a result, the drawbridge and the turrets were plastered with decorative F's and François I's symbol, heraldic salamanders.

"It looks as if it had been dreamed up by the brothers Grimm in one of their more benign moments," Rennie said. "I expect there's a troll and a captive princess." Another liveried servant opened the huge wooden door that led into the chateau's great hall, which was built of pale blue stones.

"I am the troll, and you, *gnädiges Fräulein*, are the princess."

He led her up a narrow stone staircase, confessing that he had driven out to the chateau early in the morning to familiarize himself with it, to make arrangements. "Cousin Herbert has done a certain amount of redecoration," Wolff said, taking her down a stone corridor into a low room, lit by candles in oversized brass lanterns. There was a decorative plaster ceiling, three walnut-paneled walls, and a pale blue stone floor. The fourth wall had been removed and replaced with a solid sheet of glass. "Herbert wanted a modern touch," Wolff explained.

Rennie held her breath. It was as if she were looking at an enormous, moving painting. Through the glass she could see the farmlands below, a small village in the distance, a winding river, two nuns and a priest walking up a country road. She laughed, delighted. "It makes me want to walk through, like Alice."

From a screened balcony at the back of the room, a quartet played softly while servants brought champagne, caviar. The one piece of furniture was a long, low leather couch placed in front of the glass wall. Wolff poured the champagne, a thin gold liquid. Rennie accepted the glass. "You're a romantic, Wolff."

"You're only now discovering that? My physical being comes from Father's land, deep in East Prussia. But my heart is of the South. Nothing can control it. Father has long predicted it will be my downfall."

"Oh, I think your heart will save you, Wolff."

"From what?"

"Dangerous women like me."

"Yes. You are dangerous. The Silver Rose of Berlin, *nicht wahr*? Sing to me." He snapped his fingers, and the musicians began to play "The Silver Rose of Berlin."

"Your quartet has an amazingly large repertoire," Rennie said.

"Sing to me," he pleaded. "You have no idea how difficult it was to obtain the sheet music."

"I am the Silver Rose of Berlin," she began and then found she couldn't continue. She had thought of what he had told her on the train . . . of the meat hooks in the Chancellery cellar. She went to him, putting her head on his shoulder, her arms around his waist. "Why is it I can never stop touching you?" she asked, looking up at him. "I suppose I'm afraid you'll disappear. You're so much too good, Wolff, to be true."

"I won't disappear. I promise. Der Führer says Germany's destiny is *Lebensraum*. But my destiny is you, Rennie."

The musicians finished the song and left through a door in the balcony. Wolff made slow love to her on the long, low couch, surrounded by wine coolers and dishes with silver covers.

Later, as it grew dark, they lay together on the couch, watching the lights in the village come on, as headlights from an occasional auto lighted up the narrow, winding road.

"I want you to marry me, Rennie," he said.

"But Wolff . . ."

"There is no 'but Wolff.' I want you to come back to

Berlin and marry me. Say you will, Rennie. I used to laugh in the cinema when the hero said he couldn't live without the heroine. I'm not laughing now, Rennie. I can't live without you."

"And I don't want to live without you, Wolff." He's such a boy, she thought. Such a beautiful country boy. Even the Nazis haven't been able to spoil his kindness, his inherent goodness.

He took her in his golden arms and she caught sight of his wristwatch. It was platinum and heavy and he had taken it off when they made love. It lay discarded on the floor, face up. It read nearly seven P.M. She had missed her appointment with Butch Jarman.

"What if we don't go back to Berlin? What if we keep on going? To London, New York, Hawaii?"

"I don't want to go anywhere, Rennie. I am German. We're witnessing an incredible revolution. We're going to be the greatest power on earth, without one shot fired. We have a front-row seat, Rennie. I know. The persecutions worry you. They also worry me and they worry a great many men in the party. Hitler, too, is concerned. *Kristallnacht* shocked too many people. They're going to have to stop, now. Goebbels will have to stop. Especially now that we've almost reached our goals." He kissed her. "You're not still worried about the authenticity of your papers, are you?"

"No," she said, finishing the champagne. "I'm not worried about my papers."

"Then say you will marry me when we return to Germany."

She looked at his watch again. There was still time. Butch could arrange something. After all, they were in France, not Germany.

The thought of Germany, of Kimmel, filled her with a terrible fear. But going on to a new life, one without Wolff, scared her even more. She imagined life without him would be like her idea of death: no color, everything relentlessly, forever gray. The truth, she realized, was that wherever Wolff was, life for her would be in color. Without him, it would be lived in tones of black and white. Life would be like death.

She stared out through the glass window. All that could be seen now were pin dots of light. "I'll marry you, Wolff, when we return to Germany," she said.

Butch was waiting for her in the servants' common room on the garret floor of the Ritz. He looked only a little less controlled than usual. "I've been waiting for hours," he said.

"I'm sorry, Butch. I was detained."

"Unavoidably detained," he corrected her, standing in the center of the cheerless room.

"Yes," she agreed, "unavoidably detained."

"You're going back with him, aren't you?"

"Yes. Don't tell me I'm making a great mistake, Butch. I know I'm making a great mistake. Still, I'm going back. Is Lizbeth still here?"

"She said she didn't want to leave without saying goodbye. She knew from the start that you'd be going back with him."

She went past Butch into the low-ceilinged room Lizbeth was sitting in, on the edge of a green and faded wingback chair. The small window was like a picture frame; the view like a tourist's painting: Paris by night. A brown suitcase—one of Nick's expensive discarded overnight bags —held all her belongings. She wore the black dress with the torn collar. The room smelled stale but hygienic, as if it had been washed down with antiseptic.

"He loves me," Rennie said, not able to look at Lizbeth.

"Does he know you're a Jew?" Lizbeth asked, putting aside, for once, her knitting. When Rennie didn't answer, she said, her voice going shrill, "No. Sure he don't. How could he know you're a Yid when you don't even know it?

"You've never seen the inside of a *shul*. You're a free-thinker. A German. It's an accident you're Jewish. Sure, you're totally assimilated, a regular Boche. Look at you. Who would know? *Shiksa*. That hair and those eyes. Even the way you move. What Jewess ever had slim hips and breasts like that? Himmler himself wouldn't know. You're a full-blooded *goye* now, no?"

She stood up and moved close to Rennie, her finger—old and shriveled with arthritis—pointing. "Your father thought he was a *goy*, too. Hobnobbing with the Kaiser's son. Ah, you all forgot you were Jewish. It took Adolf Hitler to remind you.

"And don't go thinking Hitler likes you any better because you look like one of his. He hates you more than he hates me. I'm the *yiddler*. He knows where he stands with me.

"But you, you're a different piece of cake. You're what Goebbels calls on his radio the enemy within. And when the day comes that your SS boyfriend finds out what you are, then you'd better watch out. Because he himself is going to load you on the *Viehwagen* and send you to the camp."

"He wants to marry me."

Lizbeth stepped back. "He doesn't want to marry you," she shouted in a hoarse whisper. "You! You're a Jew, a Hebe, a kike, an *Untermensch*. He only wants to marry what you're pretending to be.

"I feel sorry for you, Rennie. Yes, a poor, uneducated, skinny old bag like me feels sorry for you. You have no tradition but a borrowed one. You've lost your past, so you can't have any future. And you, you want to marry him so you'll have an identity. You think you'll be a person again. You'll sit in church and wear a swastika around your neck and you'll have his *goy* children . . ."

"He can't have children."

". . . and you'll close your eyes while he and his Nazi pals make the rabbis clean out their toilets with *t'filin* and prayer shawls.

"You're a coward, Rennie. You love him? You don't love him. You're only frightened. You can't leave what you've always known. You can't take the risk of starting a new life.

"So, good. Go. Marry your *sheygets*. But for me, you no longer exist. You are dead for me, Rennie." Staring at Rennie with her narrow, shrunken eyes, she put her hands to her chest and tore another rent in her collar. "As I mourn your father, so I mourn you."

She turned away from Rennie and faced the wall. She put her handkerchief over her thinning hair and began to intone the kaddish, the Jewish prayer for the dead.

Rennie ran past Butch Jarman and took the gilded elevator down to the fourth floor, to the rooms overlooking the garden. She took off her clothes and got ready for bed. She didn't lock the connecting door.

But long after Wolff had made love to her, long after he had gone to sleep, his head on her shoulder, she lay awake, listening in her mind to Tante Lizbeth chant those terrible words *Yis-gad-dal v'yis-kad-dash sh'meh rab-bo* . . .

19

Rennie suffered what she self-diagnosed as a "strange malaise" during those first days of her return to Berlin. Wolff, amused, said she was reading too many French novels. Privately, she agreed.

She enjoyed the act of cutting the pages nearly as much as the actual reading. Her father had given her, when she was fourteen, a Lalique knife for that purpose. She wondered what had happened to that knife. She wondered, idly, what had happened to all the things in the house on the Lentzeallee.

It was there, when she was depressed—or when there were situations she wanted to avoid—that she would spend the day in bed, not eating, drinking tea, cutting and reading her way through one of Colette's realistic romances.

She did just that during her first and second day back in Berlin. She used an old dress dagger that had once belonged to the hero of the Battle of Mars La Tour, Wolff's grandfather, to cut her way through *Chéri* and *The Last of Chéri*, having bought cheap editions just before the North Train left Paris. She had read them before, but propped up in Wolff's four-poster, with a wind from the east rattling the two sets of windows overlooking the Tiergarten, she found them comforting.

Wolff had had to spend those first days—and then, it turned out, his evenings as well, with Ribbentrop and Goebbels and lesser lights, giving them a detailed report of his conversations with the French.

"Will you have to fight when there's a war?" she had

asked him when he returned to the flat sometime after midnight after his final debriefing.

"There won't be a war," he said, undoing his tunic collar. "If there hasn't been war by now, there never will be. There's no reason for war."

"*Lebensraum*," she said, not liking the word, disliking the concept—more living space for Aryan Germans—more.

"After Poland, Hitler will have his *Lebensraum*." He took off his trousers, dropping them onto the floor, pushing the cut pages of *Chéri* aside, getting into bed. "No one is going to war over Poland." He made love to her and she believed him.

On Wednesday, while Wolff was attending a luncheon for King Boris, she got an unwilling Walter to give her the keys to the two-seater and drove to the Kleiststrasse. The knowledge that Hitler was now going to swallow up Poland—with or without war—made her feel alienated and alone. Wolff believed what they told him. She needed to be with someone who chose to believe very little. She needed Lillie.

Lillie held her close, tears streaming down her cheeks. She had called Lillie the moment she had returned, but she hadn't been able to bring herself to see her until now. She had felt that she had betrayed Lillie by coming back, that she had done her some disservice.

Rennie looked at her as Lillie pushed frizzed strands of escaping red hair back into place with one hand and with the other dabbed at her tears. She stood in front of the oversized portrait of herself, attempting to smile. Lillie had aged in the past few months.

"You're worse than your father, Rennie," Lillie said, pulling Rennie down beside her on the Napoleonic sofa. "Another romantic. Do you know what other people, Jews and otherwise, would give to have had your chance? Do you know what they would have given? *Ach,* and you come back because you're in love."

"They would have killed him if I hadn't returned."

"Don't be absurd. He would have been demoted, at worst. Sent off to the consulate in Mexico. Hitler reserves the meat hooks for those who count." She fitted a cigarette into her jade holder but didn't light it. "And what will happen when they find out about you? A Jewess in gentile disguise? You'll spent the rest of your life in a camp." Lillie closed her eyes. For her, the idea of concentration camp was the worst punishment. She had a great fear of closed-in spaces, of forced intimacy, of regular hours.

"They won't find out, *Mutti*," Rennie reassured her. "I have my papers. A new Aryan driver's license. A document from the Anthropological Institute. Dr. Jurgen and Rosenberg himself have my measurements, my most intimate photographs. I have been certified Superior Aryan Type A Number One. Wolff is allowed to marry me and we're going to do that just after the holidays. There's nothing to worry about, Lillie."

Lillie opened her heavy-lidded eyes and gave Rennie a sorrowful look as she reached out to take her hand. "No, you're perfectly right, *Schatzi*. You don't have anything to worry about. Now you're *salonfähig*, invited everywhere. You have your Wolff, and I can see that despite everything you'll be happy. As for me, I've made my decision. Pepsi and I are leaving after the first of the year. Running the Kleist Kasino isn't so much fun these days. As soon as I can get *them* out"—she looked up at the ceiling—"I'll take Pepsi and go back to Vienna first and then maybe make a try for London." She stood up, holding the black imitation-silk wrapper with the red feather trim close to her. "There's no place I really want to go. The trouble is, *Schatzi*, that though I know better, I still feel as if I'm a Berliner."

Before she left, Rennie went up the stairs into the false attic to see Ruben. His father was trying to take the brown and white checkered cap from him as she stepped into the corridor.

"It's unsanitary," the father said, in German. "He won't take it off. Night and day he wears that damned cap."

Having kept his cap, Ruben put it on his head and smiled at Rennie. *"Guten Tag, Fräulein."*

"Guten Tag, Ruben."

She looked into the room where her father had been hidden for so long and decided not to go in. Ruben and his parents had taken it over. It didn't even look like the same place, she thought.

It was, predictably for an early December afternoon in Berlin, gray and dark when she left. Still, she wasn't unhappy. She was going to see Wolff in a very few moments. She wasn't afraid, now, of the Gestapo tortures. She was protected. She got into the two-seater and, though the rag top was up, felt chilled. She turned on the motor and let it idle for a moment while she looked into the rearview mirror to see if a U-turn was advisable.

She caught the gleam of his eyeglass first and she saw, in the rearview mirror, his shallow eyes and his humid lips, his mouth working as he sucked on a *Lutschbonbon.*

She tried to tell herself that he could be sitting in his brown car in front of the Kleist Kasino for any number of reasons, but that wasn't convincing. She tried to tell herself, again, that she wasn't frightened, that she was protected.

She closed her eyes for a moment and saw again her father's body being spun around as if by supernatural force in the cobblestoned Ku-damm side street. She saw again those anonymous men tossing his body into the cavernous trunk of the official Mercedes.

She decided not to attempt the U-turn, after all. Though she wasn't relieved when Kimmel didn't follow her. He knew where to find her.

Rennie stood in the overheated drawing room of Hitler's Bavarian Alps retreat, the Berghof, gazing through a huge window, one that overlooked the Untersberg peak. Earlier, the window had been open, letting in much-needed fresh air. But now it was closed, because the garages were directly below and gas fumes from late arrivals' Mercedeses filled the room unpleasantly.

Wolff had brought her there for the Führer's final approval. Once it was given, they could marry. She stared at the view—so pretty it seemed unreal. A proper amount of snow had fallen. She felt that everyone in that room knew who and what she was. She turned away from the Untersberg feeling that fear, that paralyzing fear, return. She crossed the huge room and went to Wolff. He stood just outside the smaller seating area, talking to Hess, looking poised and handsome and as distant as a young man on a Hitler youth poster.

Wagner was being played too loudly on the phonograph. The twenty or so guests—Hitler intimates, this was to be an informal weekend—sat in the first seating area around a glass-topped table, their conversation competing with the phonograph music.

Wolff had propped himself up against the wall where a Bordone painting of an exceptionally well-endowed woman was spotlighted. Opposite her was a Titian nude, a hugely proportioned Venus reaching out to touch the extended finger of a smiling cherub.

What impressed her most about the weekend at the

Berghof was the lack of glamour, the stultifying boredom, the middling taste of everything from the art to the food. She had heard tales of elaborate orgies. Certainly, she thought, an elaborate orgy would be preferable to all these members of the petite bourgeoisie acting as if they were on a swell country weekend at a ducal palace.

"Shall we go make love?" she asked Wolff.

"Not done. First we must have our tea." He took her hand. She had been nervous enough the night before. They had arrived, fairly late, and had been taken into the drawing room by what seemed an entire troop of SS men wearing white gloves and that stony expression that seemed to have been grafted onto all of the noncommissioned ranks.

It had taken her a moment to grow accustomed to the dark. A movie projector and screen—hidden during the day under questionable medieval tapestries—had been set up. Hitler and his guests were watching a Hollywood film a couple of years old called *Swing Time*.

Afterwards, when the film was over and the lights turned up, Hitler had taken her hand and kissed it, muttering *gnädiges Fräulein*. Eva Braun had been introduced. She looked Rennie over with a speculative eye. She wore a nile green dress, trimmed with leopard fur, cut low. It looked as if it had been inspired by some Hollywood musical heroine. Not Ginger Rogers as much as Sonja Henie. But Eva Braun seemed more like a second lead from one of those musicals. The scheming secretary who doesn't get the job or the boy.

Indeed, several of the women were secretaries, girls resembling League of German Girls models, blond and pretty with minimal makeup. One of Hitler's personal doctors, Brandt, was present, along with his wife, Anni. Bormann and Hess were the only members of the political inner circle to have arrived, the others scheduled to follow the next day.

Hitler sulked, his hands folded across his lap in his

familiar protective gesture, a swastika in the lapel of his double-breasted jacket. His dog, Blondi, licked one hand. With the other, Hitler nibbled at sweets and chocolate cookies made by his cook, Frau Manizialy.

After the film had ended, no one spoke. Hitler ate. Abruptly he looked up and went into a long monologue on the subject of Prussia. "Fine Aryan stock," he said, in his monotone, glancing at Wolff. "A German Celtic combination. I have frequently visited East Prussia. The flatlands and the shimmering birch trees seemed to me to be quintessentially German." He went on for some time about the grandeur of East Prussia, suddenly switching subjects, calling for a glass of mineral water, comparing the Poles to the African races. "Born to be slaves," he said.

It wasn't until early in the morning that Rennie and Wolff were dismissed, allowed to go to their bedroom. It was painted blue-gray, decorated with paintings of scenes from German mythology. The private bath, their SS servant told them, was made of stone and marble taken from different parts of Germany. Beside the bed was a bookcase containing French pornographic books and a signed copy of *Mein Kampf*.

A list of rules had been placed on each of their pillows.

"Are you all right?" Wolff asked. "You're not frightened, are you?"

"Of course not." She picked up the list and pretended to study it. "We mustn't smoke."

"No," he agreed, kissing her neck. "We mustn't smoke."

"We can't talk to the servants."

"That," he said, pulling her dress up over her shoulders, "would be disastrous."

"No letter writing. No diary keeping."

He put his hands around her, caressing her skin. "Perish the thought."

"No whistling. Hitler hates whistling."

"So do I." He turned her around and began to kiss the back of her neck.

"No cosmetics," she said, holding the list up in front of her, reading from it. "No 'coloring material' on the finger-nails."

"I'll force myself to refrain," Wolff said, drawing her down onto the bed.

"All the women tonight had 'coloring material' on their fingernails."

"They are to face the fingernail squad in the morning." He kissed her again, taking the rules, crumpling them, throwing them with accuracy into the slate wastepaper basket.

Later, she lay in the bed, smoking, watching Wolff sleep as she thought of the boring people in the other rooms. And of how dangerous they were.

Early in the morning Wolff had to attend a private interview with Hitler. During lunch—when Himmler, Gö-ring, and Goebbels arrived with their aides—there was a large-scale meeting.

Eva Braun had taken charge of the nonworking guests, herding them down into the staff bowling alley where she had *San Francisco* shown, commenting freely on the acting, singing, and dressing styles of Gable, Spencer Tracy, and Jeanette MacDonald, whom she disliked.

She wore another nile green outfit, again trimmed in fur but accented with two gold clips to emphasize her breasts. It seemed an odd choice for daytime wear. She seemed an odd choice for Hitler. Rennie would have guessed he had a glamorous film star for a mistress; or a woman of power. Not this blond Bavarian girl, with her excess social poise.

Because of the weather—more snow had fallen—tea was served in the drawing room rather than in the teahouse, some half hour away by foot. White-vested SS men silently provided each guest with tea or coffee and a variety of sweets.

"I have a pleasurable announcement to make," Hitler said, after having indulged in a considerable number of his cook's pastries. He stood up, his hands, as usual, protecting his sexual organs. He looked, Rennie thought, like a prosperous businessman, a trifle chubby and not nearly so affable as he liked to think.

"General von Danzig, Wolfgang, has this morning asked for and received permission to marry his charming fiancée, Fräulein Nacht." He walked across the room carefully, drawing her to him, kissing her on both cheeks. "You are the ideal Aryan maiden, *gnädiges Fräulein*," he said, smiling. "I expect at least one dozen blond children from this union." He turned to his guests. "These two youngsters are our future. Look at them carefully. They are the cornerstone of our Thousand Year Reich. We must have a proper toast."

He nodded to his manservant, Heinz Linge, who led a troop of white-vested SS men into the room, all carrying chilled German champagne, crystal glasses.

"To that happy couple," Hitler said, his eyes taking on a glassy, self-hypnotized stare, his voice rising. "One thousand years from now, your children's children shall raise their glasses to you, in praise for keeping the racial strain pure."

Glasses were touched. Everyone drank the too-sweet champagne while Hitler drank mineral water. "I have arranged a special engagement gift for you," Hitler said, giving his empty glass to Heinz Linge, turning to them. "I know you must want to be alone on this sacred occasion. Perhaps tonight will witness the beginning of the continuation of a great German name." He smiled as Eva Braun joined him. "Captain Werthauer will escort you to the Eagle's Nest. It is yours for the entire night."

The captain, whose head was shaved and scarred, told them that their luggage had already been attended to. He bowed, clicked his heels, and led them down into the garage and to the military transport waiting for them.

"Doesn't Hitler know," Rennie whispered, as the vehicle began to climb the snow-covered mile up to the pavilion Hitler had had built high in the mountains, "that you cannot have children?"

"I arranged to have that kept from him. We couldn't have married without his approval, and if we couldn't breed children, he would see no need for us to marry."

The Eagle's Nest was a squat, massive structure, a gallery of Roman pillars surrounding a huge glassed-in circular room. Rennie found it oppressive. It was both too modern and too ancient, like some precivilization tribal meeting place. In addition to central heating, there was an enormous fire burning in the grate.

Werthauer clicked and bowed and *heil*ed until Wolff dismissed him. Chilled despite the fire and the heat, Rennie stood at the windows, the blue fox jacket over her shoulders. The air was so clear she could see Salzburg and its neighboring villages in the far distance.

"The view from your cousin's chateau was less grand but more intimate," she said as Wolff joined her. France seemed years ago. Above them rose a horizon of mountains and peaks while below them lay pastures and forest, lightly covered with snow.

A little to their right, hanging over the Eagle's Nest like a constant threat, was an abrupt wall of gray naked rock.

"I feel as if we've been sent up here to breed, like two animals," Rennie said.

"But we're all alone here," Wolff told her, surprised she wasn't happy. He couldn't have asked for a better engagement present. He thought the Eagle's Nest was dramatic and romantic. "I regret we can't have a child, Rennie. It is my only regret." He kissed her. "I thought you wanted to get away from der Führer's guests. I thought you wanted to be alone with me."

"We're not alone. Behind that rock, about to descend upon us, are a million beasts. The moment we close our eyes they're going to ravage us."

"We won't close our eyes."

He began to kiss her, but she turned away, found her purse and a Nigeria, and lit it. "You don't suppose I'll be guillotined," she said, inhaling. "This is my second cigarette."

"Are you crying?" he asked.

"No."

He put his arms around her. "There's nothing to be frightened of."

It had grown suddenly dark. She looked at him in the reddish light from the fire. "I wish you weren't so handsome, Wolff. I wish you weren't so innocent and believing."

He tried to draw her down to the bearskin rug that lay in front of the fireplace. "No," she said. "Don't move. Stand there by the fireplace. I have something to tell you and I won't be able to tell you if you're touching me." She rested her head against the cold glass of the bay window. She wanted to get as far from his warmth as possible.

"I am not an Austrian, Wolff. I am German through my mother and Polish through my father and Jewish on both sides. My father was Nick Jablonski, recently killed by the Gestapo. At least I think it was the Gestapo. Three men in trench coats gunned him down in an alley off the Kudamm, so one can be reasonably certain it was the Gestapo.

"And I, Wolff, am wanted by the Gestapo. For what I think could be classified as serious interrogation. To marry me, Wolff, would be high treason. A crime against the Reich as well as against the Nuremberg Race Laws.

"And don't say they won't find out. Kimmel, I am certain, knows. He's waiting for the appropriate moment. He considers you a far worse enemy than me. You'll end up in the Chancellery cellar, Wolff."

She closed her eyes, saw the butcher's meat hook, and then opened them to stare out at the slab of rock facing her.

She felt him approach her. He switched on an overhead
light. She turned, and in the sudden, harsh illumination
she thought he was horrified, that the arm he was stretching
out toward her was going to hit her.

Instead it encircled her and he pulled her to him. "My
darling Rennie, do you think I would have brought you
here if I was afraid of Kimmel? If there was the least
chance of his harming you? Do you think I would have let
you come back from France if I hadn't been certain you'd
be safe? And don't you know I've been aware, all along,
who and what you are? I may be an innocent, but I'm not
a fool." He laughed. "I was certain you knew that I knew.
You wouldn't speak of it so I didn't."

He kissed her. "The persecution is almost at an end. I
told you: Goebbels went too far with his *Kristallnacht*. Too
many of us objected. In the beginning a scapegoat was
needed to bring the people together, but now there are so
few Jews left, so many of Hitler's goals have been reached,
there is no longer any need for *Judenrein*."

"The Race Laws?"

"Goebbels's propaganda."

"The Jews in the camps?"

"Adolf Eichmann is constantly meeting with Jews from
Jerusalem. Eventually they'll all be resettled there."

"The Jews who have died for no other reason than that
they were Jewish?"

"We've been in a war, Rennie. A war without arms. But
still, a war. People have had to get hurt. There have had
to be some casualties. It wasn't fair or good or moral that
most of those people were Jews, picked from superstition and
ignorance. But now it's over. Goebbels is on his way out,
I'm certain. There's nothing more to worry about."

"Kimmel?"

"Even if he accused you, who would believe him? You
are safe with me, Rennie."

And though she had promised herself she wouldn't, she

allowed Wolff to make love to her in the Eagle's Nest. She could see the great ugly gray rock outside the bay window, looking as if it were about to fall on them and crush them under its weight.

The following day, after breakfast at the Berghof, Willie brought the official Mercedes around to take them back to Berlin. As they drove away, she saw Himmler walking along one of the numerous paths that surrounded the Berghof. And as he walked, he seemed to be giving all his attention to a man who, from the back, looked remarkably like him.

It wasn't until the Mercedes made the sharp turn for the final descent that the two men about-faced and Rennie saw who Himmler's companion was. He wore his leather trench coat, his monocle, and his joyless smile. Kimmel nodded to her pleasantly as he continued to talk to Himmler.

21

After the Berghof there was a bittersweet intensity to their lovemaking. It was as if they suffered from incurable hunger; as if they literally could not get enough of one another; as if they were preparing for a long fast. They spent each night making love. In the morning they woke with blue smudges under heavy-lidded eyes, their skin raw and sensitive.

Rennie, continuing to experience her "strange malaise," would return to the bed after breakfast and read French novels until noon. Their marriage had been set for the day before Christmas. It was to be a registry affair, with only Wolff's friend Hugo von Niedermeyer and Lillie Froelich in attendance. Meanwhile, she felt like a kept woman, a character from one of the novels she read.

Wolff seemed, if not depressed, distracted. Hugo had been suddenly but temporarily transferred to Vienna and had had to make a hurried good-bye, promising he would return for the wedding.

Wolff told her that a great many changes were being made in the Foreign Office. That there was a possibility, after all, that he might get a post in South America.

"Brazil?"

"No, Argentina." The head of the South American German news agency, Transocean, was ailing. Wolff thought it was just possible he might replace him. "Wouldn't you like it in Buenos Aires?" he asked one morning in mid-December, sitting next to her on the bed.

"Infinitely. But would you? I thought you wanted your

front-row seat to the great Pan-German revolution." She reached up and buttoned the collar of his tunic.

"We could have a villa by the sea."

So he is worried, she thought. He's worried about me. Someone must have said something. Or found something. Kimmel. He had found an irregularity in her papers, a fact that didn't mesh. Wolff wouldn't be promoting South America if it weren't something substantial, something to be concerned about.

After he left, she stayed in bed, drinking the chocolate Walter had prepared for her, for once unable to distract herself with the goings-on of the French demimonde, circa 1926. Her mood suddenly changed. There was nothing to worry about. She was being neurotic. If there was something really wrong with her papers, Kimmel would have acted by now.

She got out of bed, deciding she would go to the Kurfürstendamm and shop for a green dress with leopard trim. She would have to have something new for her trousseau. And afterwards, she would go to the Kleist Kasino and spend the afternoon gossiping with Lillie and Pepsi.

She got the keys to the two-seater from Walter, who handed them over and bowed formally. He treated her now as if she were a temporary conqueror, just passing through —but still, one to be obeyed.

As Rennie drove to the Ku-damm, she thought about the dress she would buy. She felt both lighthearted and lightheaded. After all, she said to herself, if I'm going to be a Nazi wife, I might as well look like one.

She parked the car near the Café Kranzler and felt— only for a moment—ill again. Kornwasser's office was only a few steps away. She thought about going in, about finding out about that strange malaise, about her odd mood changes. She waited for a moment, and when the nausea didn't go away, she walked across the side street where her father had been killed, resolutely forcing herself not to think about his death. She stepped up the two blue stone steps and went in.

She had been to him on two or three occasions as a child and the medicinal smell of the paneled waiting room with its posters and magazines and maple furniture made her feel sharply nostalgic. She felt an almost devastating need for her father's comforting hand.

Nurse Gruppe, important and oversized in her starched white uniform, was impressed by the old fox jacket and the nearly silver blond hair. She asked who had recommended the Fräulein, and Rennie said Frau Goebbels. Nurse Gruppe folded her hands across where her waist had once been and said she thought the doctor would see her immediately.

Kornwasser, looking no older and no more competent than Rennie remembered him, stared at her from across his beautiful desk. He put a pair of gold-rimmed pince-nez on, not recognizing her, a little overwhelmed by her presence. He studied the note and the chart Nurse Gruppe had sent in with her.

"You are complaining of nausea and dizziness, Fräulein. We must have an examination. Tests. You understand, I am a modern, thorough doctor. You look healthy, but one can never tell."

He waited while she removed her clothes behind a white-enameled wooden screen. "I've examined you before," he said, surprising her. "Have I not?"

"Yes," she called out. "But I was nine years old, and then my name was Jablonski."

"Dear God," Kornwasser said, but regained his composure as Nurse Gruppe came in, closed the screen, and waited as he examined the new patient.

"Are you all right?" he asked, after Nurse Gruppe had left, while Rennie dressed behind the screen. "I mean are you . . ." He hesitated. "It is illegal for me to treat a Jewess."

"There's nothing to worry about, Doctor Kornwasser. I am completely Aryanized. Inside and out." She pushed the screen aside and wished he didn't look so frightened. Doctors were supposed to be beyond fear. But it was clear that this one wasn't. He had been her father's friend, but he had none of her father's insouciance.

"You have not polluted your surgical tools, examining an *Untermensch*," she reassured him. "I am very much an *Übermensch* these days. My name was never Jablonski. It has always been Nacht. You mustn't worry."

He looked at her with anger and distrust. "Very well, Fräulein Nacht. I shall have the results of your tests later this afternoon. Where shall I send them?"

She told him she would call, that she expected it was a flu. He smiled at her naïveté, in spite of his nervousness. "Flu" was a Berlin prostitute's euphemism for being pregnant.

She felt better after her visit to Kornwasser but decided she didn't really want a green dress with leopard trim after all. She drove the two-seater through the gray Berlin streets carefully. She had a sudden, devastating need to see Lillie, to be held in those long, thin arms. There was a parking space in front of the Kleist Kasino. It was as if it had been reserved for her.

Kimmel sat in his brown staff car, watching two men drive nails into boards over the ground floor windows, the red door. They were sallow and no longer young, SA men who were never going to get much farther than they had.

Kimmel got out of his car when he saw her.

"What are they doing?" she asked him, conversationally.

"*Heil Hitler*, Fräulein Nacht. A pleasure as always, to see you. You seem a bit pale, but the weather has been—what shall we say?—against us."

"What are they doing?" she asked again, her voice rising.

"It had to happen sooner or later, *nicht wahr*? Jewish cabarets have been banned for years now."

"Lillie isn't Jewish."

"She harbors Jews. She has long been suspected of aiding and abetting enemies of the Reich. Only last night we uncovered a nest of Jewish traitors in a tricked-up hiding place above the attic in the cupola. You wouldn't have believed what was in that attic, Fräulein Nacht. Beds. A shortwave radio. Chamber pots." He laughed, seemingly at the memory of the chamber pots.

"What else did you find?" she asked, her voice a whisper.

"A good many things. That black pervert who worked here. Someone saved us the trouble of taking him in. We found him in the alley. *Ach,* what a bloody mess."

She wanted to shout, to scream. But she couldn't. She opened her mouth but no sound came out. The horror—she suddenly and definitively knew—had caught up and enveloped her.

She turned and ran past the SA men and up the stairs that led to Lillie's flat, half expecting Kimmel to shout out for someone to stop her. But she entered Lillie's drawing room undisturbed. It was empty. The Napoleonic sofa, the tubular tables, the morris chair, the beaded curtains, were all gone. Even the painting of Lillie had been taken. It was as if Lillie had never lived there.

As she walked through the empty rooms, her heels making a fearful noise on the bare wooden floors, she wondered if she hadn't somehow come up the wrong stairs, gotten into some other flat. Even the stove in the kitchen, the ancient icebox, had been removed.

She looked into the bedroom she had shared with Lillie and saw where they had broken through into the false attic. She forced herself to walk up the stairs. She didn't know what she had expected to find, but the fact that there was also nothing there horrified her. The folding table with the green-visored lamp. Her father's davenport. The Telefunken. It was all gone. The floors even looked swept, as if the Gestapo had cleaned up after themselves.

She walked along the corridor to the room Ruben and his parents had occupied. There, in the corner, they had left one thing behind. It was Ruben's brown and white checkered cap, his passport to acceptance by English boys. She nearly heard him say *"Guten Tag, Fräulein,"* and she put her hands to her mouth, forcing herself not to vomit. The nausea, the sickness—that "strange malaise"—had returned with full force, and she wondered if she wasn't seriously ill, if she had some cancer, some rare disease. If Tante Lizbeth's God wasn't making her pay for her luck and her love.

She dropped Ruben's cap onto the clean wooden floor and returned to the drawing room, to the window overlooking the Kleiststrasse. She forced herself not to think. Below, the SA men continued to board up the cabaret's windows and door, ineptly, so that from her vantage point it was like a silent comedy. Kimmel was now leaning against his car, watching them with a distracted amusement.

The worst pain, she realized, was that she wasn't going to be able to cry. She couldn't cry. And what the hell had they done with Lillie?

"Rennie! *Mein Gott,* you have a long face. Cheer up." Marlene, the obliging Goose Girl, came into the drawing room and sat next to her on the windowsill, exuding her own special odor of cheap perfume, Woolworth powder, and perspiration. "Good things are happening in this world. Listen to me, Rennie. I have to tell someone about my luck, and it might as well be you. This flat is mine now. Yes. And quite a nice, spacious flat it is, isn't it? Better than sleeping in a room with my sister and her good-for-nothing *Scheiss*-kicker of a boyfriend.

"You know, La Froelich barely let me set foot in here. And now, suddenly, it's mine. Kimmel has given it to me. I know," she said, misreading Rennie's expression. "He's nothing much to look at. But still, he has influence, power.

"In a week, he says I can reopen the cabaret, but this

time I'm to be the manager. Oh, stop giving me that long look of yours. I've learned to play the game, too." She looked over Rennie's shoulder, through the window down at Wolff's two-seater. "Perhaps not as well as you, but still, good enough, don't you think? And the best is, Kimmel says I never have to dance again. What luck. What damned good luck."

Kimmel was resting his rump on the brown staff car, selecting a candy from a *Lutschbonbon* box decorated with a picture of Magda Goebbels and her children. Kimmel studied the photograph for a moment and then smiled at Rennie as if she were a young acquaintance of whom he was especially fond; as if he were an old and honored friend of the family.

Rennie nearly smiled back. She felt as if she had known him forever. She, too, leaned against the brown staff car, resting one foot on the running board. "Are they all dead?" she asked, conversationally.

"Just the black one. And of course the Jews." He offered her a *Lutschbonbon*. She chose a red one, holding it in her hands for a moment, running a finger along the raised swastika. And then she allowed it to slip through her fingers, to fall into the gutter. "Were you the executioner? Was it fun? Did the boy struggle? Pepsi must have struggled."

Kimmel looked down at the red candy in the gutter for some moments and then, his eyeglass reflecting the gray sky, his thin, damp mouth turned up in his customary smile. "It is better they died the way they did, Fräulein. There are so many ways to die. Infinite numbers of ways to die. Most of them not nearly as agreeable as the way they died. Believe me, *gnädiges Fräulein*, it is better."

She moved a little away from his car; from him. "And Lillie?" she asked, though she wasn't at all certain she wanted to know.

"Fräulein Froelich?" Kimmel asked, with the greatest of

good humor. "Would you like to see her? Wait, one moment, Fräulein Nacht." He said a few words to the comic SA men, who stood at attention while he spoke, and then he came back to where Rennie was standing. She was attempting to light a Nigeria, but her hands wouldn't stay still.

He lit it for her with a lighter in the shape of a pistol. When he pulled the trigger, a small blue flame shot up. It was a boy's gadget, and she realized that Kimmel reminded her of a boy, too; a grossly overfed, overgrown boy.

"We should take the general's motor, do you not agree? One never knows what might happen if we left it unattended in this neighborhood." Like a bully on good behavior, he was being overly solicitous.

He offered to drive, and she handed him the keys. Her mouth felt dry and sweet, as if she had eaten the candy. She smoked her fragrant cigarette, staring out the window as Kimmel drove silently, carefully, up the Martin-Luther-Strasse, east on Unter den Linden, and over the Spree, entering the neighborhood which began just behind the Opera: old Berlin, where the Jewish quarter was located.

For once she wished that the rag top was down, that they were in an open car. She imagined she could smell the yellow soap Kimmel had used on himself that morning. She wondered if she was going to faint, but the thought of Lillie—alone, in prison, possibly tortured—kept her in control.

She finished her cigarette as the car stopped by the main entrance to the Jewish cemetery in the Grosse Hamburger Strasse. Her uncles—killed in the war—were buried there. For a moment she thought he was going to take her into the cemetery, but on the opposite side of the street was a gray anonymous building which was known to belong to the Gestapo.

They walked up half a dozen gray stone steps and passed through a series of doors, not stopping at a high desk where a man in civilian clothes, wearing a party armband, looked

up from the ledger he was writing in. The hall was narrow
and too well lit. Kimmel opened a door that led into a
small, windowless room and waited until she had gone
inside.

"I shall be back in a moment," he said, giving her his
smile, shutting the door after him, leaving her alone in the
harshly lit room. She chose one of the brown-painted insti-
tutional chairs lined up neatly against one wall and started
to riffle through her purse, searching for another Nigeria,
when the door opened. Lillie came in and stood still for a
long moment, her eyes adjusting to the hard, relentless
light.

She looked infinitely tired, a decade older. She had been
allowed no makeup. Without her penciled eyebrows, with
her once geranium red hair fading to a colorless brown, she
seemed like an improbable doll, much too long and naked,
standing in the center of that official room, hugging herself.

Someone closed the door and Rennie went to her, putting
her arms around her, holding her close.

"What I must look like," Lillie said. "Thank God they
don't believe in mirrors." She began to cry, her too-thin
body shivering through the shapeless brown cotton dress
they had forced her to wear.

"You mustn't," Rennie said. Her own eyes were dry. "I'll
go to Wolff. He'll . . ."

"I'm not crying because there's no rouge on my sand-
paper cheeks," Lillie said, holding on to Rennie for a moment, then stepping away, accepting Rennie's handkerchief,
sitting on the edge of one of the grim chairs. "I'm not
crying for me. I'm crying for them. They forced me to
watch." She looked up without seeing Rennie. "The two
parents went like sheep. Kimmel's men threw a rope around
one of the exposed beams in the attic and they stood on
chairs. Then the men kicked the chairs out from under
them.

"The boy kept worrying about his cap. They knocked it

off and he kept worrying over it, asking for it in Yiddish, even while they put the noose over his head.

"They took Pepsi down to the alley. Kimmel explained he didn't want any blood. Pepsi was fighting, but they kept hitting him with the butts of their revolvers. Finally, they tied his hands behind his head and his feet together and threw him facedown in the gutter. Then one of them carved a swastika in his back with a hunting knife. At first all I could see were the red dots coming through the white dinner jacket, outlining the swastika. And then, suddenly, it was all red. I screamed. *Gott im Himmel,* how I screamed. And no one came. Not one person.

"But Pepsi didn't scream. They called him an animal, but he died like a hero. I told them they were the animals. I begged them to hang me, to kill me, to carve a swastika in my back. But they said I wasn't Jewish. I had only been contaminated. They have a better solution for me."

"Lillie . . ."

"You mustn't worry about me, *Schatzi.* I am not even to be tortured. I am a special case. An Aryan. I'm to be sent to a work camp." She closed her heavy-lidded plaintive brown eyes for a moment, and Rennie remembered her saying how much she loathed and despised work camps. "Not a prison camp, mind you. A work camp. I'll be fine. I always am. In a few months I'll be back in Berlin, looking for a handout, asking you, this time, to put me up. You will put me up, won't you, *Schatzi?*"

She opened her eyes, and they filled with tears. Kneeling by her chair, her arms around her, Rennie said, "I'll book the best suite in the Adlon, *Mutti.* But there won't be any need. Wolff will . . ." But she never did say what Wolff would do, because the man in the civilian suit with the party armband came in and said that the interview was over.

"You mustn't worry, *Mutti,*" Rennie called as the man led Lillie Froelich away. "I'll talk to Wolff. Wolff will help

us. Don't worry, *Mutti,*" she continued, after the door had
been closed. *"Mutti. Müttchen.* Mummy!"

She stared at the door until Kimmel opened it. He tried,
without success, to take her arm. She forced herself to
regain her balance, to walk quickly and quietly and evenly.
But she found herself holding her breath until she was out
of the Gestapo building and across the Grosse Hamburger
Strasse and into Wolff's car.

"Is she really going to a work camp?" Rennie asked
Kimmel, even though she knew she shouldn't have, that
she was giving him an opportunity she needn't.

"Who knows?"

He stood in the center of the wide street, between the
Jewish cemetery and the Gestapo building, watching the
two-seater until it disappeared. Then he reached into the
pocket of his leather trench coat for another *Lutschbonbon*
and went back into the building to prepare for what he
thought of as the next step.

22

"What are you doing home in the afternoon?" she asked, sitting up in the four-poster bed.

"I'm to have the rest of the day off. It seems Ribbentrop and Goebbels have no use for my particular talents today." He opened the collar of his tunic and sat next to her, pushing aside the cut pages of the novel she was reading, taking her in his arms, kissing her. "How do you feel?"

"Just a touch of my 'strange malaise.'"

A week had passed since she had seen Lillie in the Gestapo building on the Grosse Hamburger Strasse. Surprisingly, it had taken Wolff that long to find out there was nothing he could do, that Lillie was indeed being sent to a newly established camp near Munich, where I. G. Farben was building a plant to manufacture artificial rubber. "She'll be fine," he reassured Rennie. "I. G. Farben isn't going to mistreat its workers. It needs them too badly."

He removed his tunic and his trousers and stood over her. He pulled the bedclothes aside. "You're so beautiful," he said. He stared at her body for a long time, as if he were contemplating attempting a painting of her. Then he bent over her and began to kiss her, touching every part of her body with his lips. "Storing up memories," he said, when she laughed, when she asked him what he was doing.

His body temperature seemed especially high, the touch of his skin nearly burned her. He made love to her differently than he had in the past weeks. Then it was as if he were burying himself in her, using their passion to forget everything. Now it was as if he had suddenly developed a

new sensuality, a new language to express his love. He
stared at her like a man going blind, storing up visual
memories. He touched her everywhere—with his hands, his
lips—as if he were never going to be able to touch her, kiss
her, again.

Afterwards, as she lay in his arms, he pulled his watch
across the night table and looked at it, and then casually
asked if she had been to a Ku-damm doctor called Kornwasser.

"As a matter of fact, yes."

"Why did you go?" She tried to sit up, alarmed, but he
held her to him, kissing her forehead, holding her still.

"My strange malaise. I was feeling especially ill that day.
He took a few tests and told me, when I remembered to
call back, that I was 'fit as a fiddle,' there was nothing
wrong with me bed rest and proper diet wouldn't cure.
How did you know?"

She managed to break away, sitting up, looking down at
him. He closed his eyes. "It seems Dr. Morell was wrong,
as usual, when he examined me during my SS medical
examination. Unless there's been another man, and I don't
believe there has." He opened his eyes and looked up at
her. "You're a month pregnant, Rennie. Or nearly so. Kornwasser reported you and your condition to Section II 112,
the SD department of Jewish affairs.

"Luckily, Hugo is back from Vienna and saw the report.
He couldn't risk suppressing it, but he managed to tell me
about it. His section chief gave the information to his
opposite number in the Gestapo, who connected you to me.
They know—"

"We're going to have a child?" Rennie interrupted, looking at him, pushing the butter-blond hair from his eyes,
kissing his lips carefully, as if he were suddenly fragile.
"What a terrible time to bring a child into this world."

He took her hand, holding it to his lips. "They're coming
for us in a little while." She put her hand to her mouth,

trying not to scream, not to show the horror she felt. "There's a way out. You mustn't worry." He sat up. "Listen to me, Rennie. You have to leave Germany without me. Allow me to be taken." He held her to him. "No. Be quiet. Let me finish. I am going to claim that I had no idea you were Jewish, that you were Jablonski's daughter. I'll say you were using me. I will denounce you. Hugo's destroyed the Rennie Nacht file. There's no hard proof against me. Besides, Hitler and Göring will want to believe me. In the end I'll be let off. They'll send me to Argentina or Mexico. You'll join me and we'll be together with our child. You know, that was my only regret, and now it's gone."

"I won't leave you, Wolff. I couldn't live having left you. We've got to try to get out together."

"You don't understand, darling." He took a breath and held her by her shoulders. "Listen. If you stay, then they will kill both of us and our baby as well. My only chance is if you leave, if I'm seen as your victim." He had tears in his Mediterranean blue eyes as he clung to her, as he kissed her.

"You wouldn't lie to me now, General? You wouldn't let me live the rest of my life as a coward, would you? That would be a worse torture than even Kimmel could devise."

"I love you so much, Rennie, there are no words to tell you."

"I'd rather die than live without you, Wolff."

"My only chance," he said, holding her close for the last time, "is to get you to the American embassy in the next twenty minutes."

"If this is a noble ruse to save me, I'll never forgive you, Wolff." She kissed him and they held on to one another for as long as they dared.

Wolff's official Mercedes, with Willie at the wheel, pulled into the courtyard of the apartment building of the Mat-

thäikirchstrasse, stopping on the far side of the *Hausmeister*'s
conical structure. General Wolfgang von Danzig was seen
helping a woman in a blue fox jacket with a rakish fox
hat into the passenger compartment. He stood back as
Willie suddenly drove off at breakneck speed, crossing the
city and heading south on the Avus. It took nearly forty
minutes to catch up with the Mercedes. The men who did
so found Walter sitting in the passenger compartment. He
was wearing black trousers and a black turtleneck sweater.
Next to him on the seat was a blue fox hat and a matching
jacket, neatly folded.

As Walter, in the fox jacket and hat, was stepping into
the official Mercedes, Rennie—in Walter's raincoat and cap
—was running through the *Hausmeister*'s below-ground flat,
stepping out onto the Matthäikirchstrasse through a side
door, walking half a block to the Bellevuestrasse, where a
dark blue American auto was pulled up to the curb.

Butch Jarman was in the back. "I understand," Rennie
said, getting in, joining him, "that you and Wolff, together,
are going to make an honest woman of me."

"You don't have to be brave, you know," Butch Jarman
said. "You could cry."

"I'm not going to cry. I don't cry in Germany."

Within the hour she was Mrs. Butch Jarman, with a
marriage certificate and an American passport attesting to
the fact. Immediately after the short, dry ceremony she
and Butch were taken to Tempelhof Airport and put aboard
the late-afternoon plane for Paris.

Their passports had hardly been glanced at, a fact that
the middle-aged *Stabsfeldwebel* in charge of Tempelhof passport control had to answer for during a long and not
pleasant night.

"Shall I give you a word of comfort, Herr Baron?"
Kimmel asked, as his men searched the flat. He himself was

sitting in an upholstered chair, his small yellow hands folded across his paunch. Wolff stood at the mantel, looking like an unwilling host, not a little bored with his guest.

"I think you deserve a word of comfort, so I shall give it to you, Herr Baron: she has indeed escaped. She's in Paris with an American passport, and there's little I can do about it. Not now."

Wolff continued to stare up at the painting of the Battle of Mars La Tour. "*Wo sind Sie denn?*" Kimmel asked. "Where are you? I've given you wonderful news, Herr Baron, and you act as if I'm not here. As if I don't exist." He sighed theatrically and got to his feet. "She is married to Herr Jarman. She is going to go and live in America with him. She will have a marvelous life, no?"

One of his men entered the room and said something to him. "*Ach,* I don't even have the consolation of personally conducting your interrogation, Herr Baron," he said, putting his hands into the oversized pockets of his leather trench coat. "There is to be no interrogation. No trial. *Kristallnacht* has made Goebbels permanently publicity shy.

"But there is, of course, to be a punishment. Der Führer is angry, and who could blame him? A member of his inner circle has dared to flout the Race Laws—and so publicly. And imagine: Hitler kissed a Jewess in his own private retreat. In front of his greatest friends and associates. He gave her his blessings. Oh, der Führer feels his most sacred trust has been compromised.

"You are to be hanged, Herr Baron. Not hanged like some common criminal. No, the highest sort of hanging has been reserved for you. You are going to be hanged from a meat hook in the Chancellery cellar.

"And I do have one consolation, Herr Baron. Der Führer wants your death photographed, and I am to be in charge of the photography. What do you think of that? I'll be able to watch as they place you on the hook. The initial pain is said to be exquisite. And then, of course, I shall be there as you struggle to get off. Don't think you won't. They all do. It's a reflex action, I'm told. And the more you struggle, the deeper the point of the hook goes in.

"Oh, there is no doubt, Herr Baron, that I am looking forward to watching you die, to recording your death for posterity and der Führer's enlightenment. They say you always had an inclination to be in the cinema. Now, finally, it shall be fulfilled."

Kimmel executed a half bow as Wolfgang von Danzig was taken out of his flat on the Matthäikirchstrasse. Before he followed, he went into the general's bedroom and found the photograph in its silver frame that Wolff had taken from Lillie's drawing room.

Kimmel stared at it for some time and then put it in his leather trench coat pocket. His small fat hand grasped the thin silver frame. The glass broke under the pressure, but Kimmel continued to clutch it long after the bits of glass had dug into his soft yellow palm.

Butch had tried to find a quiet hotel for her, but all the
quiet hotels in Paris were overflowing with noisy refugees.
She ended up in a suite at the Ritz, overlooking the Place
Vendôme. She said she didn't think she could have stood it
if the rooms had overlooked the gardens.

The tiny *sous-directeur*, Marcel, was apologetic. He
wrung his hands. He couldn't bear the thought that Madame
Jarman (née Jablonski and so recently Nacht) had to hear
the traffic on the noisy Place Vendôme. As soon as it was
humanly possible, he would move someone, shuffle one of
the emigrés from Prague or Vienna. Madame Ritz would
be desolate if Nick Jablonski's daughter and Henry Jarman's daughter-in-law didn't have solitude.

Butch stayed with Bones Marrow in a flat on the Rue du
Bac that was filled with books, whiskey bottles, and stray
girls. Using his father's influence, he managed to book
Rennie and himself on the U.S.S. *Norfolk*, which was to
sail at the end of the week from Bordeaux.

But Rennie was refusing to sail.

She was eating a brioche, sipping at café au lait when he
went to see her. She ate and drank as she stood looking out
at the Place Vendôme. She wore the black sweater and
trousers she had worn when they had tried to go to Italy
together. She gave him a wan smile. She asked if he had
eaten.

He said that he had and sat on the arm of the one
upholstered chair in the sitting room. "Will you leave? It

238

has all been arranged. It has all been double arranged. It wasn't easy, Rennie. A great many people want to leave Europe."

She put the brioche down and found a Nigeria. "It's not as if it's safe for you in Paris," he went on, lighting it for her. "Every other German in Paris is an SS man and every third Parisian is a would-be collaborator." She smoked steadily, staring out the window at the traffic. "What did the doctor say?" he asked, after a moment.

"You know French doctors. He advised plenty of milk and bed rest. French doctors advise plenty of milk and bed rest if you have a hangnail."

"Will you leave Paris, Rennie?"

"I won't leave without him, Butch."

"He's dead, Rennie."

"I don't believe you."

"There was an official dispatch."

"They had to save face by saying he's dead, but they wouldn't really kill him."

Butch put his hand in the pocket of his tweed jacket and fingered the envelope he had received that morning. "I have fairly conclusive proof."

"What is it?"

He removed the envelope from his pocket and hesitated.

"Don't be ridiculous. I'm a big girl now."

"It's a photograph," Butch said, and Rennie realized why he seemed so peculiar. For the first time since she had known him, Butch Jarman was frightened.

He opened the envelope and removed a color photograph of great clarity and precision. He put it facedown on the table between them, holding his hand over it as if it were alive. As if it might escape.

"May I see it?" she asked.

"I can't let you. I'm afraid you'll miscarry or have a breakdown or both." He hesitated and then he said, "It's a photograph of Wolff hanging from a meat hook. He wasn't quite dead when it was taken. Kimmel sent it. He wants it to destroy you. I'm not going to let it."

He took the photograph and tore it into a great many pieces, throwing them out onto the Place Vendôme. She wanted to chase after them, to put the pieces back together again, but the wind scattered them as if they were funeral ashes. She felt that she had been right. Life without Wolff was gray and deadly, no color anywhere. She stared out the window long after the fragments had disappeared, finally allowing herself to realize that Wolff was lost to her forever. He would never touch her again. He would never kiss her again. He would never make love to her again. She didn't know how she was going to live in such a gray world.

"When do we leave?" she asked, some time later, in a voice that made Butch want to go to her, to comfort her. It was a voice filled with despair. "When can we leave?"

Once again they traveled on a train together in a private compartment. It took ten hours to reach Bordeaux, the train making frequent stops to pick up and let off the refugees who crowded it. They spent the night at the Hotel Splendide. Butch drank too much at the closed-in terrace bar, surrounded by rich French, Americans, and Brazilians, all anxious to get to New York.

On the second night out, Rennie surprised Butch by coming to dinner, sitting quietly next to him, listening to the ship's orchestra attempt a Chopin polonaise.

"I'm going to live, you know," she said, taking his arm. "I never doubted it."

"I did. I brought Wolff's pistol with me when I left Berlin. It was blue steel and very beautiful. This afternoon I threw it overboard. I want to live for the child. Sentimental, but there it is. Our baby's going to be a living criminal act, a direct defiance of der Führer's sacred Race Laws." She lit one of her fragrant cigarettes and turned away. "I'm going to bring our baby up to be a Jew."

Her grandfather was waiting for her in New York. He had had a half-million dollars put away in the Chase Bank when he left Austria and half a million dollars seemed to go a long way. Rennie was to come to Miami, to take her place among the other rich refugees who had escaped from Germany and Austria.

She refused.

Oskar argued with her that first night in his suite at the Waldorf until, unexpectedly, Lizbeth emerged from one of the wallpapered bedrooms. She wore a new black dress that was destined, over time, to look exactly like the old one. It's collar was ripped but only in one place, where she mourned Nick Jablonski.

Rennie had been returned to her. She held out her thin arms. "You're not eating enough for a young lady who's going to have a baby," she said in Yiddish, kissing Rennie, calling her *tatela*.

Lizbeth managed to get them both transport to Palestine. "She wants to have her child there," Lizbeth told all inquirers. "You want to put up an argument?" No one did. Rennie's grandfather, Oskar, went back to his pink house on Miami Beach just a little relieved on the day Rennie and Lizbeth set sail.

Rennie had a last, final conversation with Butch on the deck of the ship. It was little more than a tramp steamer with few amenities.

"Not exactly deluxe," she said as they watched the last of the freight being boarded. There was a pervasive smell of oil and men and rotted fruit. Butch could hear Lizbeth down in the cabin, *yiddling* with two Polish Jewish refugees also on their way to Palestine.

"You could stay here," Butch said. "As my wife. I would be a good father to the child. I would be a good husband."

The captain, who was too thin and well-shaven to be a captain on such a ship, came and told Butch, politely, that he had to leave. Rennie walked with him to the ramp which led to the dock.

"No, Butch," she said in English. "You deserve better than me." She kissed him on both cheeks and held his hand for a moment. "I'm spoiled goods, Butch. You'll find your film star here in the United States. I'm no film star. I'm a German-Jewish refugee, a little pregnant, on her way home."

Butch left the pier and had dinner with his father, who appeared to have decided that Hitler wasn't perhaps the man Lindy thought him.

"He doesn't seem to have much common sense," Henry Jarman said, appraising his lobster before attacking.

"Who?" Butch wanted to know. "Lindbergh or Hitler?"

"Well, neither of them, when you come to think of it," Henry said. And then Butch began to cry. Not just tears but great, thundering sobs. Henry left his place at the far end of the rosewood table and went to his son, holding him, comforting him in a way he hadn't had to do since Butch was a boy.

"What are you crying for?" Henry Jarman, concerned, asked.

"The Silver Rose of Berlin," Butch said, after a long moment.

Later

She tried to analyze the emotions she was feeling but couldn't. Returning to Berlin after ten years, one would expect, she thought, to feel something.

She riffled through the deep pockets of her borrowed black mink coat, as if she could find what she was looking for caught up in the red silk lining. The coat was on "permanent loan" from Alon's mother, given to her the year before when she had had to go to New York for that nervous-making, surprisingly successful first showing of her work.

Rennie wondered if a man was ever going to give her furs and thought not as she came up with a cigarette, a Lucky Strike. Smoking had become difficult with the war. The fragrant Nigerias had disappeared. She lit it with the limousine's lighter, inhaled, and allowed her head to rest on the leather upholstery. Like the cigarette, the car was American, crafted with a Spartan luxury reminiscent of Butch Jarman's Packard.

She had spent an evening in New York with Butch and his very pretty society girl wife. They had been charming and generous, buying one of her paintings for an astronomical amount of money, making certain that the "right people" came to the opening, which was well publicized in the newspapers and magazines Butch had inherited from his father.

Still, she very nearly dreaded his occasional letters. Butch Jarman was a perfectly decent man, a good friend. But he was associated with too much pain. When she thought of him, she wanted to cry.

She smoked steadily as the Cadillac made its way into Berlin. Where was the hate, the anger, the fear she had expected and, in some ways, come to find? All she felt was a slight distaste, as if she had blundered into a not quite clean restaurant.

But everything was clean. Immaculate, as Tante Lizbeth would say. Though there were gaping holes in the urban landscape—entire blocks had disappeared—the rubble had been neatly piled, the sidewalks freshly swept no matter how cracked and damaged they were.

They've cleaned it all up, she thought. For a second, she saw her father's body being put into the trunk of the Mercedes. They always were very good at cleaning up.

She put out the cigarette and forced herself to focus on the buildings, on this new devastated, neat Berlin.

The section she was being driven through hadn't been badly damaged. She remembered the brown middle-class houses, the awninged shops, the wide avenues. Berlin had always been an ugly city. But once it had had a raffish sort of charm. And later, a sinister sexuality. Now all it seemed to have was a burnt-out orderliness.

It took her a moment to figure out how to work the electric windows; when she did, she pressed the appropriate button and the glass slid halfway down, allowing her to take a deep breath. The air was still delightful. She didn't know whether to be angry or relieved. They used to say it was the rivers and surrounding forests that gave Berlin air its buoyancy. The concentration camps, the ovens, had been kept away so the acrid odor of industry, of burning bodies, wouldn't pollute Berlin's crystalline air.

"*Berliner Luft*," Rennie said, aloud. The chauffeur, who wore some sort of Allied uniform but was certainly German, turned. "*Meine Dame?*"

"Sorry," Rennie said, in English. "I was thinking out loud." She wasn't going to speak German. She would not. She looked past the driver at the chrome Art Deco woman sparkling at the end of the long, khaki-painted hood and remembered when a silver swastika was the more usual adornment for a Berlin limousine.

Where are all the swastikas? she wondered, trying to find a building erected in the thirties, trying to locate a cornerstone. As the car pulled onto the Kurfürstendamm, she recognized the gray stone building of flats in which Kimmel had wanted to install her. Then, in 1938, it had been brand-new. She found the "1938" engraved in a concrete plaque, but where the obligatory swastika had been was a recent, blank, smooth space.

"The swastikas are all gone," she found herself saying to the driver whose dark, knowing Berliner's eyes met hers in the rearview mirror.

"*Es geht um die Wurst,*" he said, laughing.

She almost laughed, too. "The sausage depends on it." She had forgotten how she had enjoyed Berlin's ironic humor. Of course the sausage depended on the swastikas' disappearance. Everything in this divided postwar Germany depended on the disappearance of the once ubiquitous *Hakenkreuz.*

She turned her attention back to the Kurfürstendamm, where there were too many women mixed in with the American, French, and British servicemen. The women weren't thin, exactly; but they weren't well fed either. They had a pasty, tough look to their skins. They wore tight skirts, bobby socks, high-heeled shoes with ankle straps.

The survivors, she thought. And then she thought that she, too, was a survivor and almost felt remorse.

The Cadillac pulled up in front of the hotel, which had been a restaurant the last time she had seen it. The manager came down the carpeted steps to greet her. "*Gnädige Frau,*" he said, waving young porters about. He had a small, weasel face and a beautifully tailored black-market blue suit. "*Willkommen.*"

Instinctively, she didn't like him or the smile. A decade before he would have been clicking his heels together noisily. The blue suit would have been a black uniform. But the smile would have been the same.

"Is my husband here?" she asked in her Anglo-English.

"I am sorry," he answered, his narrow eyes carefully moving up and down her body, appraising it and the mink. "But no, madame, the general is still in conference. He left word that he shall meet you here for luncheon. In your suite. If you will permit me?"

He led her through the new, tasteless lobby into the new, tasteless elevator. She remembered the Adlon, the Kaiserhof, drinks at the Eden. Berlin had become a small, provincial sort of city, no longer deserving a grand hotel. The thought didn't comfort her. Her quarrel, after all, wasn't with Berlin.

She found herself in a suite of rooms filled with heavy, modern furniture. A small balcony overlooked the Kurfürstendamm. "We are the finest house in Berlin today," he said, pleased with himself and the suite and the porters bringing in her luggage.

She moved to the doors which led onto the balcony. She was still never in a room when she didn't feel the need to be near a window, to look out.

"The last time I tried to get into your 'house,'" she found herself saying, "it was a restaurant, and there was a brass sign on its door which read, JUDEN SIND HIER NICHT ERWUNSCHT. I gather the policy has changed."

He looked at her for a moment as if she weren't there. "Will there be anything else, madame?"

"There's been quite enough, don't you think?" she said, immediately regretting it. He stowed the complimentary champagne—French, she noticed—in the wine bucket on the dresser and retired with dignity.

Germans always retired with dignity, Rennie thought,
remembering newsreels of a dramatically slimmer Göring
being urbane and witty at the American prosecutor's expense at Nuremberg.

She went into the bedroom and lay down, fully clothed,
on the too-soft bed. She shut her eyes and saw Göring,
not as he had been at Nuremberg with the tan uniform
hanging about him but as he had appeared at the Kleist
Kasino in the new pale blue uniform he had personally
designed for the Luftwaffe.

Fat Hermann, the *Eckenstehers*, the corner boys, had
called him, affectionately. They had called Goebbels the
hunchback, not so affectionately. He had been undersized
and he had limped and he had had a piercing nasal voice
that used to blare out from the radio horns on the street
corners. He hadn't been hunchbacked at all. He had merely
been malevolent.

She opened her eyes. She wasn't going to think of them.
She wasn't going to think of any of them. She was in a
new, defeated, divided Germany. *Der schöne Adolf* with
his cobalt blue eyes and pale, unhealthy skin—with that
inappropriate boyish manner he had sometimes possessed
—didn't exist.

And neither did the Prussian baron with the ancient
Junker heritage and the butter-colored hair and the body
temperature that was just a degree too warm. Certainly,
Wolfgang Konstantin von Danzig no longer existed, except
in her mind.

She sat up and allowed herself, like a magazine heroine,
to examine herself in the mirrored wall. She was different
than she had been ten years before. That Rennie had been
charming and innocent and naïve. This Rennie was chic
and urbane and genuinely sophisticated. She didn't care,
anymore, if people liked her or not. She was more interested in truth than affection. She was, she knew, more
beautiful than ever.

"It doesn't help," she thought, allowing herself a smile. But it was difficult to look into a mirror in Germany, in Berlin, and not cry. The telephone rang.

"Don't tell me," she said, answering. "I know. We're not to lunch together. You're just coming to a monumental agreement on Paragraph Three, Section 'a' of the preliminary agreement, and you can't, as much as you'd like to, get away."

"I'll be there in half an hour."

"No," she told him, relenting. "I'm perfectly fine, Alon. You know how I am after a plane flight. I need a little sleep."

He hesitated. "I swear I'll be there by four. Not one moment later. We'll have dinner. We'll make love."

"You do take a girl's breath away."

"I wanted to be at the airport. I know how you feel about Berlin . . ."

"I don't feel any way about Berlin."

There was a pause. "I'll be with you at four. I love you, Rennie." He rang off, and she knew from his tone that he was reassured.

He was in Berlin, engaging in a German-Israeli reparations "dialogue." He and his opposite number were attempting to figure out how much the Germans owed the Jews. "No one can count that high," Rennie had told him. He had been in Berlin for what seemed like months but in reality was only a fortnight. She hadn't known she would miss him so much.

She forced herself to get off the too-soft bed, to redo her makeup in the dressing room's neon-lit magnifying mirror. She stared at herself and wondered if she shouldn't change her dress, her shoes, her hairstyle. She began to brush the silver blond hair and then tossed the brush aside, took a deep breath, and went through the series of doors that led to the elevator that took her to the hotel's grill room.

She remembered, without wanting to, a black joke from

the other time. "They're serving Jews at the Kaiserhof today," one fellow alerted another. "Tell them to save me an end cut will you?" his pal replied.

The joke made her feel ill, frightened. She allowed the maître d'hôtel to show her to a dark banquette, to provide her with an elaborate menu printed in English and German and French. She didn't open it. She didn't want pigs' knuckles or Wiener schnitzel or sauerbraten.

She ordered an omelet and a glass of white wine and looked around her at the serious diners, mostly in uniform, literally breaking bread, talking between and through bites. Except for the color and the cut of the uniforms, they might have been the same clientele the hotel, then a restaurant, enjoyed a decade before.

The Germans who sat at their captors' tables seemed especially earnest. That earnest quality was why, she thought, the Germans are so efficient at the little tasks and such bumblers when it comes to the really big jobs. They hadn't wiped out the Jews and they hadn't conquered the world and they hadn't even checked Communism. *Au contraire,* as Lillie would have said.

Lillie. She allowed herself—well, she had no choice—to think of Lillie. After the war, as the immigrants streamed or trickled in to Israel—depending on the vagaries of British and Allied policy—she had waited for Lillie to turn up. She had been certain Lillie would come to Israel to find her. She had sent letters to everyone she could think of. She had had neatly typed notices put up at all the displaced-persons centers. She had offered rewards and, later, hired investigators.

Eventually it became clear that Lillie wasn't coming to Israel and that she wouldn't ever be found.

Then Rennie had learned of the ledgers the Germans had kept, those leatherbound books that listed each inmate in each camp, their vital statistics, their employment, their inevitable date of death. The Russians had them.

So while Alon was in Berlin, politely arguing fiscal compensation for loss of life and limb and mind and property, he tried to arrange for her to see the ledgers.

At first the Russians had balked. But then they decided she was potential propaganda material: an up-and-coming Israeli artist being allowed, by the generosity of the Communists, to conclude a ten-year search. She didn't care how the Russians used her. She simply had to know.

The following day she was to be taken into the Russian sector to finally lay Lillie's ghost to rest.

She found she couldn't eat the omelet after all. She signed the check and made her way back to the suite where she lay on the too-soft bed and tried, unsuccessfully, not to remember.

She had a fitful night's sleep. Alon had risen at six and tiptoed about, noisily. She knew he wanted her to get up, to talk about the reparations, to reassure him that she wasn't going to sink into a long fit of melancholy because she had returned to Berlin.

She watched him through half-closed eyes as he emerged from the bathroom and stepped into his blue cotton shorts. His legs were tan, muscular. He put on his tieless uniform: khaki jacket and matching trousers. No diplomat's morning coat for him. He was considered tough, a hard-hitting Israeli, a graduate of the Irgun school of diplomacy. Which certainly meant no general's uniform, either.

She watched as he studied himself in the mirror, needlessly brushing his short black hair. He was manly and handsome, and he often got his picture in the papers. She closed her eyes when he turned away from the mirror, felt his lips press against her forehead, and waited for the outer door to close before she sat up, reflecting that she had been destined to marry a general.

She had met Alon in 1945 at a party in Jerusalem celebrating the end of the war. He had been quick, demanding, loving, sexual. She had married him three weeks later. He was a considerate husband, a strong, affectionate, effortless father to David.

At the thought of her son, that irrepressible David, she smiled. If anything, he was too much an Israeli, chauvinistic to the point of myopia. So proud that his stepfather was a general; so proud to be an Israeli.

But he had butter-colored hair, Mediterranean blue eyes, and stood a head taller than anyone in his class. He would grow up, she knew, to look like a model for that *Popo mit Schwert*—naked hero holding sword—sculpture Hitler had been so fond of. He would grow up to look like that ultimate Aryan of Nazi mythology. It was an irony only she and Tante Lizbeth could share.

She thought of that ancient, ageless Tante Lizbeth, who was more than likely feeding some terrible food of her own concoction to David in the bright kitchen of the house in Jerusalem, and she found herself wishing that she hadn't returned to Berlin, that she hadn't had that need to be certain about Lillie.

The American sergeant who was driving her to the rendezvous point attempted to make conversation as they rode up the Kurfürstendamm in another khaki limousine, past the smoke-blackened spires of the *Gedächtniskirche*, and through the Tiergarten, along the Bellevuestrasse.

The blocks of expensive, ancient flats on the Matthäikirchstrasse were gone, already replaced by stark white office buildings. It was a relief. She didn't want to see any personal monuments.

The Russian and the American soldiers exchanged papers and halfhearted salutes as she transferred into the Russian car. The driver didn't attempt to make conversation as he drove into the Russian sector, which seemed deliberately poor and gray.

She was surprised when he stopped on the Friedrich-strasse in front of what was once Göring's Air Ministry and was now a dreary government office building. Two silent men in gray business suits met her at a reception desk and led her to a huge green-painted room with blacked-out windows. Half the room was taken up by narrow stacks of books reaching to the ceiling, which desperately needed replastering. The other half contained wooden library tables at which a dozen elderly men and women were studying.

She was shown to a seat at a table and waited a long fifteen minutes until a pile of red leather ledgers was placed in front of her. She wanted desperately to smoke but saw from a sign over the entrance doors that she couldn't. She wondered who the other people were, if they were after the same sort of information as she. A very old man two tables away was crying quietly, sitting perfectly still with a ledger held open in front of him, tears rolling down his cheeks.

Finally, she opened the ledger in front of her. In the very first volume she found Lillie's name, her camp number, her occupation (laundry worker), the date of her death: 9/3/42. Rennie held her breath as she studied those firm, handwritten numbers, barely faded. She stood up without closing the ledger, pulling her furs around her, and made her way to the entrance, where her escorts were waiting.

"Are you ill?" the younger one asked.

"I should like to go back now," she said, not answering, thanking them at the car, allowing the Russian driver to take her up and around Unter den Linden, which was being restored. Outside the War Memorial soldiers were changing guard, goose-stepping. With one part of her mind she wondered why that particular step had been kept; she wondered why she still found it so threatening.

As she began to cry, she thought how Lillie would have hated working in a laundry, how she had hated any sort of

domestic work. She imagined Lillie ironing SS uniforms and
tried very hard to stop crying.

The driver had evidently been instructed to give her a
little tour before returning her to the West. There was a
desultory crowd of Russian soldiers in front of the Branden-
burg Gate, looking like soldiers at liberty in a dull town
anywhere, smoking stubby cigarettes, wisecracking. The
ledger hadn't said what Lillie had died of. Anger. Disappointment. Boredom. Fear.

The car stopped for a moment in front of the pile of
rubble that had once been Hitler's Chancellery and she had
the one gratifying idea of the entire day: now she could
properly mourn Lillie. There were to be no more false
hopes. She dried her tears with her hands, wishing she
hadn't forgotten a handkerchief, remembering when she had
taken a vow never to cry in Germany again. Well, she
had broken a lot of vows in her time.

And she had cried when she had arrived in Palestine.
And she had cried again when David was born. And again,
so recently, when Israel was born.

Now, she told herself, I cry at the drop of a hat. She had
said to Alon that it was a sign of increasing age, but he had
said it was a sign of increasing humanity.

She changed cars at the rendezvous, and while the drivers
again exchanged papers and documents, she saw an old-
fashioned *Wurst* kiosk. She asked the American if she had
time to stop and he said, "You can have all the time in the
world, baby."

They stood together at a round wooden table, along with
half a dozen soldiers, eating the hot sausages, drinking pale
beer. The sergeant insisted on paying.

Father would have approved, she thought, biting into her
second *Currywurst*, remembering the last time Nick Jablonski had eaten a Berlin *Wurst*, a quarter of an hour before
he was gunned down in a Ku-damm alley. She finished the

sausage and the beer in the paper cup and thought, Father would have said that despite everything, *"Berlin bleibt doch Berlin."* Berlin is still Berlin.

She asked the sergeant if he might make one more stop and he said he would make as many stops as she wanted and if she had a thirst on he knew a tiny *Lokal* on the Uhlandstrasse. . . . He was a little too old to be a sergeant and a little too fat, and so she winked back at him and said that she wasn't thirsty, that she only wanted to revisit a favorite place of hers.

He laughed when he pulled up in front of the Kleist Kasino. It looked much as it once had, its cupola weathered, the front door recently painted. The sergeant told her it was Off Limits, a bar for the boys.

"The boys?"

"They dance with each other."

She smiled as she got out of the car. How Lillie would have enjoyed that. Not to mention Pepsi.

She stepped into the familiar, small entrance hall. The leather curtains were gone but the smell was the same. Gin and perspiration and cheap scent. Rennie took a deep breath. For her this was the genuine *Berliner Luft*.

She went into the room that was once the cabaret and was now the dance hall. It was dark and empty except for a fat, blond woman sitting on a red leather stool behind the familiar, bamboo bar, laboriously rolling coins into bank packets.

"Tea dance don't start until five," she said, without looking up. "And the bar don't open till four."

"I only wanted a look around." Rennie took off the dark mink coat, letting it fall on one of the barstools.

"Be my guest." And then the fat, unhealthy-looking woman looked up and said, with a little shriek, *"Mein Gott!* The Silver Rose of Berlin. Imagine, to still look like that. What luck! You always had such luck, Rennie."

"Marlene?"

"The one and only." She laughed, good-humoredly. "I don't look much like a Goose Girl now, do I? Every time I thought I had any luck, it ran out pretty damn quick, I can tell you."

"Kimmel . . ." Rennie said, more easily than she would have thought.

"He wasn't so bad, that one. I can't say he made my life a bed of roses, you understand, but he wasn't so bad. Until the end." She took a cigarette from a pack on the bar and stuck it between her overlipsticked lips. "He's alive, wouldn't you know? Working in the Russian sector, for the secret police, they say. And if the Americans win the next war, he'll be working for the FBI. You wait and see if I'm not right." She lit the cigarette and looked at Rennie again, shaking her head. "Listen, you want a cup of coffee? Genuine American ersatz. Wait. It will only take a moment."

She walked with difficulty into the room behind the bar, and Rennie closed her eyes, once again seeing the stage and the blue spotlight and Lillie in her bugle-beaded gown, her geranium red hair going in every direction, her big brown eyes knowing and sad.

"Whatever happened to your general?" Marlene asked, as she boiled water on a hot plate and opened a tin of Sanka. "I still think about him, would you believe it? What a beautiful man! What a gentleman!"

Rennie opened her eyes, but still she saw Wolff as he had kneeled before her that last afternoon, memorizing her body with his eyes and then his lips. She could almost feel his too-warm body, the touch of his hands. He was as real to her at that moment as he had been for the past ten years. It was always as if he had just stepped out of the room, for only a moment.

Butch should have shown me the photograph, she thought.

It couldn't have been any worse than what I imagined.
Perhaps if I had seen it, I wouldn't still be haunted by him.
As he was then. Innocent, charming, wonderfully, roman-
tically loving. That perfect *Junker* knight. He's never grown
old for me. He still has his butter-colored hair, his beautiful
muscles. If I had seen him go soft, fail in business, grow
cynical . . . well then maybe I might have gotten over him.

"You still love him, don't you?" Marlene asked, sliding
a chipped china cup across the bar.

"I love him as much today as I did on the day I left
him." Rennie found she was crying again. She turned and
stared at the shadowy room, remembering when she sang
her song there. Lillie's song. And despite Marlene, all the
ghosts came back. "Oh, Lillie. Oh, Father. Oh, Wolff," she
whispered, allowing the tears to run down her face. "What
I wouldn't give to see you all again."

Marlene handed her a nearly clean handkerchief. "The
bloody Führer," she said, coming around the bar, putting
her arm around Rennie's shoulder. "That bastard."

"I have something to thank the Nazis for, though,"
Rennie said, blotting her eyes. "I realized it earlier when I
saw what the Russians had left of the Chancellery."

"What's that, kid?"

"I have the Nazis to thank for my being Jewish. If it
hadn't been for Hitler, I wouldn't be anything. I would
have assimilated. I would have become one of those European women who suffer, vaguely, from anomie, without
roots or traditions or beliefs.

"I'd be living in London or New York or—who knows?
—Argentina. Hilter's madness—Germany's madness—gave
me my sanity. I know who I am now. A Jewess. An
Israeli."

She smiled, and Marlene thought it was the saddest smile
she had ever seen. There were new tears in those remark-
able silver blue eyes as Rennie said, "Not that I still

wouldn't give it all up—not that I wouldn't give everything up—for Wolff."

As she was leaving, Marlene stopped her and ran back into the little room behind the bar. "The boys like them," Marlene explained, placing a tissue-wrapped package in her hand. "Take one for luck."

Marlene watched as Rennie stepped out into the dim November sunshine, the dark mink coat on her shoulders, the chubby sergeant racing around the limousine to open the door for her. Marlene remembered another time when she had watched Rennie leave the Kleist Kasino with a fur on her shoulders, when she was going motoring with her general.

Marlene would have traded places with her in a second on that day ten years before. But she wasn't at all certain that she would now. Rennie was more beautiful than ever, but there was a new and devastating sadness within her that seemed as if it would never go away.

The reparations meeting ended, unexpectedly, on schedule.

Throughout the flight back to Jerusalem, Rennie held the gift Marlene had given her the previous day. When Alon asked what it was, she took it out of its paper wrapper. It was a white rose that had been dipped in silver dye. She pinned it to the lapel of his khaki jacket.

"The last silver rose," she said.